FATOS LUBONJA

THE FALSE APOCALYPSE

FATOS LUBONJA

THE FALSE APOCALYPSE

From Stalinism to Capitalism

Translated from the Albanian by John Hodgson

istrosbooks

First published in 2014 by Istros Books
London, United Kingdom
www.istrosbooks.com

©Fatos Lubonja 2014
Translation ©John Hodgson, 2014

ISBN: 978-1908236197

Supported using public funding by

ARTS COUNCIL ENGLAND

LOTTERY FUNDED

This book has been selected to receive financial assistance from
English PEN's Writers in Translation programme supported by
Bloomberg. English PEN exists to promote literature and its understanding, uphold writers' freedoms around the world, campaign
against the persecution and imprisonment of writers for stating
their views, and promote the friendly co-operation of writers and
free exchange of ideas.

ENGLISH PEN

Education and Culture DG

Culture Programme

This work programme has been funded with support from
the European Commission. This communication reflects
the views only of the author, and the Commission cannot
be held responsible for any use of which may be made
of the information contained therein.

FOREWORD

By Andrew Gumbel

For a while, in the mid-1990s, Albania was as fascinating and tragic a place as anywhere on the planet. Imagine a jail break, only on an unimaginably large scale. Three million people had broken free from decades of repression, poverty and near-total isolation under the paranoid dictator Enver Hoxha and his successor, Ramiz Alia, and they were in a frenzy to make up for lost time. Certainly, they yearned for an open society, a market economy, democratic institutions – everything that could propel them closer to the living standards of their European neighbours. But they were also impatient for more immediate satisfactions, to bring in a "boatload of money" as one Albanian friend of mine liked to say, and live like kings for a change.

The pent-up creative energy was palpable. Many Albanians were street-smart and worldly. Some had acquired first-class educations, supplementing the politically tainted rigours of their formal schooling with smuggled books, tapes, contraband television signals – whatever could help them break through the artificial walls erected around them. Poverty felt like a needless aberration they could overcome now with just their wits and sheer force of will. After the nightmare of Stalinist totalitarianism, of labor camps, prison cells and an omnipresent fear, what new challenge could possibly stump them? They had natural resources, a temperate climate, a beautiful coastline and a population hungry for self-improvement. Decades of enforced collectivism made the lure of individual action irresistible. If they had to lie, cheat, steal, betray and trample over each other to get what they wanted, then so be it. Wasn't that the way of the world? The Albania that emerged from the communist era thus became a teeming laboratory of illusions fostered and dashed, of optimism and abiding suspicion, of staggering ingenuity and monstrous corruption. When I first visited, as an eager and wide-eyed young reporter in the spring of 1995, I found it all exhilarating and oddly endearing. Tirana, the capital, was a maze of crumbling buildings and rutted streets filled with garbage and broken concrete where wild dogs prowled at night. Yet it was also covered in satellite dishes and "kiosks", makeshift structures erected on street corners and in public parks in imitation of Italian terrace cafes, where you could order peach schnapps at eight in the morning, conduct business, meet friends and, if you so chose, linger late at night, at a piano bar without a functioning piano, and dance to Bulgarian bootlegs of *Careless Whisper* and other western hits.

There were the disjointed signs of progress: a spanking new Coca-Cola bottling plant, a luxury hilltop restaurant financed by Kuwaitis, a picket-fence neighbourhood near the U.S. Embassy with perfect lawns and red-flagged mailboxes. And then there was the giant hole in the centre of town, the legacy of a Kosovo Albanian investor who had promised a luxury high-rise hotel, driven around in a white Rolls Royce raising millions of dollars and absconded with the lot.

Tirana at that time was a city where everyone was living beyond their means. Everyone had an angle, a scam to pull, a bribe they were willing to pay, a corner they were happy to cut. There were fewer than ten miles of smoothly paved road in the entire country, yet the streets were choking with Mercedes and BMWs, many of them stolen in Italy or Greece with the connivance of organized criminals and sold for a few hundred dollars on the beach outside Durres, a short drive from Tirana. The country's biggest brickworks produced exactly twenty perfect bricks a year – the twenty it was obliged to submit for official certification – and sold the rest to gullible foreign investors who invariably had to throw them away and start again.

Government contractors paid such large kick-backs to maintain the dangerously low-slung telephone wires, or to repair the street drains, that they could no longer afford their own work materials. A few days or weeks later, they'd be bidding on the same job all over again when their jerry-rigged solution broke down at the first hurdle.

To the outside world, curiously, this looked like an acceptably slapdash path to progress, in line with other former communist countries in Eastern Europe muddling their way towards free-market capitalism and an open society. In 1994, the World Bank dared to imagine Albania as a "small haven of peace and economic growth" – dependent for the moment on foreign aid and remittances from Albanians living abroad to keep its economy afloat, but heading emphatically in the right direction. Sali Berisha, the charismatic Albanian president who presented himself as a strident anti-Communist, won praise for his determination to purge the country of sinister remnants of the past and for accepting the economic "shock therapy" prescribed by the IMF. In certain conservative circles he was hailed as "the last Thatcherite".

In truth, the European powers and the United States weren't paying nearly enough attention. Their priority was to prevent the violent collapse of Yugoslavia from causing further shockwaves across the Balkans, and the only thing they really wanted from Berisha's government was a promise not to stir up ethnic Albanian tensions in Kosovo and Macedonia. Berisha gave them that promise. They failed to notice, or more likely chose not to care, that Berisha, far from throwing off the mantle of Enver Hoxha's authoritarianism, was busy donning his own version of it. Soon after cementing his grip on power in a convincing election victory in 1992, he purged his party of anyone who challenged his authority, including many of his closest allies; he imprisoned the leader of the Socialist opposition,

Fatos Nano, on corruption charges after a bogus trial; and he turned the secret police, known as SHIK, into his own political enforcement bureau.

The economic growth the international community found so promising was built less on Thatcherite free market ideology - not even the banks were private - than on Albania's involvement in criminal rackets. According to multiple observers in the intelligence and law enforcement worlds, the country was smuggling guns and oil into the former Yugoslavia in defiance of United Nations sanctions and allowing the transshipment of heroin and other illegal drugs to Western Europe. Berisha's Democratic Party was directly implicated in sanctions-busting through its ownership of the country's oil distributor, Shqiponja. Many of the rackets were said to involve members of SHIK, along with at least two senior government ministers. The government was also closely tied to the country's largest private company, VEFA, which held a stake in a wide variety of economic pursuits: supermarkets, chicken farms, publishing, financial services and, according to intelligence sources, international arms trafficking.

The political climate became ever more stifling in the run-up to elections held in May 1996. Berisha wheeled in one European dignitary after another to burnish his democratic credentials. Even as a car bomb detonated outside a VEFA supermarket in Tirana, Berisha pinned the blame on his political adversaries, without any actual evidence, and the police swooped on Albania's leading opposition newspaper and detained the entire staff for an afternoon. On election day, ballot-stuffing by Democratic Party officials was so widespread and so blatant that some districts reported 100 per cent turnout and a 100 per cent vote for the party even as people stood in long lines still hoping to cast their ballots. Some of the vote totals were later adjusted to make the theft a little less glaring. But the opposition parties pulled out of the election anyway, saying the climate of intimidation and foul play was overwhelming and there was no prospect of a fair outcome.

At a massive demonstration in Tirana's Skanderbeg Square the next day, the police moved in with batons to bludgeon protesters without provocation and haul several prominent opposition figures off to jail. They did this within full view of visiting dignitaries holed up at the Tirana International Hotel only some of whom seemed to think anything was seriously amiss. The election-monitoring arm of the Organisation for Security and Cooperation in Europe issued a critical report, but it was not critical enough for a group of monitors from Norway and Britain who felt compelled to issue their own, much more scathing dissident statement. No European government challenged the legitimacy of the vote; a number of commentators were willing to point fingers at the same shadowy subversives and diehard communists cited by Berisha as the real threat to social order. Only the United States expressed real displeasure, but opinion in the U.S. embassy was split between a pro-Berisha ambassador and more critical voices on her staff. Comically, one of those who shouted loudest in the Albanian government's defence was a British conservative activist, Anthony Daniels, who was himself picked up by the police in Skanderbeg Square - an understandable mistake, he said - and continued to make excuses as he was thrown into the back of a car next to the opposition's leading economist and showered with baton blows en route to his holding cell.

Many Albanians were furious at the international community's failure to raise a stink about the theft of their fledgling democracy. While the Americans were growing markedly more impatient, the calculus in other western capitals didn't change: as long as Berisha provided what they wanted, they were prepared to give him more or less free rein. What nobody yet realized was that the stolen election was a prelude to a far more serious crisis.

Hajdin Sejdia, the Kosovo Albanian who had promised a high-rise hotel in central Tirana, didn't just bilk a bunch of investors. His fund-raising scam was, in effect, Albania's first pyramid investment scheme – a promise to deliver big, all the better to rake in more cash to steal. Other pyramids soon followed. Some were started by prominent small-town businessmen who had the trust of the local population, others by large companies like VEFA, with political connections and the clout, it was said, to tap into the revenue streams of Greek and Italian gangsters. It was hard to know with any precision what the financial basis of the schemes was, or how they managed to pay out interest rates of 6 percent per month and rising. Folklore and crowd-pleasing stunts took the place of hard information. One scheme in the port city of Vlora sponsored a beauty contest. Another, in Lushnje, lured a former Argentian World Cup star, Mario Kempes, to coach the local football team. Yet another scheme, in Tirana, purported to be the rags-to-riches brainchild of a gypsy shoe factory worker, known just by her first name, Sudja, who bought out her company when it was about to go under by convincing small investors to place their faith in her and hand over their life savings.

Albanians didn't necessarily believe such colourful stories, but they entrusted their money to the schemes all the same, on the basis that they enjoyed government backing. The rumours about them being money-laundering facilities for organised crime made them, if anything, more attractive. If the mafiosi of Sicily, or Naples or Bari were pouring in their drug money, or if – as one elaborate theory had it – the schemes were financing illicit oil exports to Saddam Hussein's Iraq, why shouldn't Albanians reap the benefits?

Until the stolen election of 1996, the pyramid schemes were Albania's dirty little secret, barely discussed in public and certainly not advertised to visiting foreigners. Afterwards, they became Berisha's biggest political raison d'être. "Vote Berisha and everyone profits!" read a poster widely distributed around Tirana - by VEFA, in its capacity as a billboard publisher - ahead of local elections in October 1996. For a short time, everyone did just that. Imports starting flooding into the country; businesses expanded; the housing market took off; there was a mini construction boom. VEFA ran an advertisement showing a man walking into one of its supermarkets with one bag of money and walking back out with four. Even Hajdin Sejdia made an unexpected return and started paying off the investors he'd cheated years earlier – by investing his own money in other pyramid schemes. Edi Rama, an artist and outspoken opponent of Berisha's who would later launch his own political career, observed bitterly that the president had fed Albanians the illusion that they could be rich without being free.

The end came swiftly, first with the lifting of UN sanctions on Yugoslavia in October 1996 and then as that revenue stream dried up, in a few desperate weeks from December 1996 to January 1997. Sudja raised her interest rate to a staggering 100 per cent a month, only to announce from the balcony of her dilapidated apartment building in Tirana shortly afterwards that the game was up. The other schemes quickly followed her into insolvency. Rrapush Xhaferri, the most prominent businessman in Lushnje, a small town 30 miles south of Tirana, was arrested as the last of the millions he'd collected from his friends and neighbours dwindled to nothing. The two policemen charged with the arrest

11

shared a nervous last cigarette before clapping him in handcuffs, because they knew they'd never see their life savings again. Bereft of everything, the town rose up in revolt, and when Berisha's right hand man, the Democratic Party president Tritan Shehu, arrived to denounce the protesters as members of a "terrorist-Stalinist clan" - his idea of restoring order - he was hit over the head with a tire iron, held hostage for several hours in the Lushnje football stadium and, so the story goes, symbolically silenced with a leek stuffed in his mouth.

Soon, the entire country was in turmoil, and Berisha's government increasingly resorted to intimidation and force to try to bottle up people's fury. In Lushnje, revenge for Shehu's treatment took the form of special policemen in hoods bursting into people's homes at three in the morning and rounding up suspected trouble-makers. In Berat, 20 miles further south, suspected anti-government subversives were crammed into a single room in the burned-out police station and beaten. In Tirana, Edi Rama was approached by members of SHIK, the secret police, late at night and pummeled with knuckle-dusters. A leading opposition politician, Ndre Legisi, was pulled out of his car and beaten so badly it was feared for a time he'd suffered permanent brain damage.

The fury, however, could not be contained. By early February, Vlora was in flames, and the crisis had claimed its first death. Over the next month, the south of the country slipped from the government's grip entirely as bands of young men looted police and army weapons depots and chased hapless officials away with Kalashnikovs. In Kucove, rebels seized a fleet of MiG fighters from a military airport. In Saranda, near the Greek border, they seized a warship. Tirana fell under near-martial law, with a strict curfew and a stifling presence of paramilitary police. The death toll rose into the hundreds. From any perspective, this was a living nightmare: the country was being ripped apart, piece by piece, and it seemed nothing could stop the momentum toward total destruction.

This is the terrifying story Fatos Lubonja tells in *The False Apocalypse*. Lubonja is perhaps the closest thing Albania has to an intellectual conscience: a former political prisoner, publisher, writer and activist who has never been afraid to offer his frank opinions, even in the depths of the Enver Hoxha years, and certainly does not hesitate to denounce Berisha in these pages as a man cut from the same authoritarian cloth as Hoxha – a dictator at heart with only the rhetoric of a democrat.

Lubonja captures the brooding, nervy mood in Tirana that took hold as the crisis deepened in those first few months of 1997 - the hastily convened meetings, the calls to action, the abiding fear of government thugs bursting in at any moment and arresting, maiming or killing people; the frantic attempt to understand what was happening before all was lost entirely. His narrative illuminates the desperation of Europe's least known country in its hour of greatest need. And it makes clear that Albania is, in all senses, a small place, where everyone knows each other and almost every relationship has a history tainted by mistrust and fear stemming back to the Hoxha era. The civil conflict that erupted in 1997 could not help but have a peculiarly fratricidal edge. The slights and losses were deeply personal, as was the lust for revenge.

And yet Albania did not tumble into the abyss, not entirely. The collapse of the pyramid schemes was a jolting wake-up call, a realization that people could not spend their lives simply buying coffee, whisky and Mercedes, as one Tirana lawyer put it to me at the time. Some Albanians continued to fritter away their days in video bingo parlors, but most of the country redirected its overwhelming bitterness and anger towards the government, and towards Berisha in particular. The rebels' message was crystal clear. As long as Berisha remained in power, the country would continue to burn.

The western powers understood this with painful slowness. For months after the stolen election of May 1996 and even after the pyramid schemes had collapsed, I had diplomats lecturing me on the virtues of continuity in a time of a crisis. In mid-March, that philosophy came to fruition in the form of a government of national unity, in which Berisha remained as president and a colourless middle-ranking Socialist, Bashkim Fino, took over as prime minister. Having tried and failed to retake the south by force, Berisha appeared to think he could outmaneuver his new rival and use the unity government as a cover to restore his diminished authority. But he was deluding himself, and the rioting only intensified.

By this point, the south was not so much the stronghold of an organized rebellion as an embodiment of complete anarchy. Young men high on raki and marijuana drove around in stolen cars at high speed and unleashed automatic weapon rounds like they were Steven Seagal or Chuck Norris in one of the action movies reliably broadcast by Italy's Canale 5 and consumed avidly across the Adriatic. In the north, meanwhile, Berisha had authorised the opening of weapons depots to his own loyalists. In the absence of some providential outside intervention, bloodshed beckoned on a massive scale.

Two outsiders made the essential moves towards a resolution. The first was the former Austrian chancellor, Franz Vranitzky, who arrived as the OSCE's special representative and convinced Berisha that he could not resolve the crisis through force alone. And the second was Italy's prime minister, Romano Prodi, who largely sidelined his own ambassador in Tirana, Paolo Foresti, who had been Berisha's biggest champion, and organized an ad hoc United Nations force to pacify the country. Both men then pressed Berisha to agree to new elections. The gambit worked: the violence subsided, new elections took place at the end of June with remarkable smoothness, the Socialists swept to power and Berisha, understanding that the eyes of the world were on him, stepped aside with barely a murmur.

It's impossible, of course, to speak of happy endings. At best the outcome was a happy middle. The Socialists were so flawed and corrupt in their own right that they opened the door for Berisha to stage a remarkable comeback - he served eight years as prime minister, starting in 2005. Berisha and Edi Rama remain locked in a furious rivalry, not least because Rama, running on the Socialist ticket, beat him at the polls in 2013 and took over the premiership. Both, in their different ways, have tested the patience of the international community. Over the past 18 years, the country has clawed its way slowly back from the brink – first through IMF-administered life support and then through a slow and painful process of political and institutional reform. Clearly, there are no shortcuts to building a new society.

Fatos Lubonja's continuing anger and melancholy over the events of 1997 are obvious. His book reads, even with the distance of the years, like an urgent series of dispatches from a battle that is, in some sense, still simmering. Albania carries a heavy historical legacy and has many wounds to salve. As for that boatload of money my friend dreamed about, the country is still waiting.

Andrew Gumbel, August, 2014.

In modern tragedy, not the hero but the chorus dies.

-- Joseph Brodsky

PART ONE

Chapter I

The Sugar Boat

Kindergarten Nr. 19, where Fatos Qorri had found a roof, had been built in the Soviet era, the 50's. It was a neoclassical building of red brick, entered through a three-arched porch that supported the central first-floor balcony. The kindergarten, as a building and an institution, had flourished for a couple of decades and then decayed over time until, after the fall of the regime in the early nineties, it was virtually derelict. The front door was torn off and most of its rooms were empty, their children long gone. The back yard was used as a rubbish dump by the residents of the neighbouring apartment block, because by this time even the rubbish was no longer collected. Some illegal extensions to another apartment block behind the kindergarten made it impossible for any private vehicle to come in to remove the garbage, and a battle had begun between the apartment dwellers who continued to throw out their rubbish, and wild nature itself, which tried to cover it with various kinds of vegetation of which wild figs were the most rampant. The most common visitors to the yard were street dogs and cats, swarming in packs over the refuse that stank foully in hot weather.

Like many similar public buildings, the Kindergarten had become a refuge for the homeless during the upheavals and the mass exodus that accompanied the fall of communism. Its rooms were quickly shared out among six groups of people. Half the ground floor, a classroom with toilet and annex, still functioned as a kindergarten, kept going by the teachers who wanted to hold onto their jobs. The family of Qorri's friend Daut Gumeni, a former political prisoner who had served twenty-four years, lived in the other half. Qorri himself was on the first floor above Gumeni and opposite him lived the former owners of the land on which the Kindergarten had been built, and who had moved in to protect their property. A divorced woman had taken the head teacher's office in-between, and opposite her lived a pensioner who had once been the caretaker.

So here in these six living spaces, some of the most acute social problems that followed the fall of the communist regime were brought together: the need to house the former political prisoners and the families the regime had interned in remote villages, the issues of compensation for expropriated landowners and of accommodation for the elderly who had lost their old people's homes and of divorced women who were no longer protected by the state, which had compelled their husbands to share an apartment with them. There were also the problems which arose from the employment of teachers who had lost their work places and of the pre-school education of children whose families had nobody to care for them.

***

Winter was particularly hard, because the rooms were large, with many wooden windows whose frames were now rotten with age. The wind pierced their cracks like a knife. The inhabitants warmed themselves with electric heaters, whose wires hung in the air and were attached directly to the poles outside, but power cuts were frequent and their heating was never adequate.

That night too, Qorri turned on the fan heater as soon as he returned home, noticing that the furred blades were making an increasingly loud noise.

Every evening he wrote a little fiction in order to clear his mind of the tensions of current events he wrote about for the newspapers. These were now becoming extremely worrying, and he was less and less able to ignore them and switch to the imaginative plane of fiction. When nothing fresh came to him, he would turn back and read everything he had written so far. He was writing the summary of a novel that he intended to call 'The Sugar Boat,' based on the story of a small pyramid scheme that a cousin of his had started. It had collapsed some time ago, but without the commotion that the fall of the big schemes was now causing.

The arrival of a boatload of sugar, whose sale would pay off all his debts, was the last deception used by the mastermind of the pyramid scheme to palm off the daily demands of his creditors. Qorri had made this boat the focal point of the novel, a symbol of people's hope and trust in the victory of capitalism over the reality of socialism. The arrival of the sugar boat would solve everything.

Notes for the novel 'The Sugar Boat':
Description of Luli's house and his arrival in Tirana after 44 years:

In the time of King Zog this neighbourhood had been one of the smartest in Tirana. The new rich had built these now dilapidated villas. At the fall of communism it was not considered an attractive neighbourhood.

Luli returned to Tirana in 1990 and found his house at the start of the street still standing, but its peeling stucco made it hard to imagine that this had once been the home of one of King Zog's senior civil servants.

But this is how Luli found his father's house, which he had left behind when he escaped from Albania in 1947. Yet he could no longer recognize it in this ugly building.

Luli was one of the first to return from abroad after communism fell. His relatives welcomed him like a god, although

21

there were few people left in the neighbourhood who had known him as a boy.

After the war the whole family had been viewed with suspicion because Luli's elder brother had fled the country in 1944 and settled in America. After Luli escaped, his father was interned in a remote village for several years and when he was allowed back to Tirana he sold cigarettes in a kiosk.

Now time had vindicated him and Luli's escape was viewed in a different light. His relatives were slightly hurt by the fact that their beloved Luli had forgotten almost all their names, even the names of his uncle's sons with whom he had grown up.

People found excuses for him. He had escaped when he was very young and the poor man had struggled hard to get where he was. Now he was a millionaire. His first successful business had been in New Zealand, they said, and now he traded throughout the world.

He himself said that he could have made no other choice. He had either to forget everybody or to pine away yearning for his relatives like his brother, a poet, who had spent his entire life writing pathetic verses of homesickness until his death from cancer in the United States a few years previously. Luli frankly admitted that his soul was not a poetic one like his elder brother's.

Meeting the President:

Luli was even granted an audience with the last communist president, Ramiz Alia. Now that Albania was opening its doors to the capitalist world, one of the president's principal tasks was to meet businessmen who wanted to invest in the country. The television news reported on the meeting and revealed that Luli wanted to buy the privatised handicrafts enterprise with its excellent lines in knitwear. Luli wanted to turn the entire organization into a woollen-wear manufacturer. New Zealand wool had an excellent reputation.

He could ship the wool from New Zealand and the cheap workforce of Albanian women could produce knitwear for export to Europe.

He stayed a short time and then returned to New Zealand where he had his family and principal business.

Mimi and Vera:

Before Luli returned, the neighbourhood had recognized his younger brother Mimi as the owner of the house. In his career as a construction engineer Mimi had risen no higher than middle management. He married late in life after an appalling incident in which a spurned ex-girlfriend had gone to his house late one evening, called him to the door, and thrown acid in his face, blinding him in one eye. Nobody knew what had so embittered this woman, whether Mimi had done anything more than break off the relationship, but people considered her a crazy woman, and Mimi her victim.

Later he married Vera, but they had no children. There was only a cat and a dog at home.

Luli's second visit:

On this second visit, Luli stated that he had come purely on business, but his first duty was to attend the funeral of a close cousin. At the ceremony the mourners were totally distracted by a beautiful woman whom Luli brought with him. Returning from the burial, the dead man's family and friends did not talk at all about their memories of the deceased, but only about the charms of Luli's companion. She was a lovely young mulatto, whose hips, breasts, and full lips drew everyone's attention. Nobody knew if Luli was separated from his first wife or not. He said that their children were scattered all over the world, one in Japan, one in Australia, and a third in the United States.

A few days later, Luli declared he had started a business partnership with a company in Slovenia, and would import household appliances. Such an idea seemed miraculous to the Albanians, who had just emerged from the penury of communism. Electric stoves, refrigerators, and Gorenje washing machines started to arrive. But Luli's main business remained in New Zealand, where he had built up his life, and in the United States, which was his trading base. His visit to Albania, he said, arose from a sense of duty to his long-suffering fellow-countrymen, and in giving work to his brother. Mimi became the firm's manager in Albania.

Founding the pyramid:

Soon after Luli's second visit, Mimi was understood to be paying interest on the dollars he had collected. For every $1,000 paid to him, he would pay out $75 per month. Mimi said that the money was given to Luli, who set it to work in his large-scale businesses throughout the world. Luli's profits in the western world were rumoured to be colossal, and 7.5 per cent a month represented a modest return.

The myth surrounding Luli, combined with Mimi's moral credibility, convinced all their relatives it was safe to invest their money. Some had only $500 to deposit and some had thousands. Mimi welcomed them all with a show of courtesy, and Vera carefully wrote down the clients' names and the amounts and dates of their deposits.

At first everything went miraculously smoothly. Some depositors of small sums of $500 to $1,000 lived for the whole month on the interest they received, because $50 a month was a substantial income in the first years after communism. But it was rumoured that some people had deposited more than $20,000 with Mimi. He was trusted to such a degree that people begged him to take their money and some even asked their relatives to intervene to have themselves included on Mimi's lists.

Mimi himself kept a low profile. He did not open grandiose offices like VEFA or Gjallica: firms calling themselves finance houses that were set up at the same time. He said that he took his friends' and relatives' money only as a favour to them, because Luli had no real need of it.

For a while Mimi behaved very properly, paying the monthly dividend on the capital placed with him. Very few people withdrew this dividend, except for needy people who had paid in small sums. The depositors watched in fascination as the sums grew every month. Those who had put in $1,000 calculated that the $75 interest of the first month increased the second month's dividend, and so on, until within a short time their $1,000 had become $2,000. Investors of $10,000 were delighted to find they had $20,000. And so for a long time Mimi accumulated more than he paid out.

Mimi and the big pyramids:

When the big pyramid schemes appeared, Mimi poured scorn on them. They produce nothing, he told everyone who would listen, while continuing to praise his brother's trading ventures.

But the strength and reputation of the big pyramid schemes grew fast. They advertised in the newspapers and on State television. The word 'Holding' which the largest firm VEFA added to its name, exerted a magic power. The Albanian economy was entering the great global market, and now had its very own 'Holdings'.

But after a while, people noticed that Mimi was becoming dilatory in paying interest on request.

Mimi's swift collapse was caused by the growth of the big pyramids. These wonder-working firms increased their interest rates. Anyone who owned a small apartment could sell it for $10,000, invest the money, and within a year buy another apartment twice the size. People flocked to them to deposit their money.

Mimi became increasingly behind in paying back the money that his depositors had invested, and now wanted to withdraw. At first he paid only the interest, but then had to suspend these payments too. A strange psychological phenomenon was apparent among the majority of people who asked for their money but were sent away empty-handed. In the beginning, they did not argue or even question the reason for this delay. They seemed scared to look beneath the surface. They were frightened of waking from their dream.

Bad news:

Soon afterwards, bad news spread through the family circle. A relative returned from a visit to Slovenia with the information that Albanians there knew Luli as a prodigious gambler who spent his days in the casinos of Ljubljana, and that the mulatto was not his wife but his current mistress.

However, the family decided not to believe this report, instead ostracizing their cousin and accusing of him of jealousy because his own business venture had failed.

The same mentality was at work in the case of the big pyramids. The more the word "pyramid" was used to describe these unstable financial schemes, the more people sought evidence to convince themselves that they were not fraudulent. They liked to be called 'creditors' and hated the word 'debt'. And anyway, who was in 'debt' to whom? Some said that the long-standing depositors were in debt to the recent ones, and all the depositors were simply debtors and creditors to one another.

Others disagreed: No, it couldn't be true. They were not merely taking the money of those who deposited it later. The interest they withdrew came from the investment of their money, or perhaps from some other source. After a time, to counter these ominous rumours, word spread that these firms were in fact laundering money. Apparently, the state was aware of this and was even abetting the laundering of money because high-level politicians had also deposited their cash. These allegations of state support had, it seemed, persuaded some people who had resisted the temptation to lodge their money with Mimi, to transfer it to the big pyramids of VEFA, Kamberi,

Xhaferri, and Sudja.

The Sugar Boat rumour is born:

Finally Mimi could no longer palm off his creditors with extensions and postponements. He told all those who came to withdraw their cash that their money was invested in a huge boat laden with sugar that Luli had bought and was bringing to Albania. He assured them that Luli had traded very successfully in sugar and this boat would bring all his profits. He put off everybody who asked for money with the story of the Sugar Boat, which now circulated amongst the investors as a sign of hope.

The elections approach:

As the democratic elections drew near, the ruling party boasted that the economy was strong and successful. The opposition, fearful of losing votes, said not a word against the pyramid schemes, even though people had started to grumble about them. Mimi himself lambasted the big pyramids, but his voice was not a public one.

The ruling party won the elections with the help of the pyramid schemes. The election campaign was adorned with the logos of finance houses such as Gjallica and VEFA Holdings.

The Dutch cheque:

One creditor, who has already become a daily visitor to Mimi's house, came back with the news that a part of the boat's cargo had been sold and Mimi had received a cheque from Luli for several million dollars in order to pay his accumulated debts.

The creditors' spirits revived. Those who had doubted the honesty of Mimi and Luli experienced a pleasurable thrill of guilt. How could they have imagined that Luli and Mimi, boys from a good family, could ever sink so low as to swindle money from their own relatives? The keenest investors promptly started counting up their money and their virtual profits for the entire period.

Mimi and Vera run away:

Their disillusionment was swift. Mimi told some of his relatives, who came to withdraw their money, that he was setting off for Holland because a problem had cropped up and the cheque was being held at a bank there.

Shortly afterwards Vera was discovered to have left with him. Some people still hoped for his return with their money and even said that Mimi and Luli had joined the Sugar Boat, which was on his way to Albania.

But the hopes of even the most optimistic crumbled when the first big pyramids fell. Mimi had been a swindler. Even the Sugar Boat had been a fraud. Mimi had used his reputation and the good name of his family to deceive them. Rumour had it that he had not even been a good husband. The woman who had thrown acid in his face now seemed to have had justice on her side. He had been recruited by the state security service long ago. His defenders said that he was a victim of his brother,. Luli was the real fraudster who had exploited his family's reputation and the prestige of the West.

***

Qorri read his notes so far. He had already imagined the novel's denouement, in which creditors would attack Mimi's house after he had escaped without trace. The creditors who had claimed to have deposited more than $200,000 with him would announce that the house belonged to them, and a deadly quarrel would break out among them, with some drawing guns and ready to kill rather than surrender the property.

But what was happening around him went beyond anything in Qorri's notes. Reality beggared the writer's imagination. The more eventful life is, the less room there is for creativity, he thought. Perhaps Balzac was right; that a novel lived through is one less novel written.

28

Where history begins, fiction stops short. In this novel, he had found in the 'Sugar Boat' a metaphor that organized the narrative and lent wings to his imagination, but the events that he was living through, so tangible and unpredictable, seemed to have demolished the edifice his imagination had constructed.

Chapter II

At Noel's

Qorri often spent the evening at Noel's bar in the hope of finding a friend for a chat before he went home to Kindergarten Nr. 19. As usual, on that cold evening in January 1997, he tied his bicycle's front wheel to the railings at the entrance to the bar and plunged into the semi-darkness of the staircase leading to the basement. But even as the noise of conversation and the odours of cooking emerged from the doorway, he could not rid himself of the worry that Noel's had lost its usual easy and hospitable warmth over the last few days.

Noel's was one of the few bars without the aluminium, plate glass, and perspex with which the Albanians, in their frenetic desire to catch up with the times, filled their first post-communist, private cafes. The counter was constructed of the standard red bricks commonly used in communist buildings. The tables and chairs were wooden, with red baize tablecloths. On the walls were racks for utensils like in Ottoman houses, and on these were placed a couple of traditional musical instruments - a *çifteli* and a *lahutë*, some radios dating back to the war, an ancient Singer sewing machine, and other objects that recalled pre-communist Albania, as if in an attempt to bring it back. On one wall and on the bar's round central pillar were black-and-white photos of world-famous actors, and a few from socialist-realist movies.

Noel's was both in the centre of the city and in a slightly secluded corner, and its semi-basement premises could be passed unnoticed, although the wooden door opened onto a well-known street of old Tirana, where some of the leading state institutions in Albania's brief independent history were situated. Immediately opposite the entrance was the gate to the former Royal Palace, faced with white marble. For most of its history, this had been the Palace of Pioneers, because King Zog was forced to flee from the invading Italians shortly after it was built, and after the war the communists had turned it into an institution for the education of the children of Tirana. To the right of the palace and adjacent to its yard was the mansion of the feudal Toptani family, one of the few Ottoman-style houses remaining in the city. This house still contained the Institute for the Preservation of Public Monuments, as it had in communist times. Next came the Academy of Sciences, a royal residence in the time of the monarchy, and a little further on was the Parliament, a 1950s building in the Soviet neoclassical style. To the left of the Royal Palace was the National Art Gallery built by the dictator in the 1970s.

Noel's side of the street also had plenty of buildings that had made history. On the right was the National Theatre, built by the Italians during their occupation, where the Albanian language was first spoken on the stage in the capital. A little further down was the Interior Ministry, which retained not only its former function, but also its frightening aura invoked from the time when it had been one of the main links in the chain that bound the country in 50 years of communist dictatorship. To the left of Noel's and less than 50 yards away, was a building that had just started to make history, the headquarters of the ruling anti-communist Democratic Party, the PD.

***

The story was that the proprietors had been unsure what to call the bar. Their first idea had been 'The Milky Way', after the street's nickname in communist days. This was not because of some imaginative association with the stars above, but because here the citizens of Tirana had stood in line before dawn to buy a bottle of milk or yoghurt from the dairy. However, this unpleasant memory was put aside and the name 'Noel's' was chosen. Most people thought that this was the name of the proprietors' son, but his close friends knew that the name recalled the democratic movement of 1990, which had started at Christmas-time.

The bar's location, special atmosphere, cheap snacks, and good-quality spirits attracted the most diverse clientele in all Tirana, from leaders of the governing PD and police officers from the Interior Ministry, to members of the nascent opposition to the ruling party, which had emerged from divisions in the democratic movement. Actors from the National Theatre came after performances, as did artists working on exhibitions at the gallery, members of the Academy, and journalists. There was also the solitary figure of Robert Shvarc, the famous translator of German Jewish origin, who continually argued with those who sat down at his table if they said çifut for Jew, a word that, he insisted, should be buried along with communism and replaced by *hebre*.

***

Qorri had reason to be worried as he descended the stairs to Noel's. During the last two or three months there had been disturbances in Tirana following the bankruptcy of one of the large pyramid scams. On several occasions, crowds of people who had lost their money had waited for hours at the counters of the offices where they had made their deposits. When they received nothing, they had taken to the streets in fury to protest. But there they had encountered the rubber truncheons of the police, who had orders to disperse them immediately. The confrontations were becoming increasingly violent, and it was now a tangible fact that the entire machinery of the State, the police, the secret service, the State television, the prosecutor's office, and the courts had all been put on an emergency footing to prevent these outbursts of rage. Suspicious groups of plain-clothes forces had also been seen in the city, and were said to be militants of the PD, mostly from the same region as President Berisha. These thugs dispersed the crowds with particular savagery. Demonstrations in the main squares had been forbidden and people trying to organise gatherings were pursued and arrested. Finally the government, in its efforts to prohibit assemblies, had decided even to cancel the football championship.

It was true that most of these people acted spontaneously and without any political motivation, out of despair at the loss of their money. The opposition was fragmented into several parties, of which the largest was the former Communist Party. So far they had confined themselves to denouncing the State's acts of violence, but the government was increasingly concerned at the prospect of the opposition giving a political direction to the citizens' anger. So every State television news broadcast included interviews with people calling for the maximum punishments for anyone causing disturbances, and the courts were handing out prison sentences to anyone 'endangering the country's stability.'

Qorri was an outspoken opponent of the government himself. After his release from his political imprisonment just before the first multi-party elections in March 1991, he had become secretary of the Albanian Helsinki Committee. In this role, he had been quick to criticize human rights violations by the new government, which was composed of communists who had turned into anti-communists led by Sali Berisha, a one-time party secretary. As a journalist Qorri had consistently urged opposition to Berisha's authoritarianism. With things as they were, words had the power to spur people into action, and the most incisive articles were in the newspaper *Koha Jonë*, for which Qorri wrote.

Recently, more high-level government people had been coming to Noel's, amongst them even the police chiefs who had crushed the demonstrations. The courteous proprietors smiled at everybody and did their best to preserve the atmosphere of the early '90s, when the bar first opened. Even the police chiefs didn't look as if they had just come from state business, but seemed to be there only for leisure, taking a break from a spot of lucrative trafficking. But recent events were bound to make their impact even here. Qorri's table and the police officers' tables were now islands that did not communicate except through the owner and his wife, who passed from one to another to serve them. At one time, Qorri would join a table if he saw one of his friends from prison, even if he now worked for the police. Hard times were not easily forgotten. But the distance between them had now increased, and when his fellow-prisoners now shared a table with other people, they preferred not to take notice of one another. Common enemies and dangers had brought them together in the communist prison, but their common hope of freedom had now evaporated and they were no longer looking at a common future. They were now in opposing camps, and their enemies were each other.

***

Qorri entered and looked around the crowded bar with its thick fug of tobacco smoke. In one corner there were police officers, and beyond them some young actors from the theatre. Shvarc was at a small table against the central pillar of the bar along with Dita, a fair-haired young actress who admired the famous translator.

At the bar's most privileged table in a distant corner, was Dashamir Shehi, the Deputy Prime Minister and a leader of the Democratic Party, who had a serious taste for brandy.

Qorri found a group of friends at the table closest to the door. There was the painter Edi Rama, who was visiting for a few days from Paris, where he had a scholarship, accompanied by his wife Delina, whose resonant voice radiated energy; the painter Lad Myrtezaj; the actor Artan Imami with his wife; and the beautiful singer Rovena Dilo. They had all been part of the anti-communist movement at the start of the '90s but had now broken with the governing party. Besides Rovena, they had all signed a petition composed of intellectuals who were against the rigging of elections that had taken place the previous year, after which the opposition deputies who joined street protests were beaten up in Skanderbeg Square.

Qorri took off his three-quarter-length coat, his scarf, and the beret that he wore tilted on the back of his head. The buzz of the conversation was about a skirmish between the police and demonstrators near the premises of a pyramid scheme named Sudja, after the woman who ran it. This Roma woman, whom nobody could have imagined as a creator of financial pyramids, had become famous. Her creditors, waiting in vain for their money, had demanded that Sudja should come out and explain. She finally appeared at a window and announced, 'I will give you an answer when I have consulted with the person in charge. But you will have to wait because I am going on holiday tomorrow!' The news that Sudja was leaving 'on holiday' fell like a bombshell on the waiting people. This was an end to any hope of them receiving their money. They took to the main streets in fury, shouting anti-government slogans. They wanted to know who was the 'the person in charge'. In the cafe, the word was that this person was probably Prime Minister Meksi himself.

Rama was often carried away when he started talking, and loudly ridiculed Sudja's holidays. Some people from nearby tables, including one of the policemen, turned their heads. At Rama's table they lowered their voices.

'Good that you've come,' Rama said to Qorri. 'I met those people from the Alliance today. They all said that it's time to act, and the opposition has to lead the protests. After Sudja's, all the pyramids will fall one by one.'

The Democratic Alliance was a party formed by disillusioned intellectuals who had been the first to leave the PD. Everybody around the table supported the Alliance. Rama said that the Alliance leaders had told him they were ready to co-operate with the former communists to create a front against Berisha before it was too late. But they wanted

35

Qorri, a well-known former political prisoner, to joint this front. They had also talked to Kurt Kola, the chairman of the Association of Victims of Political Persecution, who was willing for this association to take the initiative to create this new front.

'I'm not the right person for this job,' Qorri told them.

'Why not?'

'I don't think I have the talent for leadership. I've supported the Alliance in my articles, and I've just drafted a declaration and a protest on their behalf.'

'What about?'

'Demolishing Berisha's claims that he knew nothing about the pyramid schemes. That's what they're saying now: they knew nothing. How can't they have known? Berisha has done all he can to find out about us, and yet he never looked into the pyramids! I've put down the facts, the advertising for the pyramid schemes on State television, the threats from their bosses before the elections that if any other party came to power, people wouldn't receive their interest payments, and the election campaign with the cars and flags with the symbols of Gjallica and VEFA. So my conclusion is that these people are incapable of solving the crisis, and they can't deceive us by arresting a couple of crooks. All the Albanian political parties have to sit down at the table.'

'And what about the protest letter?' Delina asked.

'We've sent it to Voice of America, and a copy to the U.S. Embassy too. Their correspondents in Tirana are bastards. It's a scandal, how they report. They're totally in the service of Berisha. When the crowds are being forcibly dispersed, they even openly drive about in police and secret-service cars.'

'OK, but what did the embassy say? Do they know yet that they shouldn't support this government?'

'Forget it,' Artan Imami interrupted, trying to keep down his heavy, resonant voice. Rama used to tease him about this, often saying, 'You're all mouth.'

36

'Why?' his wife asked him.

'Because the ambassador is of Italian origin. She's a good friend of Foresti, the Italian ambassador, one of the closest people to Berisha.'

But Edi Rama reverted to his conversation about the Alliance. "I wrote an article too in Paris," he said to Qorri, "but as soon as I came back here it seemed so out of date. Events were snowballing. Articles and statements aren't useful any more. You have to take action."

'Leave me alone, I've started writing a novel about the pyramids,' Qorri replied. 'It's called 'The Sugar Boat'.'

'Never mind the Sugar Boat. A boatload of people is drowning right here.'

At this point, Deputy Prime Minister Shehi stood up with two characters from his table, came up to them, and stopped. He was drunk, and spoke with the characteristic ambiguity of drunken men in whom affection and aggression are hard to tell apart. 'The government is paralytic,' Edi whispered to Murtezaj, who was sitting next to him. Shehi sensed they were talking about him and wanted to stay, but the owner of the bar escorted him to the door.

'I'm a Tirana boy, born and bred,' Shehi shouted as he left, his voice thick with drink. What did he mean by this? Was he setting himself apart from his boss, President Berisha, derided by his opponents for his origins in the mountain fastnesses of the North? Or did he want to show that he belonged more to Tirana than anybody else in the bar, and so didn't give a shit about them?

Qorri didn't stay long, but before he left, he went to Shvarc's table to say hello. He had known the translator since childhood. He had a fixed image of him, sitting alone for hours on end in the Café Tirana, alone with a book or a notepad and a cup of coffee in front of him. Even long ago he had intrigued Qorri. He wore a trilby hat like the communist leaders, but on him it looked different. He was not an Albanian, but a Jew born in Sarajevo who had come to Albania with his parents when he was very small.

37

Shvarc was rarely enthusiastic about anything, but it was hard to tell if this was his nature, because he had never felt totally at home in Albania, or if it was because of the way life had treated him. It was hard to work out if he was without friends or simply kept himself to himself. Was he lonely or solitary? He sparked into life only when he talked about the translations he was working on.

But Shvarc was not indifferent to the drama of the pyramid schemes. With that irony of his, that only those who knew him could distinguish from earnestness, he was telling Dita the story of an Albanian who had deceived a Jew, keeping him in his cellar and taking money from him for several months after the war was over.

'But we're the only country that protected the Jews,' said Qorri, using the word çifut, just to tease him.

'The word is *hebre*!' said Shvarc staring at him angrily.

Qorri knew that he could continue this conversation with Shvarc all night, so he stood up and said goodbye to everyone at his table. The others were staying a little longer, because Artan Imami, the only one with a car, was going to take them to the house of Edi and Delina, where Myrtezaj lived.

It was very cold outside. Qorri hurriedly untied his bicycle from the railing outside Noel's and set off, holding the handlebars with one hand and clutching his overcoat tightly to his chest with the other. As he negotiated the potholes on the streets of Tirana, he thought of the proposition put to him by the people in the Alliance. He was wary of entering politics, yet he was not sure why; whether it was because of its dangers or because he did not have the passion that would make him heedless of these dangers. He decided that the second reason was the more valid.

Chapter III

Knuckledusters

The next morning, still in bed, Qorri heard Ben Kumbaro calling him from below in an ominous voice. He went to the window and saw Ben with one leg over the crossbar of his bicycle, his expression more sombre than usual.

'What's happened?'

'They beat up Edi Rama and Lad Myrtezaj, knocked them round the head with knuckledusters.'

'When?'

'Late yesterday evening as they were going home from Noel's.'

'How bad is it?'

'They're out of danger, but it's serious. Especially Edi.'

'Where are they?'

'The hospital stitched them and sent them home.'

'So their lives aren't in danger.'

'No.'

Qorri put on his overcoat, rammed his beret crookedly on his head, pulling it more firmly than usual from behind, and hurried downstairs. He unlocked his bicycle from the banister and set off with Ben for the house of Edi Rama's parents, where Edi had gone after they discharged him from the hospital. Some unknown men, hooded and masked, had been waiting for him in a dark place near Edi's apartment, just past the place where Artan Imami, had dropped him in his car. They let Delina go and attacked the other two with knuckledusters. Lad had escaped lightly with a cut on his head but they gave Edi a much rougher time, and he arrived in the hospital with deep gashes in his scalp

39

and a broken nose. He was now improving, but was in deep shock, and his head was swathed in bandages.

Qorri listened to this story from Ben, perched on his bicycle, and racked his brains for the reason behind this attack. He was also fearful for himself. He recalled the faces of the police chiefs at a dinner he had recently attended, and the drunken expression of Deputy Prime Minster Shehi as he left Noel's. These were the people that must have given the signal for the attack, yet Qorri did not want to believe it. Did they know about their conversations with the Alliance and their plans to create a united front? Did they want to crush this front before it was even born? He would rather believe that they had been attacked because of their quarrel with a neighbour in the apartment block opposite, who had complained after seeing two artists dancing naked in their house, on the grounds that that this outrage to family values had obliged him to keep his curtains drawn. But that had been a long time ago, last summer. No, it was naive to think that this attack was not linked to what was happening all over the country. It was a sign and a threat to them all.

For the past three or four years, Berisha's media had been stirring up hatred against intellectuals who protested against the PD's behaviour since coming to power, calling them anti-Albanian, traitors, spies and homosexuals. They had even dreamed up new labels such as 'Greco-Slavic-Orthodox', which summed up the vulgarity that had taken root in the first anti-communist political party. Edi Rama had been among the first to be attacked for his writing. Now that the government felt threatened, it was translating hate speech into direct action. But who had selected Edi Rama, and who had carried out the attack? Was this the impulsive act of some fanatic emboldened by the climate of hatred, or had it been done under orders? Unfortunately, the second possibility seemed more likely.

***

The home of Edi Rama's parents, an apartment on the third floor of a communist-era block, was open to visitors as if to receive condolences. Visitors came and went in the living room and kitchen, while Edi himself lay in one of the bedrooms.

Qorri went in to see him. As he approached the bed, he was afraid he would be unable to bear the sight of Edi's disfigured face. And so it turned out. Edi's face was horribly blackened and swollen, half covered by two bloodstained bandages in the form of a cross over his broken nose. His black eyes were barely visible on either side. Even his lips were grotesquely swollen. He struggled to speak but in vain, but only a kind of stutter came from his mouth. A wave of mixed emotions swept over Qorri, of a kind he had rarely experienced, like a failure of the nerves under the assault of all those contradictory feelings of horror mixed with despair, pity, and powerlessness to respond.

He did not stay long but returned to the adjacent room where he found many friends and acquaintances.

'We've got to do something. Something has to be done,' he heard Delina say, to him and to everyone there.

Qorri stood doubtfully, as if waiting for someone else to take a decision.

'All I can do is write an article in *Koha Jonë*,' he replied, seeing that no better suggestion was forthcoming.

Edi Rama, after being attacked, had done something that impressed Qorri greatly, and was a gift to the press. In the disfigured state that he was, his face smeared with blood, he had not waited for the ambulance but had knocked at the door of a neighbour, a photographer, and asked him to take his picture. Qorri picked up the shots that the photographer had developed that same night. Blood trickled down Edi's brow and from his nose, where the knuckleduster's blows had fallen, and spread over his face, staining his white open-necked shirt, and dripping onto his trousers. Yet the man who had

41

suffered these bloody blows was still on his feet, reminding Qorri of the legend of a murdered man who walks away carrying his severed head in his hands.

Qorri took the photo with him and asked Delina to give him a floppy disc with the article Edi had mentioned at Noel's. He mounted the bicycle he had left at the bottom of the stairs, and set off again, thinking about what he would write. He was so distracted that more than once he failed to avoid the ubiquitous potholes in the Tirana streets. The heavy traffic at that hour made them hard to avoid and several times the bicycle threw him into the air.

Chapter IV

Facing the Unknown

'Shocking Under Dictatorship, Shocking in Freedom' was Qorri's headline in *Koha Jonë* on 24th January, above the photo of Edi Rama's bloodied face. 'Men in black hoods with iron bars and knuckledusters carried out a barbarous attack on Edi Rama and his friend Vladimir Myrtezaj, the painter and lecturer at the Academy of Arts...'

The article tried to convey the public outrage, not only at the attack on two artists and intellectuals but at the national crisis caused by the collapse of the pyramids. 'People are anxious to see how the political parties will find a way out of the impasse into which they have driven the country. The barbarous attack on Rama and Myrtezaj shows that the government has opted for the path that has led Albanians throughout history to kill each other.

In conclusion, Qorri mentioned a letter that he and a group of inmates had sent from prison to Sali Berisha at the beginning of the '90s, in which he mentioned the proverb, 'Eyes see better after tears.' 'I hoped that he too would be among those who had wept. But Sali Berisha seems never to have shed a tear in the last few years. God help him!'

At the end of that bitterly cold January, the hostility between the government and the opposition reached a new pitch. Berisha had every faith in the Albanians' atavistic fear of the State. Down the generations, they had learned to be scared of three things: fire, water, and the State. Under communism this fear had seeped into their very marrow. The opposition still trusted that they would not be

43

as frightened as before, because Albania had opened up and they could not so easily be ruled by violence as they had been in the past.

Both sides were venturing into unknown territory.

The future was ever more unpredictable because of the appearance of another protagonist on the stage, whose strength nobody could assess: the furious mob of people who had lost their money in the pyramids, and whose fear had evaporated at the same time as their dreams of wealth. Recently, when the police forces charged the protesters to disperse them, they had for the first time come up against a hail of stones, along with an overturned, blazing police car.

Albanian Television's dramatic report pointed out the danger to society posed by these people and warned that the State would use all possible means to maintain order.

***

The winter cold did nothing to cool these passions, and these increasing acts of violence were a dangerous omen.

Several days after the attack on Rama and Myrtezaj, Qorri sat down to draft a memorandum for which he hoped to gather as many well-known signatures as possible.

It was time for Albania's intellectuals to state some blunt truths. The great financial deception was only part of an even greater political deception. Within a few years, the Democratic Party had transformed itself from a hope to a threat. Abandoned by its intellectual supporters, it was now a rump of ex-communists who had now turned into anti-communists, with a contingent of former victims of persecution who allowed themselves to be manipulated by a state that was crushing the first green shoots of democracy.

The stone throwing and fires were not just because people were furious at losing their money but also because their patience had been abused. They had seen the government first behave like a bandit and then set itself up as a judge. Any people who were not allowed to demonstrate peacefully would one day resort to using stones and fire. The country needed an authority based on trust not fear, and this could only come from a parliament elected by a free vote. The traditional destructive cycle of 'crime breeding crime' had to be broken.

Qorri's memorandum in this spirit was addressed to President Berisha and his party but also to the opposition, calling on them to rise above power struggles and to construct an alternative. It called on the army and the police not to allow themselves to become instruments of one political group against another, and it appealed to the whole of public opinion. Copies were sent to the embassies in Tirana. In conclusion, he appealed to people to continue their peaceful protests, avoiding outbreaks of violence and ignoring the provocations of the secret police.

The number of signatures was not large. What Qorri in one of his articles had called the 'pilot fish' (a large category of the former communist intelligentsia) were frightened. Fish of this kind have no fins to steer themselves, so in compensation nature has given them very strong lips. They clamp these lips onto sharks that carry them along until they find a pocket of warm water where they can float. These fish had now torn their lips away from Berisha, because he had left the warm waters. But he was still strong enough to punish them. So they had not attached their lips to a new host. They were biding their time.

And so there were barely sixteen signatories. Besides Qorri, they included four former political prisoners and Kurt Kola, the chairman of the Association of Former Political prisoners, and Daut Gumeni, Qorri's neighbour in Kindergarten Nr. 19. There was also the theatre producer Ben Kumbaro, as well as Edi Rama, and Artan Imami, who had been at the table that dramatic evening at Noel's.

The memorandum was published in *Koha Jonë*.

Chapter V

Proposal (In Grey and White)

Nobody knew why Berisha's opponents made the Bar West their headquarters. It was perhaps mere chance that this bar, located in the Park of Youth, now entered its heyday.

In the early '90s the opening of any private bar or restaurant in Tirana was an event. These cafés and bars, that suddenly sprouted up one after another in huts erected in public parks, were halfway houses in the transition to private property. Every proprietor tried a new gimmick, and their owners were entrepreneurs who usually had links to central or local government or paid a bribe for a permit. The most varied selection of bars and restaurants was in the Park of Youth in the city centre. The population hurried to sample every new venue, each more modern than the last, and changed their favourites from one month to the next like fashionable clothes. With extraordinary speed every square inch of the park, once the pride of the city with its tall trees and variegated greenery, was crammed with bars and kiosks. The trees and grass withered and died. Plate glass and aluminium predominated, while other bars imitated caves or grottoes. There were also arcades with fruit machines, Ping-Pong halls and discotheques. The dark alleys between them became hangouts for drug dealers and for use as outdoor urinals.

Bar West was on the northern edge of the park, opposite the Defence Ministry. It was the same street on which Noel's was situated, after it crossed the Boulevard of the Martyrs of the Nation. The bar was sheathed in plate glass that extended to the pavement and enabled prospective clients to see who was inside before entering, and also allowed customers to keep an eye on passers-by. You could leave your bicycle outside without fear of it being stolen. Inside there was central heating in winter and air conditioning in summer, both novelties in Albania.

The proprietor was a trim young lad with vertical gel-stiffened hair. He had been a wrestler in the time of communism and then the bodyguard of PD Prime Minister Meksi. But he had kept up his friendship with several deputies of the Alliance who frequented the bar. Some people said these deputies were only customers because of the many opponents of Berisha who went there. These premises gained a reputation, and their regulars gave each bar its soul and defined its political allegiance. The cafés became the nodes of a news network that spread throughout the capital city; the most powerful news medium in the country, more so than the newspapers or the sole State television channel. The network had already been established under the communist regime, and now that the cafés were more numerous, they had increased in strength and influence.

Bar West was the hub of the opposition media network. This was where journalists, intellectuals and the most media-savvy opposition politicians met. Here anti-government news was commented on and disseminated. Almost all the journalists of *Koha Jonë*, university teachers, unemployed writers and poets, and those who had turned themselves into journalists and politicians, drank their coffee there. Shvarc came here because Noel's was empty in the morning. Foreign journalists turned up, fishing for Albanian newspapermen and opposition leaders to interview.

***

On that day at the end of January, when Qorri entered Bar West, he saw an extended table from which tobacco smoke rose in even thicker wreaths than anywhere else. Around it sat a group of opposition types normally found at separate tables. Some journalists at the adjacent table had also joined the conversation.

The table's leading smoker was Meidani, the general secretary of the Socialist Party and former professor of physics at Tirana University. At the end of the '80s, the Communist president Ramiz Alia had invited him to become a member of his presidential council, and after this he had become chairman of the first electoral commission for multi-party elections, until he agreed to join the Socialist Party and became its secretary. Majko had been one of the students in the anti-communist movement of December 1990 but had switched to the Socialist Party. Some said he had done this because there had been a lot of competition in the PD at the beginning and nobody had taken any notice of Majko, and others said that he had chosen the Socialists under the influence of his father, a military man strongly connected to the old Albanian Party of Labour. He was very young, and always smiling as if delighted at having become so important so soon.

These two were both important people in the Socialist Party because they served to show the public, and especially foreigners, that the old communist Party of Labour, now called the Socialist Party, had changed its stripes and brought new people into its ranks.

When Qorri came up to their table, Majko stood up, smiled, shook his hand, and said, 'Congratulations.'

Qorri was taken aback.

'Don't spoil our day,' Majko said before Qorri could utter a word. 'We've elected you to represent the Left.'

Qorri remembered the conversation in Noel's a few days before.

'Take a seat,' they said to him, drawing up a chair.

Qorri sat down to find out more. They told him of their plan to create an alliance of all the parties and associations against Berisha. It was to be led by three former political prisoners. Kurt Kola, the chairman of the Association of Former Victims of Persecution, had agreed to be one of them. The other two would be Daut Gumeni, to represent the right-wing parties, and Qorri for the left-wing Further decisions would be made at their inaugural meeting.

'I can't give an answer now. I'll think about it,' Qorri said to them.

'Don't spoil our day,' Majko said again, speaking for them all. 'Say yes.'

Qorri looked around and his eyes involuntarily fell on a table where 'the cook', was sitting as always with 'the spook'. No doubt these two knew something about this conversation, he thought. The eyes of Berisha's security service, the SHIK, were ever present at Bar West. The powerful SHIK had inherited the aura of the omnipresent *Sigurimi* secret police.

The short, thickset 'cook' earned his nickname because he was said to have worked at one time in a students' canteen. The 'spook' was tall and bald, always making impassioned remarks to journalists about their articles. The two sat there almost all day. Both were said also to have been *Sigurimi* informers. Qorri knew the 'spook' because his brother had been in prison too. Somebody had told Qorri that the 'spook' had been forced to become an informer after his brother's arrest, but someone else claimed that he had been recruited earlier, and was partly to blame for his brother's fate. With all the rumour and speculation, it was impossible to know the truth. Everything to do with the *Sigurimi* and the people who worked for it was shrouded in secrecy. The 'spook' was the most fervent of anti-communists, like many whom the regime had both oppressed and humiliated by turning them into spies. 'You were in prison with my brother,' he had said to Qorri one day at a table in Bar West. 'And so I must tell you that I've started working for the SHIK I was out of work. But please keep this to yourself.' At the West, everybody knew that the truth was not as he had told Qorri, because he did indeed have a day job. But this job was a cover, and every day he sat in the bar on duty. It

49

was hard to understand just why people who had suffered under the rule of dictatorship looked for employment with the very agency that inherited the mantle of the *Sigurimi:* was it revenge, or simply because they could not escape its clutches? Rumour had it that the networks of the old *Sigurimi* and Berisha's secret services to a large extent overlapped. Some swore that only the controllers had changed, and that former subordinates had been promoted to controllers. It was an impenetrable underground world.

Qorri did not wait for the spook to greet him with his habitual cordiality, so perfectly simulated that anybody not in the know would think this was the last person to be suspected of being a spy. Instead, he looked across to a table at which sat Delina, Edi Rama's wife, with Rama's old friend Dash Peza and Blendi Gonxhja, his former student at the Academy. Qorri stood up from the politicians' table and went over to them. Without sitting down, he told them of the proposal put to him.

Delina almost shrieked, 'Fatos, something has to be done. They beat up Edi Rama. They could beat up any of us!'

'But Edi's run off to Paris,' Qorri said.

'He's gone for treatment until the situation calms down. He'll be back.'

Dash Peza and Blendi Gonxhja said the same. Dash was a boyhood friend of Rama. He had recently returned from America where he had tried without success to build a new life. He said he had become a born-again Christian there but this had evidently been a survival strategy, because in Albania he showed no symptoms of piety. Gonxhja was much more famous because he had taken part in the first students' strike and later had become one of the most active members of the Democratic Alliance. He was now caught between his need to make a living, his love of art, his passion for politics, and his plans to leave Albania forever. Dash and Gonxhja both insisted they were ready to help the cause.

The lack of opposition from Bar West was beginning to persuade Qorri that he might agree to represent the left in this new organisation that was to be created. But he felt no enthusiasm. He harboured doubts on which he still brooded as he left the bar.

The same doubts assailed him just as they had done before, at Noel's. He was unsure if they arose from trepidation at this dangerous enterprise or his lack of political zeal. Nor did he feel at home in this company. Could he court this kind of danger alongside people he didn't know? He believed that these were the people intellectually best equipped to bring about democracy, because they were the best educated, but what had happened to them morally during those two decades while he himself had been in prison? Edi Rama, among the instigators of this group, had fled immediately to Paris. Even at the start of the anti-communist movement he had run away to Greece in fright straight after making a speech against Enver Hoxha. This entire generation of intellectuals with their double lives, opposing the regime and yet collaborating with it, seemed to have a tendency to bolt. Their way of life had taught them never to put complete faith in what they were doing but to always leave an escape route open, and ultimately never to trust one another. In one of his articles, he had used the phrase 'grey area' which in other countries of the East denoted the region between the 'black' of the regime and the 'white' of the dissidents. Could these people be 'light grey'? In Albania, he believed, there had never been any white, but only black and grey. He did not think of the prisoners, including himself, as dissidents but victims. They served the regime by scaring the rest of the population. Hoxha's regime had been a totally black hole, unillumined by the rays of courage and hope that Sakharov, Michnik or Havel had spread elsewhere in post-Stalinist Eastern Europe. Only now, after the fall of communism, was the 'grey' divisible into the 'dark grey' of those who had risen to power with Berisha and the 'light grey' of the opponents of the authoritarian regime. But this colour chart did not cover all

51

the shades that distinguished these people from one another. What Qorri called 'light grey' had its dark patches, too. He remembered the rumours that the so-called democratic movement had been entirely a contrivance of the former *Sigurimi* and that most of its leaders had been its former agents and informers.

No enterprise of this kind could expect to rely entirely on well-known, tried and tested people. Certainly these members of this opposition were united by a need to free themselves from a regime that had violated their liberty, although each of them perhaps had their particular expectations and ambitions. Qorri could not tell where this adventure would lead: to the pinnacles of power in a future government, or somewhere very far from them.

Yet he felt he would accept their offer. He was tempted by the prospect of a leading role, and also driven by his old desire to overcome his fear of any task fraught with danger. Whenever faced with important decisions, since the clashes with the authority of his father in adolescence and his conflicts with the dictatorship and the prison authorities, it seemed to Qorri that he had always been trying to overcome fear and repress the weaker part of his nature that did not allow him to become his stronger, fuller self. That was what the dictatorship had done to people. It had made them fear to live and left them diminished. But did not these diminished selves ultimately become real selves? Fear had to be fought against, if you were not to be diminished. Qorri's relationship with fear had been decisive in his life and in the lives of people among whom he had lived, because in their society fear was the main instrument of control. It created relationships. But it was also the main obstacle to being free. Since prison, he had established a different, less confrontational rapport with fear and with authority. He was no longer so ashamed of his fear. He was more willing to accept it as a part of himself. Sometimes he even thought of fear as a mark of dignity and respect for life. Experience had taught him that the problem was not of feeling fear, but of not allowing oneself to be mastered by it. It was less a question of not falling than of picking yourself up again. This meant that he had to nurture within himself the figure of a hero that challenged fear, but without feeling heroic. More coolly considered, this hero figure was perhaps the obverse of a repressive culture based on fear.

Chapter VI

First Meeting

Qorri entered the premises of the Association of Former Victims of Political Persecution, studying the building with interest.

The architecture of the villa housing the association was like nothing else in Tirana. The eclectic 1920s style of the façade included a round protruding balcony with a conical roof above it, which added a distinctive charm. The building also occupied a special site on a small but important square where the flag of independence had first been raised in Tirana.

The villa had been built by a former Ottoman military officer who later sold it to the Italians for their consulate. During the Fascist occupation it became the seat of the *Luogotenente*. On his visit after the invasion, Ciano had looked out from its balcony on the crowds of Albanians at an organized rally in the square. In his famous diary, he mentioned 'silent students' among the throng.

Most of these students later became communists, went underground and took to the mountains as partisans. In 1944, they seized power and turned the headquarters of the *Luogotenente* into the offices of the Albanian-Soviet Friendship Association, until the beginning of the '60s, when the Albanian communists broke with the Soviets and remained loyal to Stalin. The building subsequently became the headquarters of the Veterans of the National Liberation War until the fall of communism.

The Democrats, as soon as they gained power in 1992, decided to give this villa to the recently formed Association of Former Victims of Political Persecution. But the desire to break the moulds of the past soon yielded to a tendency to emulate them. The PD was very successful in enlisting the support of former political prisoners and their families as a way of reinforcing its own anti-communist credentials. These former prisoners were required to take the places of the communist martyrs and war veterans. The ex-communist Berisha believed that they were more interested in recognition and compensation for their past than their future careers. The gift of this building was intended to mark the start of a new epoch, and invited the former victims of communist persecution to accept the symbolic role of veterans.

In addition, the only monument to communist persecution in Tirana at that time had been erected in a corner of the square in front of this very building. This sculpture was intended to represent a victim of torture, but it gave the impression of a body whose neck, at the moment of beheading, had been stopped with a cork so that its blood had spread through its body, turning its limbs into swollen lumps like inflated balloons.

The former prisoners, especially the group who from the start had rejected the PD and called them 'tools of the communists', did not like the absence of a head. Most of the former prisoners were not old men content to be honoured as veterans and pillars of moral support, but were active people of ambition. Many of them indeed subtracted their years in prison from their age, thus presenting themselves as even younger and more purposeful. But most importantly a deep gulf, created by their different histories, yawned between the former victims of persecution and the elite anti-communist leaders. When the anti-communist movement erupted, most of the victims of persecution were either in prison or internal exile, or were living quietly in obscure corners out of the way of the dictatorship. They had minimal contact with the elite, which consisted almost entirely of members of communist families, if not party members. Qorri quoted Machiavelli to describe their position: 'Stay neither too close, nor too far from the Prince... If you are too close, you may be buried in the rubble when he falls, but if you are too far you have no time to move in to take his place.' The prisoners had been too far away to play a major part in the overthrow of communism, but they felt morally superior because they had not collaborated with the regime. So the elite envied the prisoners their moral stature, and the prisoners envied the elite their opportunities for education and entry into the country's higher intellectual strata.

Quite a few former prisoners nevertheless joined the Democratic Party. Some were ambitious people who saw in it a launch pad for their careers and hoped that they could soon get rid of the communists in the leadership. Others, with lesser pretensions, joined this big party in the hope of landing a job.

But the Association, led by Kurt Kola, had broken with Berisha's party after a hunger strike started by former prisoners when the government refused their claim for compensation. The strike took place in the Association's premises and became the focus of media attention. One by one, former prisoners joined the strike in solidarity with its initiators, making the situation more complicated every day. Finally Berisha saw fit to put a stop to it. Early one morning he sent in police squads who dragged the strikers out of the building by force. After this incident the more intellectual former prisoners increasingly saw Berisha as a figure resembling the dictator Enver Hoxha, their one-time persecutor. More of them also believed the rumour that the *Sigurimi* had created the Democratic Party and that most of the former prisoners active in it were informers recruited in the camps and prisons, sometimes with the promise of release.

***

The inaugural meeting of the Forum was held in Kurt Kola's office, the room that had once been the office of *Luogotenente* Jacomoni,

56

then the chairmen of first the Albanian-Soviet Friendship Association and then the War Veterans.

Qorri was a former prisoner, but he had never been in this room. It was a large room with a parquet floor, a group of old armchairs on one side, and two tables in the shape of a T on the other. Clearly the furniture had not changed: what particularly irritated him were the T-shaped tables that created a barrier between the chiefs and their subordinates and also reminded Qorri of a hammer, one of the symbols of the regime and an instrument of brute force. Qorri had suggested in an article that this sort of furniture should be replaced by round tables, but nowhere had the old layout been changed.

Kurt's office was almost full. The first person he encountered was Rexhep Meidani, one of the regular Socialist clients of Bar West. Meidani was taciturn and listened carefully, in contrast to Pandeli Majko who as always was smiling at everybody for some reason or for none. It was hard to tell why the chain-smoking Meidani was so silent; perhaps he was sure of the support of his large party, perhaps he felt guilty for having joined this party, or perhaps it was his moderate and cautious nature. Paradoxically the Socialists were both the strongest and the weakest party seated at the T. This party formed a majority in the room. It had plenty of foot soldiers ready to enter battle, and the structures inherited from its fifty years in power. But it enjoyed minimal trust, precisely because of the past exploits of these troops. After the fall of communism the Socialist Party was a cadaver, brain-dead, drained of its life-blood, about to decompose. But this corpse had been quickly resurrected because its troops needed to survive. One hundred and eighty thousand members of the former Party of Labour were stuck without a party and without work. They were well known as people who had enjoyed privileges under the regime. Some, like Berisha, turned into anti-communists, but not all of them could join the PD, and nor would they have been admitted. Others remained loyal to a party that no longer existed, and boasted of their honesty

57

and consistency, while others left politics forever. But most became members of the Socialist Party, as the old party was to be called from now on.

Apart from a couple of others, Qorri did not recognize the other people or the parties they represented. One of the most striking figures present was an energetic, blue-eyed, white-haired man of sixty, the most elegant in the room in a blue suit, a snow-white shirt, and a blue tie with pale spots. This was Petrit Kalakulla, the chairman of the Democratic Party of the Right. He came from the long-persecuted class of former landowners. He had been the Democratic Party chairman for Tirana and agriculture minister in Berisha's government, but he had left the party early on. He had a reputation as an extremist for wanting to purge the party of communists and announcing at one of the first sessions of the PD-dominated parliament that communism in Albania had been worse than fascism.

***

Kurt, as host, talked to everybody with extreme benignity. A courteous atmosphere prevailed, and an exaggerated willingness to reach an understanding. It was as if these people had kept all their bitterness for their enemy, and to each other were uniformly smooth and sweet. Qorri wondered if this was unity against a common enemy, or the solidarity of the weak. Some treated Qorri himself with a respect that bordered on servility because he was one of the three at the head of the T.

This atmosphere could not be sustained, and the meeting was short. Those present had already announced their intention of joining together. They approved a statute that welcomed any party or association to the Forum regardless of its political programme or orientation, as long as it supported its platform for a solution to the crisis. Everybody who joined would have an equal right to speak, and to propose and sign the Forum's declarations.

Qorri and Gjinushi undertook to craft the text of the Platform, which was to appear in the press as soon as possible.

***

'This Forum isn't clear to me. What do you make of it, aren't we too much of a mixture?' Qorri said to Gjinushi as they made their way to Kindergarten Nr. 19. Gjinushi looked at him from under his bushy eyebrows and replied, 'It's a discussion table of political parties working for early elections.' They walked on a little, and he added with a chuckle, 'So don't take it into your head that we've brought you in so you can take power.'

Qorri was taken aback. His meaning was obvious. They had installed three former political prisoners as their spokesmen, but kept power for themselves. Who were 'they?' Clearly he was talking about himself, but who were 'we' at a time like this, when nobody knew how the game would end?

Qorri thought back to Gjinushi's career under the dictatorship. In 1990, Ramiz Alia had sent him with Berisha to pacify the rebellious students, precisely because he was a trusted figure. This role became his bridgehead to a future political career. Berisha had been put at the head of the anti-communists and had taken the leadership of the Democratic Party. Meanwhile Gjinushi had waited a little and created the second opposition party, the Social Democrats, which in the first years had been in coalition with the PD. Then, as Berisha gradually cemented his power, Gjinushi found himself sidelined and had joined the opposition. However, all told, he had survived longer in power than anyone else. Qorri had wondered if people like Gjinushi were the kind who, according to Machiavelli, had stayed neither too close to nor too far from the Prince: people who lived with danger and were poised to take high office. But in fact neither Gjinushi nor Berisha

59

belonged to this category. They had been close to the Prince but had known when to run away. They had betrayed him at the last moment and escaped being crushed by the rubble of his fall. These people should have fallen with the Prince, but in the absence of anyone 'not too close nor too far,' who was 'poised to take office,' they were the only people who could fill this role. That was the drama of Albania and they were the country's only chance, Qorri reflected. So this ''we' stood for the former communists who were accustomed to power, whom Kalakulla hated. But there was still a big difference between Berisha and Gjinushi, who was not a communist transformed into an anti-communist. He was subtler. He almost never looked back to the past, and neither deplored it nor glorified it, and he had formed a party whose name at least was left wing.

He and Gjinushi finished drafting the Platform, and with these thoughts running through his mind, Qorri was left alone. The roughly plastered walls of Kindergarten Nr. 19 suggested all kinds of images to his mind. This time his eyes rested on a shape resembling the profile of a man with a shock of hair. His cat Nusi, the only other resident to share his living space, was curled up asleep at the foot of the bed.

***

The next day *Koha Jonë* published the Draft Platform. It contained several of the ideas that Qorri and the fifteen other intellectuals had outlined a few days before, but this time couched in straightforward political language and issued in the name of the parties and associations taking part in the Forum for Democracy.

The most striking and at the same time most sensitive point of the Platform was the demand for a government of professionals to prepare new elections. In plain words, this meant Sali Berisha's peaceful surrender of power was the very thing furthest from his mind.

In fact this government of professionals was an ideal concept designed to carry out an ideal and impossible task: to clear up after the collapse of the pyramids, to find ways to repay the stolen money, to restore the trust of the international community and investors, to release the State television, the police, and the SHIK from political influence; to ensure the independence of the courts, and to pave the way for free and equal parliamentary elections before the end of 1997, under impartial international supervision. It was intended to be composed of people who were not implicated in the pyramids, were untainted by corruption, and enjoyed both the trust of the people and the support of all political parties. Where could you find such paragons? They did not exist.

The requirement for international observers was sufficient to illustrate the impossibility of all the other demands, because any government that could carry out these other tasks would not need international backing. It was obvious that Berisha would not accept the Platform, because if he had been able to accept demands like this, the country would not have reached its present plight. Yet Qorri thought that an ideal document of this kind had to be written. The impossible wish to see things done properly cloaked the Forum's desire to overthrow Berisha. That was vital for any progress. Meanwhile, nobody knew what was going to happen. Would the Forum function as a sum of its many parts, and what direction would it take?

Chapter VII

First Statements

The headquarters of the Association and the ruling PD were no more than 100 metres apart as the crow flies. Between them lay a park crammed with kiosks and cafes. The former prisoners gathered at tables by kiosks in front of their building, while PD militants usually sat at café tables in front of theirs. There were some who frequented both sets of tables, although the bridges between the two had been broken since the government had forcibly evicted the hunger strikers.

Nevertheless, on the same morning as the Forum's meeting, the news that the Association had opened its doors to representatives of the former communist party and would put itself at the head of the Forum reached the PD office and from there went to the Presidency, the government, and the State television. Berisha only responded publicly the next day, after the Platform appeared in the newspaper. He announced with scorn that he didn't recognize the Forum and he expressed ironic sympathy for the political parties who were reduced to seeking shelter under the umbrella of an association. It was the kind of response that expressed the contempt of the strong for the weak and disdain for a civil society that was only now taking root in the country

As if to reinforce Berisha's rejection of any kind of agreement, more and more gangs of armed civilians roamed at night, intimidating journalists, opposition leaders, and any opponents of the government. A band of masked men assaulted the young socialist deputy Ndre Legisi as he left his home and beat him with knuckledusters. Abused and humiliated, punched in the head and beaten all over his body, he ended up unconscious in hospital, in a worse state that Rama.

Every day it grew clearer that for Berisha the use of force was the only way of solving the crisis. He strove to conceal this behind repeated optimistic statements to the national and Western press. 'Everything is under control... repayment of the money has begun.' The Albanian police have acted in a manner truly worthy of a democratic society.' 'Albanian democracy has made great progress.'

In an interview with *Le Monde* at the beginning of February, Berisha was asked about the people demonstrating against the government. He separated them into two kinds, 'Some are fanatical ex-communists, and others are people who made mistakes in investing their money and do not have the courage to shoulder the responsibility themselves...' He even asserted without batting an eyelid that the bankrupt pyramids had been bitter opponents of the PD.

The Forum met every day in Kurt's office. Meidani chain-smoked and Gumeni sucked a pipe, and it seemed to Qorri that the cigarette smoke of Bar West had been wafted to this office and had settled there. These meetings felt almost clandestine. There was no heating and they sat in their overcoats, but their political nerve was strong. Every day they issued statements denouncing Berisha's lies and protesting that they were up against organized violence, that the State was encouraging gangs to spread fear and panic and that the attacks on Edi Rama and Ndre Legisi were plain evidence of the State's policy of terror because the State had made no effort either to condemn these acts or to find the culprits.

Over and over again they appealed to members of the armed forces, the judiciary, the State-controlled media, and the civil service to dissociate themselves from the instigators and perpetrators of state violence before it was too late. They insisted on the release of the SHIK, the courts, and the police from political control. They asked the European Union, the Council of Europe, and the U.S. Government to send urgently a commission to verify the state of human rights.

In their quest for allies and supporters they even drafted a letter addressed to three Albanians who lived abroad and were unconnected to one another: Leka Zogu, King Zog's son and the pretender to the throne; the nationalist Abaz Ermenji, the representative of the National Front Party created during World War II, whose leaders were scattered throughout Europe; and Rexhep Qosja as a representative of Kosovo. The letter explained what the Forum stood for, and continued, 'We invite you to join our discussion where your voice will be heard with special respect.' Ultimately this letter was not sent because events moved too fast. The first major disturbances had begun in Vlora.

PART TWO

Chapter VIII

Vlora

At whatever time of year Qorri visited Vlora, he seemed to be
seeing it for the first time. Human beings, he thought when he looked
at the bay, are granted a sense of awe in the presence of beauty which
makes up for their inability to account for such astounding caprices of
nature. How could nature be so generous as to display all its beauties
here in one place? What made possible such a delicate yet imposing
juxtaposition of sea and mountains? The peninsula of Karaburun
descended to the water like an extension of these mountains, and the
island of Sazan was an outpost of them, protecting the bay so tenderly
from the open sea and at the same time creating the magnificent
harbour that emphasized the breadth of the sea and gave the bay
something of both the energy of the open water and the smooth and
hospitable tranquillity of a lake.

With the calm beauty of Vlora in his mind, Qorri found it
hard to imagine the kind of livelihood the bay had provided since the
fall of communism. The whole country talked about it. The city of
Vlora, which lay at Albania's closest point to Italy, lived off the traffic
of drugs and human beings.

Under the dictatorship, one part of the city had expanded in
the ugly functional style of communism, but the remaining part along
the shore of the bay had survived virtually untouched. The Karaburun
peninsula and the island of Sazan were military bases. Until the 1960s,

the largest Soviet base in the Mediterranean had been situated there, but after relations were broken off the Soviet fleet had left - cruisers, submarines and all. Karburun and Sazan remained quiet backwaters as military areas, while the city had only the port and a few small fishing boats, and no tourism that might bring development. So in the first years after communism, the shores of the bay remained as unblemished as in classical times. The city's sophisticated inhabitants began to imagine the bay, one of the most picturesque in the Mediterranean, filling with yachts and tourist boats with multicoloured sails. But before the sailing boats arrived, or perhaps as their harbingers, there appeared a kind of craft that the residents of the city had never seen before. These were speedboats with what resembled two torpedoes on each side and a powerful motor at the stern. During the day they roared back and forth, showing off their capacity along the shallow shores of the bay and racing each other, watched by the curious townspeople. But at night they had work to do, transporting human beings and drugs to Italy.

Trafficking soon became the main business of the people of post-communist Vlora. They considered it totally above board, a job like any other, which required among other things, skill in duping the Italians. The owners of the boats were well known, as were their points of departure, schedules, and tariffs. Sheltered to the west by Sazan Island and to the south by the long Karaburun peninsula, the bay of Vlora was both protected from the winds and hidden from view. But it was less its sheltered position than its proximity to Italy that made Vlora not a magnet for tourists but a hub of what the West called the 'black economy'. In Albania, this was considered merely a form of livelihood, one of the few opportunities to survive in the European market.

The trafficking and the corruption in the port's customs offices, where goods entered from the West, led to an explosion of crime and also to the accumulation of big money in Vlora. After

Tirana, it was Vlora that had the most powerful financial pyramids, the largest of which was Gjallica. Some said that this firm took its name from a river near Vlora, but others were sure that it was christened after Mount Gjallica near Kukës, the birthplace of one of its proprietors. The two proprietors were rumoured to be former *Sigurimi* officers who had nevertheless given strong financial backing to the PD in the last elections. A large proportion of the trafficking bosses and others engaged in this trade had invested their money in Gjallica. This business required large numbers of people. There were the middlemen who brought together customers and traffickers and struck deals between them, drivers who transported refugees and prostitutes to Vlora, keepers of hotels and motels who put them up for one or two nights, and the young men who worked the boats. There were also officials and the police who were bribed to turn a blind eye to these activities. Trafficking became an entire industry.

Vlora, being so close to Italy and Greece, also had large numbers of migrant workers who had sent home large sums and invested them in Gjallica.

The city by the Mediterranean seethed with activity. Bars and restaurants were under construction by the beach, and luxury villas and mansions invaded the hills behind the city. Foreign journalists came, stayed two or three days, and described Vlora as a miracle of the new Albanian capitalism.

***

There had been rumours that Gjallica, the country's largest finance house after VEFA, was in trouble. At the beginning of February 1997, it declared bankruptcy. The incredulous people of Vlora heard the report on the State television's evening news and gathered the next morning in front of the shuttered offices where they had deposited their money.

It seems probable that they became a collective entity at the moment when a messenger brought the news that one of the co-presidents of Gjallica had fled abroad. A single vivifying current seemed to pass through the amorphous mass of individuals who stood outside the Gjallica office preoccupied with their own affairs, and transformed them into a single creature with a head, a body, and a soul. They waited in vain for several hours. Within two days their numbers grew to thousands. This vast throng occupied Flag Square, which was dominated by the monument to Albania's declaration of independence in this same city in 1912. 'We want our money' was the chant that united this swarm of people, proof that enormous sums had been poured into this pyramid. They demanded to speak to a representative of the government. In Tirana, Berisha's police had crushed a demonstration of this kind as soon as it started. But Vlora did not have sufficient police to confront such a crowd.

The people of Vlora protested freely for several days. Their numbers swelled. They grew angrier as their hopes of recovering their money faded and the government remained silent.

On 5th February, the government at last decided to act. Large numbers of police were despatched from Tirana with orders to disperse the protesters. Yet the threatening crowds still grew and spread to two other nearby towns, Fier and Lushnja, where the anger of many 'creditors' of another pyramid boiled over after that firm closed its offices.

That afternoon, an appalled mass of protesters found themselves facing innumerable ranks of policemen equipped with shields, helmets, and black rubber truncheons. Still the demonstrators' front line advanced. The police even had orders to shoot without hesitation. A shiver ran through the crowd when the first gunshots were heard. The front line stood still in confusion, and after a brief resistance scattered. But the harm had been done. A bullet, from who knew what weapon, had struck the 30-year-old demonstrator, Artur

Rustemi, in the spine and killed him on the spot.

The news of the killing of Rustemi spread that evening throughout the country and even abroad. The police claimed that they had fired in the air. But meanwhile it was learned that several people had been wounded that day. That night Vlora dressed in mourning.

Artur Rustemi's funeral the next day turned into a frightening demonstration of strength. The entire city performed the funeral rites, as if transformed into a house of mourning. The coffin was placed on top of a black Mercedes with a large photograph of the victim in front. The route to the cemetery was designed to pass along the main boulevard and through Flag Square. Behind the Mercedes walked 40,000 people holding national flags, chanting rhythmic slogans that Karaburun seemed to echo back at twice the volume, 'Berisha killed him,' 'Revenge is ours, ' 'Down with dictatorship,' 'Berisha killed him,' 'Revenge is ours, ' 'Down with dictatorship.'

At one point the entire cortege stopped and fell silent. The moment for the keening women had come. The lament of the women wailing over the coffin washed in waves over the limitless sea of silent people. The lament sowed hatred and the longing for revenge. It was an ill omen. After the women had finished, the throng set off again, howling even more loudly, 'Berisha killed him,' 'Revenge is ours,' 'Down with dictatorship.'

***

The news of the demonstration, the murder, and the funeral reached Tirana in two totally different versions. Albanian television was very sparing with its images and relied on reports read by the announcer, who also read out a government statement blaming the demonstrators and calling for all those who had caused disturbances to be punished. But on Euronews and the Italian channels, people saw the endless crowds and the coffin on top of the Mercedes, and heard the terrifying keening of the women. They also heard the slogans. These scenes fuelled the anger of the humiliated demonstrators of Tirana and gave them courage.

The Forum met the next day in the Association's offices. With Rustemi's murder the crisis had entered a new and more acute phase. The hope that the government would surrender without violence was giving way to a fear that the situation would slide out of control. But no one doubted that the Forum must support the demonstrators, especially as Berisha was exaggerating the danger of destabilization in order to claim the right to use force. The Forum's statement drafted at this meeting described Rustemi's murder as an act of state terror intended to scare the demonstrators. It demanded the release of the innocent people who had been arrested and appealed to the population to continue their civil resistance through peaceful protests, even if that meant calling a general strike. It also appealed to the police and army to keep order and protect public buildings and not to strike at their brothers and sisters who were demonstrating peacefully.

In order to ease the tensions, Gumeni proposed appealing to demonstrators to hold flowers in their hands instead of stones. This might paralyse the police. The Forum sent an application to the police for a peaceful protest gathering in Scanderbeg Square and an invitation to Sali Berisha, which read, 'The Forum for Democracy, representing eleven opposition parties, insists that dialogue must begin as soon as possible and asks you to meet its representatives, as a sign of goodwill.'

This invitation to dialogue, like the slogan 'flowers instead of stones,' encapsulated the contradictions of the situation. The Forum was sure that Berisha could not be toppled except by force, because he had already chosen violence to crush the movement against him, but still it appealed to people to confront the guns and rubber truncheons with flowers in their hands. Could any policy of peaceful resistance be successful in a country that had just emerged from 50 years of a cult of violence and the dictatorship of brute force? It was a tall order.

Berisha sent no reply to the request for a meeting. The police refused permission for a peaceful demonstration in Scanderbeg Square.

Chapter IX

Arrest

From Fatos Qorri's Diary
Saturday 8th February

We decided this time to do all we could to occupy Scanderbeg Square. We set a meeting place at the Catholic church on Kavaja Street, a long way from my home on foot. From Kindergarten No. 19, I had first to take Qemal Stafa Street and then cross Scanderbeg Square before reaching Kavaja Street.

At the junction at the end of Qemal Stafa Street leading to the square, I came up against police patrols that were stopping any groups of more than three people and turning them back. They let me pass, but I could not tell if this was because they recognized me or because I was alone. When I came out by the Tirana Hotel I saw that the square was unusually deserted. This emptiness at midday was frightening, as if the city's life had stopped. I did not walk straight across, which would have drawn attention to myself as the only human being in this vast space. It looked as if the police were planning on guarding it and keeping it vacant all day. I skirted round the edge, passing in front of the Tirana Hotel, the National Museum, and the square separating Durrës Street from Kavaja Street, where Hoxha's monument had once stood. Where Kavaja Street joined the square, several lines of policemen were preventing anyone entering the square. They did not stop me because I was coming out of the cordoned area. On the way to the church I saw that the alleys off Kavaja Street were crowded with people who were scared to come out on the main street because of the heavy police patrols. It seemed that the State had mustered all the forces at its command to prevent people reaching the main square. The cordon was like a tight band squeezing the city's heart, depriving it of its lifeblood. The sight suggested a world without people: the ultimate dream of dictators.

This square had acquired a symbolic meaning on 20th February 1991, when the demonstrators at the students' campus shouted 'To the square!' and took possession of it in spite of the dogs and tear gas of the police. Then came the event that marked the end of the regime: the dictator's statue was toppled. It was this spectre of occupation and overthrow that scared Berisha. He would not allow his opponents to take the square at any price.

Before reaching the church, I met the Forum leaders who were just setting off to occupy the square. I joined Kurt, Gumeni, Meidani, Kalakulla, Petrit Ishmi and many others on the central reservation down the middle of Kavaja Street. How far would we get? We were exposed to attacks from all directions. We kept our eyes peeled and each of us tried to keep calm in his own way. People emerged from the side streets as we passed and followed us, filling the roadway. If this had gone on, Kavaja Street would have turned into a human river pouring uncontrollably into Scanderbeg Square.

But we had not walked more than 200 metres before three blue police minibuses came out of the street that ran diagonally in front of us and blocked our way. Several groups of police leaped out, led by an officer who looked very young to have such a great belly. 'Paulin Sterkaj,' said someone, 'chief of the Specials.' At the moment of confrontation, both sides froze. Sterkaj apparently had orders not to let us pass that point. He stood in front of us and ordered us to turn back. 'We'll keep going,' someone replied. The police were apparently waiting for the first opposition before they went into action. Pairs of policemen instantly gripped us by the arms and bundled us into the first minibus.

From inside the bus I watched what was happening. A group of plain-clothes men, their faces savagely distorted, were beating up Kastriot Islami, the former parliamentary leader of the Socialists. This was no doubt their revenge for his statement a long time ago about breaking the Democrats' heads. These plain-clothes men are the most frightening and dangerous of all, because you couldn't tell if they were police or paramilitary gangs. On the opposite pavement 'normal' police hurled themselves against the street vendors, throwing their stalls and goods in the air. Our minibus set off.

At the second turning I realized they were taking us to the Tirana police headquarters, the same place where twenty-three years ago I had signed the document of my arrest that led me through countless prisons cells. History was repeating itself. Was this again a frightening departure into the unknown?

Perhaps because of this memory, I expected us to be separated and sent to dark solitary cells in Tirana prison. But they put us all together in a kind of corridor on the first floor, apparently a public waiting area.

This corridor and the evident nervousness of the police who received us there were somehow reassuring. Most of the officers were veteran policemen who did not seem happy to see us there. Some were clearly bewildered, and became even more confused when after about fifteen minutes other policemen brought in Kastriot Islami, who was howling due to the bloody wounds to his head and face

We did not know what they intended to do with us. None of the policemen gave any explanation. Gradually it dawned on us that that they meant merely to keep us there until after two o'clock, when we had scheduled our protest to finish.

We were relieved not to be spending a night in the cells. Now I knew there was no going back to the time of Enver Hoxha. But even this relief set in motion a fear of a different kind. They could not put us in prison, but were we now less safe than ever outside? The State could no longer imprison and shoot its opponents by legal means, but was there now a new danger of 'accidentally' being murdered?

Tirana was no longer as quiet as when they brought us in. In our absence people had still responded to the call for protests. Police cars coursed up and down Kavaja Street, where the pressure of the crowds to enter Scanderbeg Square had been greatest. Later they had arrested other people trying to reach the square from Myslim Shyri, parallel to Kavaja Street. Where this street came out near the Appeal Court, there had been an unpleasant confrontation between a large crowd of women and the police, who had pushed them as far away from the centre as possible into the villas of the former leaders' block. People had also gathered round the Shallvare apartments and in the afternoon protests had broken out at the Central Post Office. Police with helmets and rubber truncheons had used force to prevent the crowds from reaching the square.

Tirana became calmer at about one thirty or two o'clock in the afternoon, when Kurt, Petrit Ishmi, and I were released. They started with us, I thought, because we were former political prisoners and the anti-communist government wanted to show that it retained respect for us. But soon we realized that respect had nothing to do with it, because the car set off without asking us where we wanted to go.

'Where are you taking us?' I asked the driver.

'To the Socialists' HQ.'

'Why should we go there? Take us to the Prisoners' Association,' Kurt said to him.

'I have orders to take you where I said,' the driver retorted.

It was a short distance from the Tirana police headquarters to the Socialist Party. The car stopped outside the door, which was locked. Scanderbeg Square was visible from there, just as deserted as it had been that morning. We got out of the car and set off on foot towards the Association's headquarters, which was not far. But we had not gone twenty yards before a character appeared with a television camera on his shoulder and the second correspondent of Voice of America put a microphone in front of us and asked us what had happened. The cameraman, whose channel we could not identify, filmed us as we spoke. We walked a short distance, with one of them asking us questions and the other filming, and then they went away.

We crossed the empty square and turned into Elbasan Street, which passes in front of the headquarters of the Democratic Party. As we drew near, a 4x4 drew up beside us. We turned our heads instinctively to see why. The driver, a man of about thirty-five with short hair and a moustache, barked at Kurt who was closest to him.

'We'll fuck your mothers! We'll fuck your sisters! Arseholes!'

Was this some kind of ambush? I looked round to see what was happening nearby. Kurt retorted, 'Get lost, you filthy scab!'

'You wait and see!' said the man with the moustache. He revved the 4x4 and left us behind.

The car had no license plate. It must have belonged to the semi-legal fleet supposedly shared by the Interior Ministry and the SHIK.

***

At eight o'clock I turned on the evening news to see how the State television would describe the day's events. Our abortive rally was the lead story. The usual announcer said that, reportedly, the Forum for Democracy had appealed to the people of Tirana to take to the square in a protest gathering. Meanwhile the screen showed the eerily empty Scanderbeg Square that I had seen that morning and again at two o'clock. The announcer went on, 'See how the people of Tirana's responded to this appeal. The only people near the square are

Kurt Kola and Fatos Qorri, taking a stroll round the Socialist Party headquarters.' This was the film shot by the cameraman escorting the Voice of America correspondent. So this was why they had taken us out of the police station first and dropped us by the Socialist Party building.

Chapter X

Foresti

After the skirmishes between the demonstrators and police at Vlora and Artur Rustemi's murder, events became even more unpredictable. Berisha had on his side the police, the army, Albanian Television, and the entire psychology of fear inherited from fifty years of dictatorship, yet the support on which he had built his power was slipping away every day and his future looked increasingly uncertain. Would he stand firm or was he already tottering? One thing was sure: it would be hard to bring Berisha down, and hard for the Forum to rise to its own feet, without a helping hand from the West.

So for the Forum, it was just as important to win Western support as it was to encourage protests. Berisha too needed Western support, and to suppress these same protests. For centuries the Albanians, weak themselves and struggling for their survival, had been awed by the power of the West. The West was now the shrine at which Albania's politicians worshipped. They longed for the West's blessing and feared its excommunication. They also knew well that the West's greatest worry was any threat to peace and stability in the region. And so both sides, in addition to force, used the rhetoric of peaceful solutions and dialogue. This sort of Byzantine cunning had worked well under communism. Berisha, although his actions ratcheted up the conflict every day, spoke incessantly about the need for calm and stability. The Forum knew that it had no hope of success without instigating protests, but still harped on about 'dialogue,' 'discussion', 'tolerance' and 'consensus'.

Meanwhile, the needle on the West's dial was still not twitching in the direction the Forum hoped. The embassies were with Berisha. In the wake of the Yugoslav wars, regional stability counted for more than human rights. The equilibrium was delicate. The destabilization of Albania could upset the delicate balance in Serbia and Macedonia, where Albanian separatist movements were ready to explode.

The most active member of the diplomatic corps was Italian Ambassador Foresti, a short man, always elegantly dressed, and with a sensitive but animated expression. His fine-boned face was adorned with a dapper, slightly greying moustache that seemed to maintain the tension between the fragility of his diminutive frame and the incessant energy he radiated through his eyes and gestures.

The West considered that it had left Albania in Italy's care. Italy had taken the initiative to intervene with the Pelican aid operation immediately after the fall of communism. Italian investments in Albania were also the largest. Foresti had many ties not only with political leaders, but also with business and the emerging Albanian civil society. He had travelled around the country more than anyone else. It was rumoured that he had a collection of more than 300 Albanian socialist-realist paintings, given as gifts by the artists or bought at knockdown prices. He appeared frequently on Albanian television and in the press, giving advice in interviews. Some called him the State's *eminence grise,* and he enjoyed almost the authority and privileges of a governor. Berisha, who adamantly refused to sit down and talk to the opposition, found it very difficult to go against this man's advice.

Foresti had good reasons for his explicit support of the government. He considered its years of work as his own achievement. Thanks to his political ties, many Italians had invested in the country. But above all, he supported the government because this was in the Italian interest. Any destabilization of Albania, such as the opposition's attempts to unseat Berisha seemed to entail, could create a new wave of refugees heading for Italy. So Foresti stated openly that he would not talk to the opposition. Its leaders were not invited to receptions he hosted, and to other diplomats and foreign journalists he reviled the Forum as a *revanche* of the communists.

Foresti was also known to be the best friend of American ambassador Marisa Lino, who had been appointed shortly before the crisis of the pyramid schemes. Lino was also of Italian origin. As dean of the diplomatic corps, Foresti had introduced her to the intricacies of Albanian life.

But it seemed that it was more that the worry of destabilization that made Western diplomats resistant to movements for change in Albania. Deep down, the anxiety of people like Foresti about the country's stability involved a contempt for the backwardness of Albanian society. They were politically correct in their interviews with the Albanian media, but in private asked one another if the country were really ready for democracy.

Ambassadors, when they were appointed to Albania, imagined that their task would be merely to look after the interests of their own states in proper diplomatic fashion, to keep low profiles, and show respect for Albania and its people. But as soon as they landed at Rinas Airport, they found themselves the focus of extraordinary attention. The arrival of a new Western ambassador was the leading item on the evening news and on the front page of the papers. The astonished ambassadors ascribed the local people's exaggerated goodwill to the role of the West in the fall of the Berlin Wall or the quantities of cash they were supposed to bring with them. But they soon realized that there was more to it than this. It was not long before they were receiving invitations to heart-to-heart meetings with politicians, at which they learned that these politicians loathed one another and saw it as their duty to apprise the ambassador of their rival's mendacity. Meanwhile waiting journalists interpreted even the ambassador's routine engagements according to the interests of their own parties. So, like it or not, the ambassadors found themselves front-page news, enlisted as referees in the Albanians' power struggles. Some hesitated to play the part asked of them, but before long, and often out of necessity rather than any enjoyment of their almost untrammelled powers, the ambassadors accepted this role.

But Foresti took a special pleasure in his function, convinced that the Albanians needed him as a mentor; someone stronger and more mature than themselves. Churchill once said that the Italians were a puerile people in need of a fatherly hand. It was now the Italians' turn to apply this principle to the Albanians, who were still in a state of infancy, and moreover had been horribly abused under communism. Foresti, whenever he tried to resolve conflict among them, could sense the anxiety that was the dictatorship's traumatic legacy. Who was better placed than the Italians to help the Albanians overcome this trauma? Could they be left to find their own way, as some Westerners imagined? No, this would be a very dangerous experiment. Isolated from the world, had they not constructed the most monstrous communist regime in Europe? Moreover, their long-term and short-term interests rarely coincided, especially at times of political crisis. If these grown-up children were left to their group therapy without supervision, they would destabilize the region and become a haven for Islamist terrorists. The interests of the West demanded that Italy should take charge and become the arbitrator the Albanians so desperately needed.

***

Qorri, Kurt Kola, and Daut Gumeni were invited to visit the Austrian Embassy in those first days of February. For Qorri, visits to embassies were like trips to islands of another world within his own city. Everything there was different and better, just like in the West, from the furniture to the central heating that was so rare in Tirana. This made him withdrawn and reticent. Moreover, at some embassies he had met with a frosty reception, even colder than the usual diplomatic formality required. He was convinced that there was an element of disdain in Foresti's icy hand.

The Austrian ambassador and his secretary received them. Qorri looked at their suits, ties, and stiff collars, and could not help

81

glancing at their own clothes. Kurt was wearing a dark grey suit whose trousers were obviously more worn than the jacket. Gumeni's blue double-breasted suit was distinctly old-fashioned, and he himself was in casual clothes hardly appropriate for an embassy.

The diplomats' expression of polite boredom remained unchanged throughout the meeting. No smile or spontaneous gesture ever conveyed the slightest emotion. The representatives of the Forum talked about the police violence, the arrests, Berisha's authoritarian character, the urgent need for intervention in this worsening crisis, and the government of professionals that would have to prepare for new elections. They were met with piercing, suspicious looks and the first question fell on them like a cold shower: 'But what did the opposition do to warn people against the pyramids?' The subtext was that the opposition shared the responsibility for the crisis and should work together with the government to resolve it instead of inciting people to protests. The representatives of the Forum talked about the manipulation of the elections the previous year, which was one of the reasons people were so angry, but the ambassador seemed barely able to recall these events of only seven months ago.

'I don't think we saw protests then. It seems that people are protesting about their money, not their freedom, doesn't it?'

Only when they rose to leave were they granted one little smile.

A similar scene was enacted in the American ambassador's office a few days later. Yet they were pleased that Lino had finally invited them. They waited in an anteroom until the door of her office opened and found themselves in front of a woman in her fifties, her face familiar from television. She was friendlier than the Austrians, and asked them into her warm office. This made the representatives of the Forum more forthcoming. Qorri sat down, casting his eyes round the American landscapes hung on the walls.

This time they had brought with them Blendi Gonxhja who

was trying to take on the role of the Forum's secretary and interpreter. In fact, Gonxhja had come with them because he was close to the Americans and kept company with Charles Walsh, the head of USAID, whose office was in the former Enver Hoxha Museum. However, the ambassador seemed to take a dislike to this smiling lad with his slightly vampiric protruding teeth, who interpreted Kurt and Daut into halting English. Strangely, when Gonxhja mentioned Charles, the ambassador's expression became even colder.

Qorri's frequent contacts with foreign journalists had improved his English. The well-worn phrases to describe the crisis and the Forum's proposals for solving it now came to him instinctively. Lino asked more questions than the Austrians, and asked the three former prisoners about their long years in gaol. Unlike the Austrians, she also gave them some advice, 'The U.S. Government is following events with concern, because this country has suffered a lot of violence and conflict. So dialogue is very important.' But the Forum sensed that she was on the side of their opponents. They expected her face to brighten when Gonxhja said that some American friends were preparing a meeting for Qorri in the United States with Richard Schifter, Clinton's adviser, but Lino expressed no enthusiasm. On the contrary, she coldly advised Qorri also to meet the State Department's desk officer for Albania.

This discouraging atmosphere persisted even when Lino offered her hand in farewell. When they left the warm rooms of the embassy, they seemed to feel even more strongly the keen chill of that Tirana February. They set off for the Association's unheated office, casting doubtful glances at each other.

That evening, as he lay back staring at the wall of his home in the Kindergarten, Qorri tried to work out why the American ambassador had been so unresponsive. She had been particularly frosty when Charles Walsh of USAID was mentioned. Walsh was working to arrange Qorri's meeting with Schifter. He had been the first foreigner who had tried, a few months ago, to convey to the local press the serious danger posed by the pyramids. Charles was very possibly the CIA's man in Albania, and this made Lino's coldness even more extraordinary. Did Foresti exert so much influence over her? Why did she disapprove of his prospective meeting with Schifter, and recommend he should also meet the State Department desk officer? It must be because the latter had direct contact with the embassy and received his information from Lino. Obviously this information did not suggest that Albania was going in the same direction as Walsh of the CIA might be reporting. Perhaps, thought Qorri, this was not simply the influence of Foresti, but of American lobby groups. Perhaps all this was his own paranoia. Perhaps the ambassador had nothing against the Forum. Diplomats seemed to cultivate a professional opacity. They often started a conversation with the purpose of confirming information obtained from other sources, and did not produce their own interpretations. Even when they might be aware of contradictions, they rarely expressed them. They represented their countries, and their need to watch what they said in public inhibited their spontaneity. But no, Lino was obviously not well disposed to them. Qorri recalled a more forthright German diplomat who had said to him. 'I talk with you Albanians and listen to what you say but I never totally understand what goes on in your country. For me, there is always a wall behind you that I can't see beyond. I don't know what you do behind that wall.' 'It's the same for us,' Qorri had replied, 'We don't know what ambassadors say after they close the embassy gates and report back to their governments.'

As these thoughts ran through his mind, his eyes wandered to a patch of plaster like a fragment of a map, which he tried to approximate to a familiar continent. But it insisted on retaining its own unique form.

Chapter XI

The Rogner Hotel

Foreign journalists stayed at the Rogner, the first private hotel built in Tirana after the fall of communism. It occupied a site in a former park on the main Tirana boulevard, between the Prime Minister's Office, built by the Italians, and the Palace of Congresses, built by the dictator. The people of Tirana protested that it usurped one of the city's prettiest parks, and complained that whereas the two buildings on either side were built of costly marble, the Rogner was an ordinary construction covered in painted stucco. But the Austrian builders surrounded the hotel with greenery and soon it blended into the rest of the boulevard. There was no other hotel where foreigners could find familiar comforts. But at $200 a night it was also the capital's most expensive.

The Rogner's spacious lobby was decorated with rustic wood-carving, in stylized reference to both Albanian and Austrian traditions. Behind the bar, two corridors led to the rooms where press conferences were held. In those days, both the lobby and the conference rooms were always crowded. The Forum too sometimes held its press conferences at the Rogner. That morning Room A was packed tight with the Italian, German, and American press, but there were also plenty of Greek, British, Scandinavian, and Spanish journalists covering Eastern Europe. The well-known correspondents of Euronews, Reuters, AFP, the BBC, and many Albanian journalists were also present following the events at Vlora and the arrest of the Forum leaders in Tirana.

Kurt, Daut, and Qorri took their seats and the journalists positioned their microphones on the table in front of them.

Kurt began by reading a statement that the three of them had drafted late the previous evening in Kindergarten No. 19. They called on people not to give up their peaceful demonstrations every day between twelve and two o'clock. Bearing in mind the prohibition of assemblies, they suggested alternative forms of peaceful and symbolic protest, with the slogan 'flowers instead of stones'.

They called on people to turn off the State television, which was spreading hatred and disinformation. They appealed to members of parliament to be aware of their responsibilities. They asked the police to protect public buildings, keep the peace, and not to strike their suffering brothers and sisters but to protect them from the real terrorists who were roaming freely on the city streets in cars without license plates.

Questions followed. What would the Forum for Democracy do next? What did they predict happening in Albania? What did its leaders have to say about their arrest the previous day? Were they in touch with the demonstrators in Vlora? What plan did they have to recover the money lost in the pyramids?

The question about the money was the most sensitive of all. Many people were demonstrating in the hope that the Forum would return them their money. Kurt replied that this was not the task of the Forum, but of the government of professionals they were proposing.

A Scandinavian journalist with flaming red hair asked Qorri to explain the meaning of the slogan 'flowers instead of stones' when the government was using truncheons.

Qorri took this question as a provocation, and was unable to reply as he would have wished. It was hard to explain to a Scandinavian that this was a Byzantine ploy involving the encrypted subtexts essential to any understanding of Albanian politics, and whose effect indeed depended on these meanings remaining encoded. He could not say that one reason for choosing this slogan was fear of being accused of inciting violence and ending up at the bottom of a ravine, and another was caution lest foreigners should gain the impression that they posed a danger to regional stability The slogan was designed to make it increasingly possible for people to come out in public, and also to paralyse the police. In his reply, Qorri took refuge in contrasting the brutality of the government with the peacefulness of their own protests. The Forum was too responsible to respond to the government with its own kind of violence.

At the end a British journalist came up and asked for an in-depth personal interview. Qorri accepted with pleasure, for with Western journalists he often reached a level of understanding impossible with diplomats. Journalists had a professional instinct for major events and radical positions, and spoke their minds in conversations, unlike diplomats, who were like answering machines registering grievances.

Qorri set an appointment for noon at Bar West. Meanwhile, there would be a brief meeting at the Association to decide what action to take the next day. Qorri's bike route from the Rogner to the Association led along the Milky Way, where he saw Noel's door, closed as usual at that time. It was extraordinary that he had not been there since the night when Rama was attacked. Life had changed. Every moment of his life was now dedicated to this cause that had been lying in wait for him. Even a few days before, he could not have imagined staying away from Noel's for so long.

Chapter XII

Thugs

Bar West was more crowded than ever with opposition journalists and politicians. It was cold: there was no electricity, and the bar was warmed only by the breath of its many customers. As he waited for the British journalist, Qorri sat alone behind a glass partition in the centre of the café near the bar, where it was a little warmer.

The leaders of the Democratic Alliance were deep in conversation at a table to the right of the door in the main body of the café.

The British journalist arrived on time. He was a smiling, affable man in his fifties with thinning hair combed to one side. Before launching into his questions, he introduced himself, said he was trying to understand what was happening in Albania, and asked Qorri about his life. When Qorri mentioned his time in prison, he stopped him and asked more questions about the dictatorship.

They were still talking about prison when a group of seven or eight men dressed in the military camouflage of the rapid intervention forces burst through the door. They were all tall, with protruding chests, revolvers visible at their backsides and truncheons hanging by their right thighs. They marched in with a challenging swagger and sat down in the main body of the bar, very close to Qorri and the British journalist, but separated from them by the glass partition.

'Come here, mate!' shouted one to the waiter, who hurried to take their order. They called for a full bottle of brandy, and the waiter scuttled off to serve them out of turn.

These men had not come for a cognac and a coffee, and an expectant silence fell. The psychological mechanism was set in motion whereby the weak run for cover and lie low in the hope that the strong will not bother them. This merely emboldened the hoodlums to raise their voices even louder.

The British journalist, perhaps because he felt the tension even more than Qorri, or because he saw Qorri was distracted, suggested they should move to the bar next door. They went out and sat down at an outside table at the neighbouring Marlboro where it was quieter. They were no more than twenty metres from the Bar West. With these paramilitary thugs before their eyes, it was easier for Qorri to explain that such louts were the true face of the regime. The journalist found this hard to grasp, and asked again about the historical background of communism.

While Qorri was talking about the dictator Enver Hoxha, a hideous noise erupted in the Bar West. There were shrieks and the crash of breaking chairs. Qorri and the journalist stood up to see what was happening and at that moment the gang of thugs strode out. One of them, apparently the ringleader, struck the picture window with the butt of his revolver, and there came the noise of splintering glass. Qorri instinctively followed this man with his eyes, but the journalist said in a voice of alarm, 'Don't look at them, don't look at them!' so Qorri stared at the journalist instead. The hoodlums headed for the opposite pavement and disappeared in the direction of the Interior Ministry, from where they had apparently come.

***

They found the customers of Bar West numbed, shocked, and humiliated. Neritan Ceka and Preç Zogaj had been the main targets. The thugs had quickly downed a glass each and then a second and a third, and then turned aggressively to the table of the Alliance leaders. As soon as they caught Ceka's eye, they said, 'Why are you looking at us?' 'I have no business with you,' Ceka had replied. But they jumped to their feet and went up to their table. Ceka asked them who they were. 'Stand up when you talk to us!' said their ringleader. Without waiting for Ceka to move he grabbed him by the collar and lifted him forcibly to his feet. He slapped him on the face and then sat him down again, lifted him and hit him again. There were protests from a nearby table, and two of the louts drew their pistols and threatened to put a bullet in the head of anybody who intervened. Then their ringleader slapped Zogaj and swept away the glasses on his table.

'We'll fuck your mothers!' was his parting shot to the bar in general, before he led out his henchmen and shattered the window with the butt of his gun.

Listening to the story, Qorri did not want to believe that nobody had dared stand up to this collective humiliation in the very centre of Tirana. But he understood perhaps better than anyone the paralysing effect of fear. As a prisoner he had experienced similar feelings of powerlessness in front of the thugs of state power. Now, as then, his mind was torn violently in two directions. On the one hand, this was a time when they should have turned on these villains and make those hands holding the guns shake, but on the other hand he understood very well that their fear, however demeaning, was deeply rooted in the instinct for survival. And so nothing had happened, and violence and intimidation had won the day.

The British journalist had vanished. But a foreign television crew was filming the broken glass, the visible evidence of the crime. Everybody watched the camera focus on the huge jagged hole in the window between the street and the café. The cameraman filmed with total silence around him. Was this hole big enough to express everything they wanted to say at that moment? As they stared, each person seemed to see in that hole a blow to his own conscience made by that steel revolver butt.

This was 9th February 1997.

Chapter XIII

Clashes in Vlora

The rebel city in the south kept alive the universal hope that the violence of the police would not triumph as it had done in the capital. Since the day of Artur Rustemi's funeral, the people of Vlora had been protesting unhindered in Flag Square. These massive gatherings were carried by Euronews, CNN, the BBC, and the Italian television stations that were watched throughout the country, and gave courage to protesters in other cities. This was the clearest example that the media were not merely reporting events but generating them.

So the government was determined to extinguish once and for all this smouldering hotbed of conflict. Unknown to the opposition in Tirana, early in the morning of the same day when Neritan Ceka was beaten up, the government had despatched large police forces to Vlora with instructions to quash the rebellion in the city.

On the afternoon of 9th February, the people of Vlora took to the streets in protest as they had done every day, but found themselves facing a police cordon of a kind never seen before. About five thousand policemen with helmets, plastic shields, and truncheons formed a solid wall at the entrance to Flag Square. They looked more like robots than people. It was clear that occupying the square would be the measure of victory or defeat, and the mass of protesters surged forward. At the first contact between the two front lines, the police went on the offensive. Their plastic shields were more aggressive weapons than their transparency suggested, and could be used to push and crush people. The plastic -clad robots kicked, threw tear gas grenades, and hit out wildly with their rubber truncheons until the demonstrators were forced back to their homes.

Rumours spread that there had been a lot of casualties, one fatal. But nothing could be verified. The wounded did not go to the hospital for fear of being identified.

The police had orders not to leave Vlora. On the next day, 10th February, some of the victors strutted about the city with the self-assurance of men who had established law and order, boasting that they had finally broken the back of the rebel city. It was the kind of day, as the saying goes, when even the sun becomes your enemy. But the victors did not know that during the night, many of the beaten and humiliated demonstrators had stayed awake, hatching their plan of revenge. Throughout the night, strange couriers had darted through the back streets of the city, weaving the fabric of this plan. Meanwhile, not a single motorboat left for Italy. While the police from Tirana swaggered round Flag Square, the lanes of Vlora filled with swarms of angry citizens who poured into the main streets leading to the square. Soon the streets were packed.

This time it was the police who were taken by surprise. The crowds they thought they had quelled the previous day surged towards them in fury. The protesters armed themselves with stones and with any solid object that came to hand. Some had guns. They wanted revenge for their humiliation of the previous day.

Cowed by a hail of stones from all directions, the police chiefs did not dare to give orders to shoot. Nor did they have time to receive any orders of this kind. They had to respond or retreat at once. There were shots into the air from among the crowd. The police decided to withdraw, but their retreat turned into a rout. They ran for cover where they could. This left the people of Vlore free to exercise their muscle against the few policemen who thought they could stand up to them, but who were soon puzzled to find themselves huddled under their plastic shields at the foot of a wall, warding off stones that flew at them from every direction. The crowd, determined to seize and disarm them, tightened its encirclement and pelted them with stones until they dropped their guns, helmets and shields to the ground in token of surrender. When they stood up with their hands held high, the protesters hurled themselves against them, as if to tear them to pieces. But they merely stripped them of their clothes and left them free to go, walking shamed and half-naked through the city. The crowds collected the uniforms, helmets and shields in a great pile and set fire to them in vindictive triumph. A cloud of smoke rose in the shape of a giant cypress tree. The children of Vlora who had taken part in the battle danced with joy.

Berisha's police coup in Vlora had failed.

The scene with the embattled police and the burning of their uniforms, plastic shields and helmets was filmed by CNN, the BBC, Euronews, and many of Europe's leading television channels. Fuller broadcasts showed burning police cars from Tirana on the streets of Vlora, and a procession of demonstrators holding candles who went to Artur Rustemi's house to tell his family that vengeance was theirs.

Chapter XIV

Prime Minister Meksi

After Vlora's victory over the police, the two neighbouring towns of Fier and Lushnja rose in revolt. In Fier, the protesters blocked the roads and burned police cars. In the evening, several thousand people headed to Vlora to join the rejoicing there. In Lushnja demonstrators occupied the main square and tried to set fire to the town hall.

Berisha himself did not react to this escalation of the violence. He passed the buck to Prime Minister Meksi, who announced at a news conference that the government was drafting a law to provide for a partial state of emergency. He claimed that the attacks on the police stations and public buildings in Vlora were not peaceful protests but conspiracies aimed at overthrowing the State, 'scenarios to destabilize Albania,' as he put it in an interview that day with Voice of America. The police were not equipped to put down plots of this kind with force. The army would have to intervene to bring cities under control where daily life had been brought to a halt and all the roads were blocked. 'This will prevent any escalation of the terror,' the prime minister declared.

Aleksandër Meksi had taken no part in politics in the time of communism; he had been a specialist in Byzantine history at the Institute for the Protection of Public Monuments. He first appeared on the platform when the Democratic Party was born, and with his spectacles, moustache, and bald egg-shaped head he stood out among the communist intellectuals who were prominent at these events. He looked like a member of the pre-war intelligentsia, a suspect class for the communists, and indeed his family origins lay there. He seemed a person of sensitivity and refinement, lacking Berisha's hunger for power, and certainly not a man of violence. Only after he became prime minister did the public learn that Meksi's biography had indeed been tainted in the eyes of the communists, but he had done his utmost to hide this, to the point that the only persecution he suffered was a delay in the approval of his party membership. When the regime fell, he was still a probationary member.

It was nothing new for an intellectual to apply for party membership, and it became it common after Enver Hoxha's death in 1985. Hoxha's successor, Ramiz Alia, was known to be more moderate and instead of persecuting intellectuals, had preferred to keep them close by enlisting them in the party. He knew that they did not believe in communist ideals, but made it clear that they could only advance their careers by joining the party. Hoxha had been suspicious of intellectuals to the point of paranoia, but Alia was ready to offer them this kind of deal. Qorri had been in prison during the last two decades of the regime, but his discovery of this trend led him to suspect that with the passage of time the intelligentsia had become even more morally degraded.

Nevertheless, the PD's opponents did not rank Prime Minister Meksi, the former probationary party member, on the same level as Berisha, the former party branch secretary. They nicknamed President Berisha 'the caveman'. He had emerged from the nowhere-land of his home province much earlier, in Hoxha's time, when a much higher degree of fanaticism was required. He never made any distinction between his personal ambitions and 'the ideals of the party'. His colleagues at the hospital recalled that as a party secretary in the 1970s he had torn the students' flared trousers and cut their long hair. Anecdotes circulated about his manoeuvres to ingratiate himself with the higher echelons of power. Hoxha's widow, whose arrest he demanded when he took his first step on the road to president, used to tell her friends how Berisha on one occasion wormed his way through the back door of Enver Hoxha's house, with the help of the children, and had shaken Hoxha's hand. Thereafter he never greeted anyone without saying,

'Enver Hoxha touched this hand.' How could this man suddenly turn into a rabid anti-communist? His opponents insisted that his ambition knew no moral restraint. His troglodytic energy had brought Berisha to the leadership of the anti-communist movement, in preference to moderate people like Meksi. Now as a fervent anti-communist, he still identified his personal ambitions with the ideals of the party he led.

Meksi's friends reported that when they visited him in the prime minister's office, he gestured to them to lower their voices because he was bugged by the SHIK. He had been appointed to this post, they said, because Sali Berisha saw in him the right person to give a more cultured look to his government, but also someone who would never escape from under his wing. And Meksi had been able to preserve his image as a tolerant intellectual. Berisha by contrast had come down from Albania's wildest mountain region of Tropoja where a fight to the death is part of a manly code of honour. But some also accused Meksi of being a subordinate who put up with the ridiculous, bullying behaviour of his boss for the sake of personal gain, a puppy who wagged his tail for big bones. They saw him as a repellent, cowardly, and shameless person, a greater evil than Berisha himself.

The small number of Meksi's friends who were still on speaking terms with both camps told the Forum that the Prime Minister was trying to play the last card left in his hand. By declaring a state of emergency, he remained Prime Minister. But Berisha had two cards to play. Firstly, through Meksi's statement he was threatening to use the army to suppress the revolt, but secondly, he was preparing to dismiss him to cool the temperature. The power in his hands seemed to give him the advantage in a game with its many imponderable factors.

***

The day after Meksi's statement, Qorri went to his nearest newspaper vendor. The papers were sold at a street corner, spread out on the pavement. A larger group of people than usual were staring despondently at the headlines, reading a selection before buying the paper of their choice. Print runs were higher than ever before, and *Koha Jonë* had reached a 100,000 copies. The names of the daily papers had become symbols of opposing political sides, and the headlines in huge fonts inflamed passions more than they conveyed information. Not since the fall of communism had the population of Albania been so glued to current events.

The newspapers all commented on the events in Vlora and predicted that the parliament would declare a state of emergency that afternoon.

Qorri usually cast an eye first at the pro-Berisha papers. 'Vlora heads for martial law' was the main headline of *Rilindja Demokratike*, the PD's newspaper. 'Interview with Prime Minister Meksi: Albania needs good governance not instability'. 'Citizens, avoid all acts of violence and terror!' 'Far-left leaders trample on freedom and break the law.' 'Yesterday at the Hotel Rogner -- Terrorist leaders call for further violence -- Forum declares war on the State.'

'Police assaulted, forty-six injured' was the headline of *Albania*, which continued on other pages with stories headed 'Battle of stones', 'Violence returns to Vlora', 'Vlora -- state of emergency', 'Forum for Democracy escalates situation', 'Forum Representatives Defend Police Assailants, Attacks on Police Stations'.

The Forum had the majority of the newspapers on its side, compensating to a degree for the entirely pro-Berisha State television.

'Albanian flag raised in Vlora' was the banner headline of *Koha Jonë*. 'Dictatorship Shoots to Kill in Vlora', 'Protests Continue in All the Streets of Vlora', 'Flags at Half-Mast on All Houses', 'Protesters Tie Black Bandannas Round their Heads', 'Opposition -- National Mourning, Meksi -- State of Emergency', 'This is a Crisis of Politics.'

***

Contrary to expectations, after two hours' debate the parliament voted against a state of emergency in Vlora. Parliamentary speaker Pjetër Arbnori said that the 'Albanian constitutional package' did not allow the government to declare a state of emergency in a single district. The rumour that relations between Berisha and Meksi had deteriorated turned out to be correct. It was clear that Berisha would jettison Meksi. But would that be enough? People like Meksi and the boss of Gjallica, who had been arrested a few days previously, were now small fry. Hatred now focused on Berisha and his immediate circle.

Chapter XV

From Fatos Qorri's Diary
Wednesday, 12th February

We gave another news conference at the Rogner today and explained again our position on the uprising in Vlora and why we are not condemning it. We appealed to people to express solidarity with Vlora and continue to protest between the hours of one and two o'clock.

Some pro-government newspapers insisted on asking what policy we have for the return of the money. That's why people have protested, they said. We repeated that this is outside the scope of our programme. People expect an end to the crisis and we say that the solution starts with the departure of the culprits from power. A government formed after early elections must decide what comes next.

One journalist persisted with a question laced with his own remarks. According to him, we were creating commotion not to solve the crisis but to exacerbate it until we could seize power. But if the crisis is prolonged, he said, the Albanians will lose more than they gain. It was difficult to counter this argument. There was no denying that both sides are motivated by a desire for power. But if only power is at stake, we would do better to stop our campaign, because for me it is not just about money or power. It is a question of freedom.

See what happened after our news conference.

After we finished at the Rogner, we went to the Association for our daily meeting. Close to midday, we were getting ready to go out and join the people when the caretaker came to tell us that police had arrived at the gate and had blocked the exit.

We went out into the yard. The iron gate was closed, and two policemen stood on guard to make sure it was not opened. A whole crowd of policemen hung around outside the railings. They had arrived in two blue minibuses that were parked a little further off. Among the police was a tall, striking figure in plain clothes with a short black-leather jacket. With his jutting chest and a growing belly that protruded outside the open zip of his jacket, he looked like one of the thugs who assaulted us in the Bar West. I had seen him before. Whether he worked for the police or the SHIK, he was clearly in charge of this operation. I had been told that he was a relative of Sali Berisha, some said a nephew, a character with irrational and frightening personal devotion to his patron, a mixture of bodyguard, strongman, and local patriot. Everybody said he had been the ringleader behind the assaults on Edi Rama and Ndre Legisi.

But besides these warders of our improvised prison, our guardian angels were also in attendance beyond the railings: several foreign journalists were there with video equipment. One came up to the railings as soon as he saw me. I went up and greeted him. He told me that he had seen large police forces on all the roads leading to the square, shoving, threatening and beating the people of Tirana. He wanted to know why, in my opinion, they were not allowing us to leave the building. Before I managed to reply, Berisha's strong man came up to us.

'This journalist wants to know why you have shut us up in here,' I said to him.

'We've locked you in for your own protection, in case anything happens to you,' he replied.

This answer struck us as ridiculous but at the same time significant. Once again, as at the police headquarters a few days before, I realized that the regime was incapable of responding to changed circumstances. On the one hand, it could not stop itself imitating the regime of Enver Hoxha, but on the other hand, it could not, for a thousand reasons, behave in exactly the same way. Ludicrous responses of this kind were the result of this dilemma. Who, under the old regime would have said, 'We're protecting our enemies' lives'? Hoxha's police would not have locked the gates, but would have broken them open even if they'd been locked, and we would have been dragged out, thrown into cars and put into cells, and we'd have ended up with death sentences. As for foreign journalists, Hoxha called them spies and didn't even allow them into the country. Berisha is imitating Hoxha, but is scared to use violence openly and is doing all he can to show the West what a democrat he is. Quite apart from the fact that he is a hostage to Western economic aid. It is as if the spectre of the dictatorship is trying to make an appearance, but evaporates in terror as soon as it sees the foreign journalists' cameras. Yet this amateurism could still lead to a tragic end. Perhaps the reply of Berisha's thug also concealed the threat that, if we go on like this, he and his friends might do us some harm.

These cameras help us maintain our courage. We know that Euronews will report what happens, as it did the demonstrations at Vlora and the attack on Ceka. These cameras put to flight the spectre of Hoxha, whose regime was so terrifying precisely because of the media blackout. They banish its ghost even from the stubborn skulls of these attacking louts, not just our own.

That is why this matter is not just about lost money or even lost power, but a threat to freedom.

They let us out after three hours, when the critical moment had passed and people had gone home for lunch.

I am writing these notes after finishing a press statement condemning the transformation of the Association's premises into a prison for the leaders of the Albanian opposition. I ended it by repeating our appeal for all Albanians wherever they are to persist in taking to the public squares from noon to two o'clock, and calling for the right to legitimate assembly.

Thursday, 13th February

This morning before entering the Association I sat down for a coffee by one of the kiosks in the park opposite. We didn't have any meeting planned, but we usually go there even when nothing is on.

As I sipped my coffee, a message came that something was happening in the building. I got up at once and went across the road. There were two police vans and an unusual crowd of plainclothes men who we now recognize as SHIK agents. As I drew nearer, I saw a crowd of people shouting in the courtyard where we were locked in yesterday. Somebody said they were political prisoners, supporters of the PD. They were complaining about the Association and its chairman Kurt Kola making common cause with the communists, their former persecutors. Some were holding placards. I noticed a correspondent of the State television, a PD militant, with a drooping moustache, talking angrily into his mobile phone and asking for cameras at once.

It did not seem to me a good idea to go in while this hostile crowd blocked the entrance. I was also curious to hear what they were saying. A grey-haired, former prisoner was making a speech reciting the crimes of the communists. Then the State-television cameras arrived. The crowd in the yard, as soon as the cameras focused on them, brandished their placards and shouted in chorus, 'Down with communism!' 'Down with Kurt Kola!' 'Long live the Democratic Party!' 'The Association is ours!' I went nearer to see if I knew any of the former prisoners who were protesting. The first person I saw was one of the most repulsive spies we had ever had in the prisons. It makes one both weep and laugh to see how these narks have found a refuge in the ruling party and have turned into the most radical anti-communists. Nor is it obvious that their hatred is simulated. I don't know what to say.

The former prisoners grew more savage with every impromptu speech. The fixed stare of the camera seemed to stoke their fury. Suddenly one of them shouted, 'Let's get them out of here, let's get them out!' I don't know if this was planned or not. In an instant half the crowd had stormed the steps. I didn't know who was inside: Kurt certainly. I heard muffled noises, and before long Kurt and Petrit Kalakulla emerged. The Democratic Party prisoners spat at them and punched them.

I turned to a policeman, 'Why are you standing here doing nothing? Can't you see, people are being beaten, this building is under attack?' I hadn't noticed that one of Berisha's hoodlums was standing close to me, the same one who had locked us in the day before. He came up to me and muttered insults as if to himself but loud enough for me to hear, 'We'll fuck your sister in the arse.' 'I don't have a sister,' I said, turning towards him, and felt a kick in the back of the knee. I saw I was surrounded. But one of the protesting former prisoners, who had evidently not expected this affair to go so far, intervened and said 'No, no, don't hit this person,' and escorted me to the opposite pavement. I didn't know what to do next. A journalist appeared, having recognized me from the previous day, and bundled me into his car.

***

This has been a heavy blow from an unexpected direction. Kurt, Daut, and I met a few hours later at Bar West. We felt totally powerless to respond. Our first idea was to appeal to powers stronger than Berisha, to the foreigners of which he was scared. I decided that we should go together to the U.S. Embassy with Shane Muda, the secretary of the Association.

I had already visited U.S. Ambassador Marisa Lino with Kurt, Daut, and Gonxhja a few days after the creation of the Forum. I remembered our chilly reception in her warm office.

The police in front of the embassy directed us to the steel gate at the back, which resembled the side entrance to a prison. We sent notice of our arrival and waited, and suddenly the goatee-bearded photographer of *Albania*, who was said to work also for the SHIK, came up to us from the opposite pavement. I think he has the name of some mythological bird, maybe Feniks. With total lack of shame he came up to us and photographed us several times without asking permission, although he knows me. If we had told him to get lost he would have said he was doing his job. Having pinned us to the embassy railings through his lens several times, he went away satisfied.

After a while, an official responsible for human rights came to the door. I had met her once, when she had just come to work at the embassy and had asked me for information about human rights in Albania. She was a listless woman whose tedious questions bore no relation to the reality of the situation. Later she said how pleased she was to be in Albania and to have met President Berisha himself, who had welcomed her with such courtesy.

She stared at us but gave no sign of inviting us inside. We had to talk standing where we were. She said that she had been informed of what had happened and did not want to hear any more from us. We put a copy of the statement we had drafted into her hand and went away. It seemed to me totally absurd that we had knocked on the door of the U.S. Embassy, crying for protection like beaten children. The statement we had delivered to the embassy was in fact addressed to the Albanians. It described the incident with the PD's 'Black Guard', which under police protection had forcibly entered the premises of the Association, assaulted its chairman and evicted him together with Petrit Kalakulla, the chairman of the Democratic Party of the Right. We appealed to the Albanians' civil courage, asking them not to yield to these semi-fascist acts. Who knows what the diplomats say to each other after we come to their door complaining that Berisha has thrashed us. They probably can't tell the difference between the goodies and baddies, but think of us as playing one part one day and another, the next.

104

I fear that they have already made their choice: stability at any price. Shane and I were not sent packing because the ambassador had studied this matter deeply, and wished to convey the message that it was not their task to force children to patch up their quarrels. More probably, the ambassador has decided to support for Berisha.

Albanian television news has just reported at some length what happened at the Association's headquarters after I had left. 'This shows how strong we are,' said one of the leaders of the protest in an interview. The cameras then showed the locked gates of the Association and a shot of me looking as if I were trying to gain entrance. 'But the Association's door is closed to these traitors to their fellow-prisoners,' the announcer concluded.

Chapter XVI

The Newspaper Albania

The next day, the newspaper *Albania* splashed on its front page a picture of Qorri, with his beret back to front, alongside Shane Muda in front of the inhospitable railings of the U.S. Embassy. The adjacent article was headed, 'Former Victims of Persecution Expel Chairman from Building.'

Qorri hesitated before buying the newspaper to read the report, imagining the usual cocktail of disinformation, insults and blackmail. He was a prominent target of this paper and its barbs no longer stung.

'Take it, take it, this is a good one of you,' the newsvendor said.   So he had to buy it, as well as *Koha Jonë*.

The newspaper *Albania* was launched at a time when Berisha's rule was still undisturbed by protests, although his political opponents were becoming more numerous. Berisha was a dictator at heart, but a democrat in his rhetoric, because democracy was the spirit of the age. This new regime was a rough union between the soul of the dictatorship and a democratic project demanded both by the people, who were exhausted by dictatorship, and the West. Qorri, analysing this hybrid, found it difficult to tell if Berisha had devised it, or the regime produced Berisha. A part of Berisha certainly understood that he could no longer fight his opponents with the dictatorship's weapons of prison, exile, and liquidation. This quasi-democracy preferred either to silence or to buy off its enemies rather than imprison or murder them. And so the newspaper *Albania* was born, itself a hybrid, half a newspaper and half a tool of the secret services. Bashkim Gazidede's National Intelligence Service, known as the SHIK, had conceived it in order to give the secret services a hand in the political game. The SHIK itself was a hybrid creature, grafting an intelligence service under notional democratic control onto the old *Sigurimi*. At one time, the *Sigurimi* had put people under surveillance and arrested them. Now the hybrid SHIK eavesdropped and collected information, but could not arrest its opponents. It had to use other, softer means, such as blackmail. If blackmail didn't work, the SHIK could ruin someone's reputation. A newspaper was the ideal tool for this purpose. The SHIK was said to have inherited the files that listed the cover names of the former *Sigurimi* collaborators. In some cases, if someone raised a critical voice, the SHIK could reveal their activities during the communist regime, publish their *Sigurimi* pseudonyms, or the details of their dubious business dealings. They would soon toe the line. Who didn't have a skeleton in the closet? But even if the SHIK had to invent one, how would they possibly clear their name? The editor-in-chief himself was said to be a former *Sigurimi* agent. As for the funding for the newspaper, that was easily found. With the information it possessed, the SHIK had only to knock on the doors of the pyramid bosses for them to open their wallets.

Many people were intimidated by the very vocabulary of this newspaper: spy, paedophile, thief, scumbag, prostitute, drunk.

Qorri had been long been a target in the paper's sights. The paper defamed former political prisoners who opposed the regime as filthy queers who, due to the unavailability of women in prison, had buggered one another. But the vulgarity of these attacks tended rather to provoke laughter than to shock. When Qorri saw he had been photographed like a supplicant at the gate of the U.S. Embassy, he remembered Feniks, whose red beard looked so artificial that it seemed designed to illustrate the theory that beards are subconscious attempts to hide something.

Something more interesting in *Albania* was a statement by a group of Englishmen who called themselves the British Helsinki

Group, to which the paper had given the eye-catching headline, 'British Helsinki Group: Opposition on Brink of Coup d'État.'

This group was not a member of the Helsinki Federation, to which it was actually opposed. It was the creation of extreme right-wingers who claimed that Western leftists who had shown sympathy for communist dictatorships, as had some activists of the Helsinki Federation, were not in a position to defend human rights. This group saw violations of human rights principally in the crimes committed by the communists, and so it defended all the new anti-communist regimes in the East, even Lukashenko's Belarus. But its critics claimed that the group was not ideological at all but composed of a few ordinary con men who had found patrons in the new dictators.

Qorri sat down to read their statement. It supported the government's accusations that common criminals were roaming the streets of Vlora, where the public offices and schools were closed, and that former communists were trying to destabilize the country and reclaim power.

With Berisha and Meksi in power, there was some justice to the British group's complaints about the return of the communists. Qorri threw the newspaper away. It fell with its front page upward, comically distorting the picture of him in front of the embassy railings.

PART THREE

Chapter XVII

The Independent

In mid-February, while the opposing parties were both courting international support, an event tilted the scales in the Forum's favour. In Britain, *The Independent* published an article entitled 'The Gangster Regime We Fund,' written by its correspondent Andrew Gumbel after his visit to Albania.

The article began, 'The Government of Albania, Europe's poorest nation, which is now teetering on the brink of anarchy, has been drug-smuggling, gun-running, sanctions-busting and money-laundering.' The article accused the governments of the West, including Britain, of continuing to support the government despite the warnings of their intelligence services that Albania had turned into a gangster state. The journalist claimed to possess detailed proof from reliable sources of the involvement of members of the ruling PD, including ministers, in extraordinary crimes ranging from drug trafficking and illegal arms trading to large-scale sanctions breaking during the Bosnian war. One of Gumbel's sources in the Western intelligence services said, 'I find it amazing that nobody has blown the lid on what is happening in Albania, because it is truly mind-boggling,' and also told him that he had passed this information to Western governments, but nobody had wanted to know. Politicians in France, Germany, Italy and Britain continued to praise Berisha for his commitment to peace, the free market, and the democratic process. But Albania was now an oppressive one-party state. Corruption had spread at every level

109

and a gangster economy operated under the control and patronage of the State. Drug barons from Kosovo operated in Albania without fear of punishment and the SHIK organized a large part of the traffic in heroin and other drugs passing through Albania from Macedonia and Greece *en route* to Italy. According to Gumbel, intelligence agents were convinced that that the criminal command-chain reached the highest levels. They had named names in their reports.

During the war in Bosnia, the *Shqiponja* ('Eagle') company enjoyed a monopoly in the import and export of oil. It was under the direct management of the PD and its chairman Tritan Shehu, who was also deputy prime minister and foreign minister. The firm openly smuggled drugs, weapons, and cigarettes and had transported oil across Lake Shkodra, violating the embargo against Milošević›s Serbia.

Agron Musaraj, interior minister until the elections of May 1996, had finally been sacked because the United States, the only country that had maintained a critical attitude towards Albania, had told the government he was suspected of controlling the entire drugs trade, while Safet Zhulali, who was still defence minister, had used his office to facilitate the transport of weapons, oil, and cigarettes.

Gumbel also dealt with the now failing financial pyramids. These pseudo-banks that had gobbled up money from almost every Albanian family, promising unimaginable interest rates, also bore the government's dirty finger- marks. Two weeks previously, *The Independent* had reported that these schemes had kept their heads above water thanks to the influx of funds from organized crime, and were also used to launder dirty money. There were serious suspicions about VEFA, the largest pyramid, which was still operating. Its president Vehbi Alimuçaj, a former storekeeper in a munitions depot, had become rich, according to Gumbel, by trafficking weapons with the government's connivance.

Why had Europe closed its eyes to the corruption that had poisoned this country? The journalist replied that short-term political stability had been put before long-term interests. The United States had changed its position only after the serious manipulation of the elections, while many European countries had remained unruffled even by this. Indeed, Italy and Germany, Berisha's closest allies, had actively lobbied for a special agreement between the European Community and Albania, to open new credit lines. This had extended the government's credibility. The proposal failed only after some other European governments, shocked at the rigging of the elections, asked first for improvements in the country's democratic standards. Yet only two weeks ago, Leni Fischer, the chair of the Assembly of the Council of Europe and a diehard fan of Berisha, had spoken out in support of the PD and echoed the Albanian government's rhetoric about 'Red terrorists' destabilizing the country. Gumbel's sources said that these politicians were so 'dogged' in their support of Berisha that they did not even bother to read the alarming reports their intelligence services sent to them. Gumbel also mentioned valuable objects that Berisha had taken from the National Museum to give to the Queen, the British Prime Minister, and other ministers.

The international community, he concluded, had supported Berisha's regime because their priorities in Albania were mistaken, because they had poorly interpreted the nature of President Berisha's Government, and, claimed the secret service sources, out of pure stubbornness and ignorance.

This article was very different from the sort of reports about Albania published in the West while Berisha ruled undisturbed. They had conveyed the impression that Albania was making fast progress. So the West was surprised at what was happening and believed that this really was a *revanche* of the former communists. Most of the previous articles had been written by journalists after they had spent a few days in Tirana, where they had taken a look at the boulevard between the Hotel Rogner Hotel and the Tirana Hotel, and left. The articles generally opened with a paragraph about the exotic nature of the country, on the lines of 'The Albanian language is the sole survival of the Thraco-Phrygian linguistic family,' or described the Canon of Lekë Dukagjin, the still surviving age-old code of revenge. They often mentioned the admirable religious tolerance between Muslims, and Orthodox and Catholic Christians before moving on to Enver Hoxha's Stalinist dictatorship and concluding with an interview with the charismatic anti-communist president Sali Berisha or the successful businessman, Vehbi Alimuçaj.

Finally *The Independent* had described the truth of what was happening under the noses of the internationals, what the so-called Albanian transition from communism to capitalism really meant, and why there were clashes in the streets.

    ***

Qorri immediately thought of Charles Walsh. Who else could be the secret serviceman who had given Gumbel his information? Of all the foreigners that Qorri knew, only Charles had understood what was happening in Albania. A while back, he had expressed serious alarm to Qorri about the rise of the pyramids. 'There will be a catastrophe,' he had said, 'can't you understand? Can't you tell the public? Can't you write in the press?'

He also remembered how Charles was on poor terms with Ambassador Lino, evidently one of the 'dogged' politicians who refused to see reality. What would she say after Gumbel's article?

The article acted as a catalyst, accelerating all the reactions taking place in Albania and exacerbating the conflict. The government responded with a long-winded statement that suggested that the article had struck home. It expressed regret that a prestigious newspaper had fallen victim to communist slanders. According to the government, what Gumbel claimed to have learned from the secret services was only what the press of the ex-communists had been writing for the past year.

112

The next day, *Rilindja Demokratike* lambasted the British newspaper. Gumbel's article was 'intentionally insulting and defamatory.' *Albania*, in its inimitable fashion, called it a 'tale of paedophiles.' The defence minister announced that he was suing the journalist. The director of the National Museum denied that the antiques that Berisha had given to the Queen and the British politicians had been taken from the Museum. He too claimed he would be turning to the courts.

Meanwhile, the article echoed throughout Europe. Leading articles entitled 'Gangster Regime' raised the question of money laundering. In Britain, eleven members of parliament called for investigations against Berisha. He was losing international support.

Chapter XVIII

The President's Speech

Koha Jonë published a translation of the article from *The Independent* and a leader entitled 'The Eagle Losing Its Feathers'. To show that the eagle still had feathers and even claws, Berisha held a meeting with intellectuals, business people, young people, workers, farmers, and investors, which was broadcast with great fanfare on television.

'Today, when hundreds of thousands of families are in despair over the loss of their money in the financial pyramids, a minority of extremists, many of whom have not lost a penny, are trying for their own perverse and totally undemocratic purposes to turn this serious but not irrecoverable financial loss into a true national tragedy... At a time when we need wisdom, self-control and decisiveness, this small group has found the support of a few thousand followers, and is exploiting the silence of hundreds of thousands of others whose pain should not allow them to tolerate what is happening.'

Next, Berisha tried to explain how the crisis with the pyramid schemes has some about: 'Capitalist society has always involved money lending. In Albania, this was unknown until 1991. Until 1996, no political force, neither the ruling party nor the opposition, and not a single individual or institution publicly condemned what was happening or foresaw the consequences. This silence of political parties, and of experts, financiers, economists, intellectuals, and academics, and indeed of foreigners, is being explained in different ways today. I am deeply convinced that it was ignorance of capitalism and the market economy that was the reason for this long silence. But in Albania, in contrast to the other ex-communist countries, the state institutions are not implicated.'

Perhaps aware that this 'silence' was a lie, he later conceded that in the second half of 1996 the IMF had expressed serious concern over this informal market and had demanded that the dangers of these high interest rates should be made known. According to him, this was not the institution's responsibility. 'A few weeks ago, I apologized to all our citizens who would not have invested their money in these pyramids if this had been made clear to them. Why did I not warn them of the danger? The only reason was that I could not prejudge them as pyramid schemes.

Berisha claimed that the tolerance shown towards the schemes for so long was part of the government's general tolerance of independent initiatives. In Albania, money lending was considered a legal and entirely private activity, unlicensed by the State and without legal regulation, but guaranteed by the Civil Code. These pyramids had no boards of directors. He said in an interview with the BBC that Albania was building 'capitalism with a human face.' These companies also had investment subsidiaries in different fields, and the government had maintained a tolerant attitude to all investors. 'We have made every effort to be as amenable as possible. We wanted them to develop the market economy in Albania. We have never heard business people complaining about taxes.'

Some time ago he had stated that 'The money of Albanians is clean.' He claimed that this had been a warning to the fraudsters not to trifle with people's sacrifices and toil. But evidently it had been insufficient.

'Ladies and gentlemen, in conclusion I appeal to all citizens, men and women, intellectuals, business people, workers, and farmers not to allow the strength of their reaction to these crooks to turn into a psychosis of despair and destruction.

'I want to send a particular appeal to the citizens of Vlora. I express my condolences to the Rustemi and Zani families.'

'I call on the media not to exploit people's misfortunes, pain, and despair.

'I appeal to pseudo-analysts who are exploiting events and mindless individuals to refrain from slandering Albanian culture. We are a people with an ancient civilization.

'I call on political parties not to lay down conditions but to condemn violence and establish the dialogue for which I remain ready as always.

'Finally I appeal to all Albanians who believe in God, in themselves, their freedom and their future, their property, and their country and flag, to remain true to their moral principles and common sense, to their traditions and culture, and not to turn this transient set-back into an irreparable tragedy, as I trust will not happen ever. Long live Albania.'

Clearly, Berisha's speech failed to provide honest replies to several basic questions. Had his state, his police force, and his SHIK, which watched even the private lives of his political opponents, done anything to control the activities of these firms? What more important duty could the State have but to protect its own citizens from thieves and crooks? Why had the PD accepted such huge sums of money from these firms for its election campaigns?

Berisha could no longer be trusted, and his power was surely at an end. While he tried to preserve what little remained intact, the Forum hoped for the fall of the last and biggest pyramid, VEFA Holdings, whose collapse must finally drive Berisha out of politics.

Chapter XIX

VEFA HOLDINGS

Western journalists, thronging to Albania as never before in that calamitous winter, described Tirana as the 'least European' capital they had ever seen. One compared the Martyrs of the Nation Boulevard, the pride of the city, to a street in Kathmandu. The giant electronic advertisement for 'VEFA HOLDINGS' stuck to the façade of the Palace of Culture was particularly striking. 'Tourism -- Supermarkets -- Resorts -- Exclusive Events -- Storage -- Refrigeration -- Transport -- Investment' flickered in turn with continually shifting colours and images. By February, it was the only pyramid advertisement that remained.

VEFA Holdings had the reputation of a company of 'European standing'. Its headquarters were on the square named after Avni Rustemi, whose grimy bust stood in the garbage-strewn central flowerbed, surrounded by dust and rubbish. Nobody paid attention any more to this national hero. People looked at the gates of VEFA behind him, gathering in larger numbers every day and waiting to withdraw their money. Men in leather jackets, clearly secret police agents, were there to ensure the crowd did not try to storm the gates. Western journalists and cameramen also hung around the VEFA railings, filming and interviewing.

Waiting for the counters to open, people talked about the sums they had poured into VEFA and the profits they were forgoing. They also talked to the leather jackets about their misfortunes and flocked round Western journalists to tell them their woes. Speakers of foreign languages first described their own troubles and then interpreted the tragedies of others. But usually at this point they came up against the leather jackets, whose job was, as far as possible, to prevent this kind of contact.

A notice had been fixed to the railings surrounding the Firm's headquarters: 'The President can only be contacted at his own invitation.'

President Vehbi Alimuçaj's glory days were over. At one time he had lived like an Arab sheikh in the most expensive hotels of Europe, escorted by an entourage who shared his pleasures, and spending his nights with the most beautiful prostitutes. But now the crowds monitored his every movement, and kept tabs day and night on his white helicopter with the blue VEFA logo that still stood in a clearing in the park of Tirana. The presence of this helicopter was a sign that its owner had not vanished as others had. In fact, Alimuçaj had tried to flee to the United States but the Americans had denied him a visa. He had retreated for twenty-four hours to his native mountains of Kukës and then found the courage to return to Tirana to pose again as a man of power behind his desk at his fine headquarters on Avni Rustemi Square. A journalist friend of Qorri's who had penetrated his citadel had found him in a huge drawing room, with, amazingly, a piano in the corner. 'Do you fancy some music?' Vehbi had said to him. 'Sure,' he had replied, humouring him. Vehbi had rung a bell and immediately a young woman appeared. 'What piece shall she play?' Vehbi asked. The journalist shook his head indecisively. 'Play that thing of Louise's,' Vehbi decided for him, and she had played Beethoven's 'Für Elise.'

With his pot belly, bulging eyes, and fat man's waddle, Vehbi Alimuçaj was the laughing stock of half the nation. How had this military storekeeper turned out cleverer than all the trained officers of the Albanian Army, and become the richest man in the country? How could he have deceived everyone? Some people offered the simple explanation that capitalism had produced a new kind of individual with different characteristics from the socialist personality.

Hadn't these former drivers and bodyguards shown certain talents that their communist bosses had never displayed? New capitalist man, the model businessman, had a different mentality, and so should look different. This theory had plenty of adherents, but not among intelligent people. Others claimed that behind the drivers and bodyguards stood their patrons, either those from the past or newly acquired ones. Otherwise, how could these people have gained credibility? How many of the distinctly racist Albanians, would have trusted Sudja, the Roma 'boss', if they had not believed that a 'person in charge,' alias Prime Minister Meksi, stood behind her? Even when Sudja was arrested, it was rumoured that she was detained in order to prevent his name being revealed. Most people believed that these characters were fronts who shielded the much more capable ruffians who led the State. So they had trusted them, and now they turned against them in fury.

'I'm a language teacher. I put in $500. That's a large sum for me. Now I need that money because my granddaughter's getting married,' said a white-haired man, speaking French to a foreign journalist. 'All right, all right,' the leather-jacketed SHIK agent interrupted, shoving him out of the queue with the aid of his belly. 'Five hundred dollars,' the teacher shouted again, trying to make clear to the journalist the extent of his catastrophe.

'What will you do if VEFA goes bankrupt?' the journalist asked the first person in front of him. The Albanian interpreter clinging to him translated.

'If VEFA goes bankrupt, it's the end of everything.'

'If VEFA collapses, all Tirana will take to the streets, SHIK or no SHIK,' people round about chorused, speaking for the leather jackets too.

***

Berisha's political future was tied to the fate of these hundreds and thousands of people who crowded round VEFA's railings. Vehbi called them 'creditors' because, according to him, their money had been taken in the form of credit to a company that was making investments. Some people still hoped that this former storekeeper could do something. A new rumour had spread that the bosses of Sacra Corona Unita, with whom he had done business, had come to his aid, and one billion dollars in cash had been brought in suitcases loaded onto the ferries between Brindisi and Vlora and Durrës, which Alimuçaj himself owned. The government, people said, had given *carte blanche* to some Vlora traffickers linked to VEFA, to find whatever money they could to cover its losses.

From the State Bank on Martyrs of the Nation Boulevard came news that seemed indirectly to confirm the reported billion-dollar lifebelt thrown by the Apulian mafia to the Albanian billionaire. 'It is hard to assess,' a senior bank official declared, 'how much money Alimuçaj has here in Albania. He has accounts and deposits in all the banks in this country, national and foreign. There may be tens of billions. If he's starting to pay back the money, this money clearly has come from somewhere, but it's not money that has moved through normal banking channels.' The source of this money was the last thing on people's minds. The most important question was whether it would be enough to calm the streets and avert bloodshed.

The evening news reported that VEFA had begun to pay out money again, and had closed its counters only at times when the situation had become strained. The company had decided to return the small sums that were most important for ordinary people. Then it would refund investors of $5,000 to $10,000 and then $10,000 to $20,000. The entire procedure would take three weeks.

Clearly this tactic was designed to gain three weeks' breathing space, with the knowledge that anything could happen in that time. Nobody knew if money was really being paid out or not.

The next day, *Albania* ran the headline: 'VEFA Paying Back Capital Too',' but soon it was being claimed that the rumour of the opening of the counters had been spread because a group of about fifty government grandees had got back their money from VEFA, with interest. The opposition press ran contradictory reports: 'VEFA Suspends Payments,' 'VEFA Fails to Repay as Promised,' 'VEFA Faces Bankruptcy.' The confusion was growing.

A statement by the Greek interior minister poured cold water on all these conflicting reports. He declared that a large-scale drugs laboratory somewhere between Vlora and Fier was supplying Greece, Italy, and the markets of the East, and that this laboratory belonged to Rrapush Xhaferri, the chief of the pyramid that bore his name.

Xhaferri was another fraudster who had amazed his fellow-citizens of Lushnja not only by becoming extremely rich, but also acquiring fame in the realm of football. With the money he collected, he had revived the town's football team and even bought some Latin American stars who were on the verge of retirement. But this glory was short-lived. Most of these star players left because the massive salaries they were promised dried up after the first few months.

The statement by the Greek interior minister also hastened the collapse of VEFA and Alimuçaj.

Western journalists, after talking to the people gathered outside VEFA's office, returned to the Rogner to meet politicians and diplomats.

'What do you think will happen with VEFA?' they asked.

'Who knows?' came the usual reply.

Chapter XX

Rain

From Fatos Qorri's Diary

We had no permit from the police, but again we called on people to rally today in the square opposite the *Dinamo* Stadium.

I left home an hour and a half beforehand, hoping to drink coffee on the way. Before I reached the boulevard, I was caught in a torrential downpour. I opened my umbrella and broke into a run, jumping over the puddles, and made for the Rogner Hotel, which was not far from the stadium. Other people had the same idea. I had never seen the lobby so full of people I knew, but also many unfamiliar faces.

Despite the continuing downpour, I stood up to leave with several others shortly before twelve o'clock. As we headed for the main door of the hotel, I saw a group of policemen in front of me. Obviously they were there to prevent us leaving. Some of the unfamiliar faces in the lobby drew nearer -- clearly SHIK men. 'Orders from above,' said the officer in charge with an expression that seemed to say, 'What can I do?'

The procedure was the same as at the Association's headquarters, except that the hotel entrance was still open for anyone entering. We began arguing with the police. Some journalists arrived and told us that the police had surrounded the stadium square, and groups of plain-clothes men, from what we now called 'the Democratic Party's Black Hundreds', had combed the nearby cafés and bars, making threats, beating people, and ejecting them from the premises. Other leaders of the Forum had been stopped just before twelve o'clock, wherever they happened to be, and had not been allowed to move.

The torrential rain continued - a consolation for this further fiasco.

The evening news carried a report in the familiar style of the Albanian Telegraphic Agency, ATA. It stated that an illegal rally of the Forum had been planned to take place on Selman Stërmasi Square, but nobody had turned up, just some children playing football in the rain and a few sodden journalists. 'At least the organizers should have come to get wet too,' the announcer read, and added, 'The Democratic Party salutes the people of Tirana. They have understood that the Forum leaders are manipulating the situation and have ceased to support them.'

The Voice of America reported not that we'd been stopped by the police, but that at the time of the rally we'd been drinking coffee in the bars of Tirana.

So the disinformation game continues.

The attacks on foreign newspapers have been stepped up. Today *Albania* accuses foreign journalists of inventing incidents. 'Even on days when nothing happens, events are dreamed up in Vlora.' Two Italian reporters supposedly went to the seashore with a boat owner, who simulated the departure of a motorboat for them. But most of the attacks are aimed at the Greek press. According to *Albania*, one Greek reporter went to an ordinary funeral, took photographs, and published them with the claim that the police had killed the dead man. Another gathered together a group of boys to shout, 'Down with the government!' in Greek, and presented this on the evening news in Greece as a spontaneous demonstration.

The leaders of the faith groups also support the government, and have appealed for a day of prayer some time in February.

***

Kurt made a second attempt to enter the Association's headquarters after its occupation, but he found the gates guarded by former prisoners opposed to him and by police who told him they had orders not to let him in. Gjinushi suggested that the Forum should

123

move to his Social Democratic Party headquarters. We have made this move, but without much enthusiasm. It's the only party headquarters with room for us, except the Socialists, and going to the Socialists would compromise us.

The central offices of the parties that were formed in the nineties all have significant histories. The Social Democratic Party's building is a three-storey villa at the entrance to Fortuz Street built during the Italian occupation, and has a front garden with tall pine trees. The communists expropriated this villa and for some time it was an art gallery. Early in 1991, as soon as political parties were allowed, the regime gave it to Gjinushi's party. He was obviously favoured by the former communists, because this is the most lavish central office.

Seen from above, the building resembles a bird with wings outstretched and head held high. The wings have two floors and the head has three. The right wing has a large meeting room and the other consists of storerooms. On the upper floor of the right wing is Gjinushi's office with large armchairs in a corner and a desk to the side, and secretaries' offices to the left. Only the body of the building where the two wings join has a third floor, and this is where we have moved to. A spiral staircase rises from the main entrance. So we are in the bird's head. We have a small room with a desk and a phone, an upright chair, a computer where I work, and a fax machine that Gonxhja will use to distribute communiqués. Dash Peza has promised to come now and then to help us. We have the use of a larger room opposite for small meetings, and we will hold large meetings in the hall below.

The most interesting feature of our small office is that it looks out over the terrace that forms the roof of the left-hand wing. The surrounding pine trees rise above the building like a green hedge and protect it from the street and from all onlookers.

So we have more roof terrace than office. In fact we no longer need an office. In two weeks the Forum has become a myth that unites opponents of Berisha wherever they are. Not a day passes without ATA reporting some event: 'The Forum for Democracy in Vlora delivers a petition to the Vlora police station.' 'Gathering in Durrës following call by the Forum for Democracy.' 'In Cërrik at noon, several hundred people gathered in a demonstration following an appeal by the Forum.' 'In the square in front of the stadium in Elbasan, several hundred people gathered following a summons by the Forum.'

In fact it is the people who are assembling the Forum, not the Forum the people.

In the opposite camp, Berisha is trying to hang on to the small parties that are showing a desire to run away. At a meeting he held with them today there was a proposal for the resignation of the government and the formation of a new one, with some of the parties proposing a government of professionals or a coalition that includes the opposition. But there were no details of this on the news, which broadcast a statement condemning terrorism, acts of vandalism, and political manipulation. The party chairman Tritan Shehu stated that the suggestion of a coalition or a government of professionals supported by the opposition was unacceptable.

Rilindja Demokratike's headlines ran 'No Coalition with the Socialists'; 'Technocratic Administration Rejected -- Support for Democratic Government'. There was also an article about me, accusing me of saying that we are on the brink of a violent confrontation: 'At a news conference on Friday, Fatos Qorri, one of the leaders of the so-called Forum for Democracy, predicted civil war.'

In fact, I was not predicting the country's imminent collapse but warning of the danger of such a thing. Berisha's men are cooking up violence because they feel strong as long as they have the army and the police. Today they drove Rexhep Meidani's car into a ravine somewhere near Puka in the north, where he was going to meet supporters.

The second half of February has begun with tensions rising and falling. It seems that Berisha is playing this game on purpose, alternating pressure and concessions. On the one hand he holds meetings and makes propaganda statements for the benefit of foreigners, and on the other he is whetting his sword. Each day one report contradicts another. People are told that the football championship, suspended on 25th January, will resume, and at the same time that a ruling on this is expected from the Interior Ministry.

Rumour has it that Berisha's allies met a second time and demanded 'Meksi's head.' The Vlora Municipal Council, dominated by the Democratic Party, has drawn up a petition for the removal of the prime minister and the creation of a new government. On the other hand ATA increasingly reports that crime has flourished in Vlora since the police retreated on 11th February, and claims that traffickers have repossessed 135 boats confiscated by the police and have resumed the trade of prostitutes and drugs to Italy. Each boat reportedly makes three journeys each day. Five people were wounded, one seriously, in a fight with knives and guns among rival traffickers.

Clearly the purpose of these reports is to show foreigners, especially the Italian and Greek Governments, what might happen if they fail to intervene to stabilize the situation. The Greek border guards are said to be in a state of alert. Even Foresti is in feverish activity. Italy's concern over human trafficking might be much more decisive for our fate than the economic and social crisis that has us in its grip.

In Lushnja, furious crowds seized the Democratic Party chairman Tritan Shehu and held him hostage for several hours. The protesters had turned out not with flowers, as we had suggested, but with leeks, a symbol of poverty. The television showed only a few pictures of the incident but everyone says that they stuffed a leek into Shehu's mouth or even his anus. Berisha immediately set off for Lushnja in order to recover his lost dignity, and according to ATA's

126

positive spin on the visit, told the people of Lushnja that he had not lost faith in dialogue with them. He called what was done to Shehu an act of terrorism that had nothing to do with the people of the town, because the young men of Lushnja and nearby Karbunara had done their honourable best to protect him. He said he would decorate the people who had defended Shehu and that he had come to Lushnja to ask for help and cooperation in overcoming the crisis created by the money lending. But other reports arriving through different channels tell a different story - that he was welcomed with stone throwing, whistling and an attempt to overturn his vehicle. The Voice of America's chief correspondent indirectly confirmed this by reporting that when Berisha left Lushnja he was shouted at and insulted, and a rock was thrown at his car.

When asked about early elections, Berisha said that they would be held in 2000 as planned.

I often think of the years 1990-1991, because some people say that we are doing exactly what the PD did at that time. The PD brought down the communist government after destabilizing Albania for a whole year, at a heavy cost to the country. Now too there is an economic and political crisis, and we are fanning the flames. Another similarity is the regime's fear of the crimes it has committed. Then, the communists' knowledge of their crimes increased their fear of leaving power. Now too, the government appears frightened of losing power, although it is not burdened by crimes of the same severity. But there is also a substantial difference. At that time Ramiz Alia made it obvious that he wanted to make a soft landing and leave the political scene. But Berisha insists on keeping his plane in the air, although there is every sign that its engines have broken down and we are all going to crash.

Today Sabri Godo's Republican Party announced its departure from the coalition government. The Christian Democrats, who are with Berisha, also called for Meksi's resignation and called on all the right-wing parties to create a genuine democratic forum. But the strongest blow to Berisha came from within. A group of fourteen members of the PD's National Council, mainly former ministers, submitted a nine-point petition calling for the resignation of the Meksi government and the formation of a government of national salvation. They called on Berisha to dissociate himself from the political parties, play a conciliatory role, and guarantee inter-party debate. The signatories included former deputy Prime Minister Dashamir Shehi. But according to them, only the Democratic Party should form the Salvation Government.

There is not a word about the responsibilities they bear or their acts of violence. They are abandoning a sinking ship. Others jumped overboard as soon as they saw the ship entering stormy waters, and some were made to walk the plank. But these are abandoning ship because they have taken what they can and now they don't want to drown with Berisha.

'These has-beens are unhappy at losing their jobs,' Berisha replied. Perhaps he is right, but when he fails to sit down with his own party to discuss an option that is entirely in the party's favour, what kind of dialogue can he conduct with us? Clearly he will continue to rely on force.

Chapter XXI

20th February

Qorri was re-reading an article he had started a long time ago but left unfinished. He had thought of publishing it on the anniversary of the overthrow of the statue of Hoxha, the former dictator. It began with an episode from history that he had read before the dictator's monument was toppled, and which had haunted him incessantly in prison, like an impossible dream.

'The colossal statue of Serapis in Alexandria was the object of a religious cult. A huge number of metal plates had been skilfully joined to create this magnificent figure of the god. The appearance of the seated Serapis, holding a sceptre in his left hand, was very like the familiar aspect of Zeus. The superstition among the people was that if anybody dared insult the majesty of this god, heaven and earth would revert instantly to primal chaos.

'A brave Christian soldier, emboldened by his faith and armed with a mighty sword, climbed the steps. The crowd awaited the outcome of his challenge in terror. The soldier struck Serapis' face with a powerful blow, and the metal plates forming his cheeks fell to the ground. There was no sound of thunder and the earth and sky remained peacefully in place. The soldier struck a second and third time. The huge idol toppled over and shattered. Then its limbs were dragged with contempt through the streets of Alexandria...'

After this introduction, Qorri described what had happened about two thousand years later, on 20th February 1991 in Tirana.

'A vast crowd of excited people had gathered since morning on the hills of Student City, where the halls of residence were, to support the eight hundred students who were on hunger strike, demanding the removal of the name of the dictator Enver Hoxha from their university.

The regime, burdened by its crimes and exhausted by the ruined economy, felt impotent. The assembled crowds sensed this, and decided to accomplish themselves what the supine members of the Politburo could no longer find the strength to do. Someone gave a sign: if they won't remove his name, we'll pull down his monument. The crowd poured downhill into the centre of Tirana, where the nine-metre high statue of Hoxha stood.

'Events developed fast. At first no one dared approach the monument, not just because riot police were protecting it but because of the dictator's terrifying aura. A helicopter circled above the crowd, sending continuous reports to the leadership. The crowd was so huge that any military intervention would lead to a massacre. Slowly, the bravest overcame the barrier of fear that was stronger than the cordon of police, climbed onto the pedestal of the monument and threw a rope round Enver Hoxha's neck. At five past two, they pulled the rope and the bronze monument tottered and fell. The crowd's enthusiasm knew no bounds. People kissed and hugged even the police and the riot squads that had vainly tried to restrain their frenzied desire for liberty. The statue was desecrated, urinated on, hacked to pieces, and hauled to the place history had reserved for it in scenes that expressed people's boundless hatred and alienation under the dictator's cruel tyranny.

'Never before had all Albanians, from the most wretched poor to the most sophisticated intellectuals, felt so united and happy. The young men who had hung the noose round the monument and defiled it were united in spirit with the rest who were gathered round, but whose culture and self-restraint did not allow them to join in.

'It was as if the sun of freedom above Albania had come out from behind a fifty-year eclipse and now blazed forth its life-giving rays. The clouds of hatred, division and poverty seemed to have

130

vanished from the sky. What would come next didn't matter. This was a moment of eternity. The future lay waiting on the far horizon, but at that moment it was like a fluffy little white cloud to which nobody paid any attention.'

Qorri was astonished at the pathos in what he had written. He hardly recognized himself in this article. Had he since matured as a writer, or was he then merely reflecting the spirit of the times? Or could he not tell the difference? He had experienced that day from his prison cell. The prisoners yearned to be rid of the shadow of this dictator. Albanians outside the barbed wire were itching to flee abroad. Many people passed a sleepless night reliving the fall of the statue as they had seen it on television. This day would endure in their memory as the high point of their lives. Now this summit seemed to have receded into the far distance and was surrounded by black clouds.

What had happened to the Albanians now, after only six years? That little white cloud of the future that once floated gently and benignly on the horizon had drawn nearer and grown larger and blacker until it filled the entire sky. Storms were on the way. The anniversary of the overthrow of Enver Hoxha's statue found the Albanians more bitterly divided than ever before, and using the memory of this day only as a weapon against one another.

Qorri was puzzled as to how this great day lost its lustre so quickly. Of course, the tribulations of daily life were enough to overshadow even the most glorious memories. But that was not all. Perhaps, Qorri thought, truly great days are when foundations are laid, not when something is demolished. Christians celebrate the birth of Christ, not the downfall of paganism. Perhaps that was the trouble. The day had not really laid the foundations of freedom, and history had not produced any true victors. The bravest of the crowd who had surrounded the monument and thrown the rope had known only that single day's triumph. They had remained anonymous. Those who had risen to power were neither demolition men nor builders, but merely

131

collaborators with the regime to whom fell the task of clearing away the debris before it crumbled and crushed them. There were rumours later on that even the overthrow of the monument had been planned, and that the screws on the pedestal had been loosened by the agents of the regime itself, which was why it had fallen so easily.

Qorri saw now that he would never finish this piece. He shut down his computer and went out for a coffee.

***

The Forum had applied to hold another protest rally on Scanderbeg Square on 20th February. This time, it was hard to imagine Berisha denying permission. On the 16th, the Tirana branch of the Democratic Party had applied to hold a peaceful rally at one o'clock either on Scanderbeg Square or opposite the University. According to the Interior Ministry spokesman, the rally was to mark 'the anniversary of the overthrow of the symbol of communism, Enver Hoxha's monument.' The police refused to allow this assembly on Scanderbeg Square, supposedly because of the traffic and associated problems, but approved the square in front of the University. Perhaps they might give a square to the Forum too, but not the central one.

And so, as they expected, the government allowed the Forum a rally on the field of Ali Demi.

'Finally the government has allowed a rally of the opposition on Ali Demi field on 20th February, an important date in the struggle of the Albanian people against dictatorship. The Forum for Democracy invites you all to Ali Demi field. Let us protest together against the destructive policies of neo-dictatorship which have led the country to political and economic collapse.'

'Everybody to Ali Demi field at 14.30! Support the peaceful anti-government protests and the demands of the Forum for Democracy!'

Meanwhile, *Rilindja Demokratike* announced, 'Everyone to University Square to mark the Day of the Overthrow of the Symbol of Dictatorship!'

***

Qorri had never before faced such a sea of humanity. The football field, the surrounding area and even the neighbouring apartment blocks were crammed with people singing and shouting slogans.

'Seize your guns, boys, death or freedom,' was the first song.

Suddenly, instead of enthusiasm, a sensation of powerlessness in front of this great mass of people overwhelmed him. He felt that deep down this came from his own inability to communicate with them. It was not clear to him why this should be so, whether it was his lack of experience or because this kind of oratory was foreign to his nature. He usually preferred one-to-one discussions, conversations that went to the heart of an argument. He felt that the greater the number of participants, the shallower a discussion became. He had of necessity got used to round tables and discussion panels, but these didn't involve much applause. Here he faced an ocean of excited people, who needed less to communicate than to celebrate. It was a savage kind of festival, in which individual participants felt powerful precisely because they were part of a great multitude. The people there were drunk on the freedom they had gained from joining together. They had never felt as powerful as at that moment.

Another slogan burst out 'Vlora, Vlora'; 'Vlora, Vlora', and then came 'Berisha needs a length of rope.'

It was possible that every person who had lost their money was there. The wildest among them had no doubt been beaten by Berisha's police at the impromptu protests at the gates of the pyramids' offices. Qorri hoped that this swarm of people also included some who were

133

there because of the violation of their freedom, so recently won, and some who had helped to topple the dictator's statue six years before.

They were all looking towards a small rostrum on which the Forum's leaders were placed. It was as if their presence was required merely as symbols, and because without them the crowd would remain amorphous. Qorri remembered someone saying that without leaders there is no critical mass, and it is a critical mass that produces a leader. But he found it difficult to see himself through the eyes of this crowd and thought that from their point of view he cut a very small figure. The road towards freedom, for which he was struggling, led out of the crowded field, after these people dispersed and became individuals again.

Below the rostrum some television cameras focused on the Forum leaders and turned now and again towards the field.

The speeches were soon over. After all, the point of the rally was to show the massive support for the Forum. But that wasn't why crowd had come together. A voice rose from the throng 'To the Square! The Square!' With the energy of thousands of people united as never before, the crowd felt ready to conquer Scanderbeg Square. In their previous attempts, they had not been able to muster such a large number. Now they felt nothing could stop them. They wanted confrontation, and slogans could be heard that sounded like 'Freedom or death!' Yet they were also waiting for an order, an instruction from the rostrum, which did not come. For good or ill, the Forum's leaders were unwilling. They knew that the police, who had barely allowed people to gather on the Ali Demi field, would not allow them to seize the square.

At this point Qorri saw that this mass of people was now in control of events. They were a raging ocean of humanity on which he and the other leaders of the Forum were a few wretched skiffs bobbing on the surface, struggling to pull their oars and exploit this energy for their own purposes. They wanted to distinguish themselves from this mass and rise above it, but the crowd strove to absorb them and make them its head, using them to direct its own energies. Perhaps the crowd knew instinctively the best place to strike. But it was unable to carry responsibility. Someone had to act as its head.

But the connection between the Forum leaders and this crowd was not of this kind. Looking back on this day, Qorri would wonder what might have happened if the Forum's leaders had been as courageous as the crowd. Maybe blood would have been spilt at the square, but this bloodshed might have prevented even more later on.

***

Descending the steps of the rostrum, Qorri was surrounded by protesters. Some became his self-appointed bodyguards, some wanted to talk to him about their worries, and others just to see him.

At that moment the crowd parted to make way for a man rushing towards him with outstretched arms.

'Fatos! Fatos!' he cried, clasping him in a tight embrace. Qorri didn't recognize him.

'Don't you know who I am? How can you not recognize me? I'm Gjergj.'

Qorri finally saw who he was and fell speechless with disbelief. This was 'lame Gjergj', one of the most detested guards of the prison camp at Spaç, who had once beaten him and punched him with his fists. A shadow of seriousness and confusion fell across the man's face. Qorri did not say a word. It did not seem the right moment to make judgments, in the midst of the crowd, and after that embrace. He walked away silently, feeling that this encounter had alienated him even further from the people. What had emboldened this torturer to come up and embrace him? Was it just that he now thought they were on the same side? Or did he think that that they had lived together under the same sky of Spaç, and the distinction between torturer and victim struck him as unimportant? A mounting anger rose within Qorri. Whatever this embrace meant, it was not repentance. If Gjergj had felt the slightest remorse for the work he had done, he would not have greeted him like that. The embrace showed that he had not felt a moment's regret.

Gonxhja interrupted his reflections. They would have to hurry. He had made an appointment with Charles Walsh of USAID after the rally, and Charles was waiting for him in a jeep parked off the main road. Qorri and Gonxhja climbed quickly into the back. Walsh was in front beside the driver. They noticed that a car had set off just behind them – obviously following them.

'Congratulations,' Walsh said. 'It was incredible. All those people.'

At the first turn, they realized that the car behind them must be the SHIK. Walsh told his driver to take some sudden turnings in the narrow lanes. But their pursuers clung to them, so Walsh directed the driver into the street behind the embassy where nobody could follow them. This street was blocked at one end for security reasons and only cars on embassy business could enter. Their pursuers vanished, perhaps thinking they were entering the embassy. Then the jeep made a U-turn and headed for the nearby Café des Artistes. They recovered their breath in the leafy courtyard of the café. There were few customers, and nobody suspicious came in after them.

Walsh was about forty, tall and with curly blond hair, now slightly thinning. His manner was always restrained, but open and friendly. Qorri had only met him once some time ago, when he had talked about the dangers of the pyramid schemes. 'Don't you understand you're heading for disaster?' he had said. Everyone was sure that Walsh was the CIA's number-one man in Albania. Qorri had interpreted his concern over the pyramids as the anxiety of the U.S. intelligence services over a phenomenon that posed a danger to the

136

whole of the Balkans. He was fully convinced that Walsh had given Gumbel the information for his bombshell in *The Independent*.

Walsh had watched the end of the rally, surprised and thrilled at the large crowds. Qorri understood from his first words that he was among the few foreigners who were persuaded that Berisha must be removed from power, as the main source of the evil. So the conversation naturally concentrated on how this could be achieved.

'The trouble is,' Qorri said, 'that he's like a terrorist holding hostages and saying as he points a gun at them, "If you don't do what I say, I'll kill them all." How can we get the gun out of his hand before he can do any harm?'

'There is a way,' Walsh replied.

Qorri and Gonxhja stared at him, waiting for the magic formula.

'Judo,' Walsh said.

'Meaning?'

'He has to be forced to turn the pistol on himself, so that when he fires he shoots himself.'

Qorri remembered Walsh saying that before he came to Albania he had been cultural attaché in Japan.

Qorri parted from Walsh, still imagining Berisha firing a pistol and the bullet striking himself. Would it be the opposition's skill, his own lunacy, or fate that decided where the bullet would fall? Walsh hadn't offered them a solution, only a helpful metaphor.

The evening news reported that after the rally a crowd of three or four hundred protesters had headed for Scanderbeg Square. But the report concentrated not on the protesters but on the fate of the police who had borne the brunt of the crowd's aggression and had been pelted with stones. Hooligans, the report said, had injured five policemen and destroyed four of their cars. Seven people had been arrested.

PART FOUR

Chapter XXII

Hunger Strike

It was the fifteenth day of demonstrations in Vlora. In what had now become a ritual, between nine and ten in the morning and five and six in the afternoon the people marched together to Flag Square where speeches were made. The city lived on and for demonstrations, and almost everyone assembled in the square.

But the people of Vlora would never have joined together to fill the square for this collective rite if they had not been nourished by the very specific hope of recovering their money. Nobody knew how it would be returned, and as the days passed, more and more voices announced that the money was lost forever. In some people, this fostered an even more irrational hatred of the government and a desire to overthrow it, but others just as irrationally grew depressed and gave up. Those who were not demonstrating only about the lost money but were bent on using the passions of the crowd to overthrow the government began to think that the movement should be expanded if it were not to lose its impetus or become self-destructive.

For some days there had been rumours of escalating the protests with a hunger strike of students at Vlora University. A group of students announced 20th February as a deadline for the resignation of the government and the return of the money. Then they would start their fast.

***

The Forum could not determine if it were a coincidence or a premeditated plan for the students to go on strike on the anniversary of the overthrow of Hoxha's monument and on the very day of the rally on the Ali Demi field in Tirana. The organisers of the Vlora protests were in contact with Tirana, but also acted independently and unpredictably, and any coordination of action seemed to come more from a shared purpose than good organisation. Recently, events in all the towns seemed to flow and merge naturally like currents in a great river.

According to ATA, forty-two students went on strike. The opposition said sixty. They occupied classrooms on the ground floor of the university, tied bandanas round their heads, and lay in corners, creating less a public form of self-sacrifice than a media event. Strikers had to display faces distorted by suffering to feed the anger of the public. The declared reason for the strike was solidarity with the demonstrators of Vlora, demanding the government's resignation and the return of the money.

The strikers and their supporters outside were inspired by the original, legendary hunger strike of students that had led to the toppling of Hoxha's monument in February 1991 and hastened the final collapse of the communist regime. There had been several strikes since then. The most famous had been the underground strike of the miners of the Valias coal mine and the first strike of the former political prisoners which hastened the departure of the Democratic Party from the coalition with the former communists and led to the arrest of the dictator's widow Nexhmije Hoxha.

Among the people at large, these strikes had been highly emotional collective experiences. Intense media pressure concentrated public attention on the self-sacrificing strikers and plunged the nation's institutions into crisis. Faced with the destabilization of the country, the government had been forced to resign out of fear that the impassioned crowds could act as they did when they toppled Hoxha's statue.

Aware of the power of hunger strikes, Berisha was very frightened that the scenarios that he himself had used could be turned against him with the same success. Therefore he agreed to meet a delegation of the students. But like his predecessor Ramiz Alia six years before, he failed to reach any understanding with them. The old scenario was enacted again, except that Berisha was careful to show greater resilience in the face of strikes against his government.

There was every sign that he would try to end this strike by force. He was helped in this by the fact that, in contrast to the strike of 1991, this one was being held in Vlora, where, according to the government, it was being organized by a minority, manipulated by traffickers and former *Sigurimi* agents.

***

ATA reported that the students had been given blankets and were guaranteed medical aid, and that the police station had sent personnel to guard the building. The report also cited inside sources claiming that on the first day there were no concerns about the students' health.

On 22nd February, ATA again carried a short report: 'The students' strike continues. Their health is good, except for one student who during the night had a temperature of 37.5°C. On Friday one student left the strike and was replaced by another. The students are satisfied with the conduct of the police.'

Every day, huge numbers of demonstrators joined the strikers' relatives in the square in front of the university. The most articulate among them made speeches, calling on the crowds to continue their protests until their demands were met. They sang songs and chanted, 'We want our money!' and 'Down with the government.' When they got tired of shouting in chorus, other orators climbed onto the improvised rostrum and made more speeches.

Qorri did not like the fact that the strikers' aims contained a contradiction that had already prompted disagreements within the Forum. They demanded both the resignation of the government and the return of their money. He thought that the government should either return the money or resign, and the question of what money was left should be investigated by the government of professionals or the new one to emerge after elections. He had always opposed any pledge to the return of the money because it seemed to him a false and impossible promise. For him what was most important was to bring down the government, which had to be punished for the catastrophe it had caused. But after a press conference at the Hotel Rogner at which he and Kurt Kola had said that the Forum did not promise to return the money, both their own people and their opponents had attacked them. Berisha's press, to discourage the demonstrators, carried banner headlines, 'Forum Does Not Promise Return of Money.' Within the Forum Qorri and Kola were accused of political naivety, because if they did not promise the money they would lose support. This caused the first rift in the Forum, and on the following day some journalists close to individual Forum leaders had written that the three former political prisoners should resign their positions to make way for tried and tested politicians.

There was something else about the strike that troubled Qorri, which also had to do with the false promise to return the money. The students were in fact eating, and this was not a genuine hunger strike. The same had been true of earlier strikes. Everyone knew they were eating, both the organizers and the government. No act of self-sacrifice was taking place. The strike was a kind of theatre acted out by both sides, but which both sides pretended to believe in, and indeed experienced as if it were real. Could anything genuine come out of this sham?

These doubts running through his mind were much weaker than his faith that he was working for a just cause. Truth and lies, pretence and honesty coexisted in the movement, sometimes within the same person. Many people had joined the movement unclear whether they did so because of the money or the violation of their freedom, for the sake of power or in a genuine effort to solve the crisis. Ultimately, was there any clear distinction between play-acting and an authentic event?

'This sublime step shows that Albanian youth has resolved to act in order to change the destiny of the nation, to liberate the country from corrupt politics and the irresponsibility of the ruling party.'

'The Forum for Democracy strongly supports the students of Vlora and their political and economic demands. We appeal to all the students of Albania to express solidarity with them through peaceful demonstrations of all kinds, from boycotts of classes to hunger strikes.

'The Forum appeals to the people of Vlora and the entire country to support the young people of Albania.'

On 23rd February, Gumeni, Gjinushi and several others went to Vlora and repeated this call from a rostrum among the fervent protesters. The language seemed to seek to give meaning to the students' action. Yet, when Qorri thought of how they were secretly eating, it seemed to him that the strike was stillborn.

Meanwhile, reports soon arrived that students from other cities were preparing to start strikes in solidarity with the students of Vlora.

***

On 24th February, a group of doctors reported that the health of the students had deteriorated. Seven of them had been admitted to hospital, and others were showing serious symptoms. Nobody could tell to what extent this report was accurate or fabricated. It was the aim of both sides to dramatize the harm done by the other. ATA countered with a report that groups of demonstrators around the university were launching increasingly wild slogans for the resignation of the government, and threatening to burn down the District Council and the city's courts if they didn't strike too. On 25th February, the strike committee reported that fourteen students had now been admitted to hospital.

***

Berisha continued his feverish activity to prevent power slipping from his grasp. He visited Elbasan, Peshkopia, and Shkodra, and then set off for the south. In Gjirokastra he expressed his gratitude to his supporters for their 'civilized' attitude. He said that their stand was a deserved response to all those who pursued anti-Albanian, anti-democratic, and careerist aims at the expense of honest people. He told them that the Council of Europe supported the State institutions.

But the main piece of news from his visit was his reply to a question about early elections and the president. 'The elections,' Berisha said, 'will be held in due time, and that is in 2000.' The idea of 'first the constitution, and then the president,' he added, was mistaken because the country required leadership. The president would have to be elected by the deadline of 9th March.

The message was that Berisha, regardless of what his opponents wanted, had decided to get himself re-elected and had no intention of letting go of power. This added fuel to the flames.

***

By 26th February, the seventh day of the strike, there were fifteen strikers in hospital, and the strike committee claimed that the condition of the others was worsening. The students insisted that they would not give up their strike before their goals were achieved. Both sides seemed to be preparing for the inevitable showdown. The entire south was racked with conflict. Tractors blocked the road to Memaliaj after an inhabitant of the town was arrested in the demonstrations.

On Thursday, 27th February, Meksi stated in parliament that the country was on the brink of macroeconomic instability: the collapse of the currency, inflation, and a budget deficit. The Foreign Ministry denied the reports by some foreign media, including Reuters, that rapid deployment forces had been sent to Vlora. These malevolent slanders of extremists, the ministry stated, had seriously radicalized the situation in the city.

Chapter XXIII

The Left and the European Right

Qorri could not believe his ears. The announcer of Albanian Television, his voice slightly more strident than usual, was reading a report that twenty-eight British MPs had submitted a petition against the motion of a group of Labour members criticizing the Albanian Government. The long report quoted extracts from the petition, which stated that the MPs 'supported the measures proposed by the British government, the Conservative Party and the honourable member for Chertsey and Walton to help Albania in its continuing transformation into a democratic and free market state.' They added, 'We point out with concern but not with surprise that the honourable members of the Labour Party have also signed petitions in support of communist dictatorships in Afghanistan, Cuba, and Nicaragua.' The Conservative MPs also supported a statement by the British Helsinki Human Rights Group, according to which 'the Albanians should be congratulated on creating a multi-party democracy,' and condemning the foreign observers, who, according to the group, were old friends of the Stalinist regime of Enver Hoxha. They also criticized the Albanian Section of the BBC for reporting every criticism of the PD and its government, while passing over in silence the statement of the British Helsinki Group.

In its next item, Albanian Television reported that the Foreign Ministry had charged the BBC with having accused Albania of breaking the oil embargo against Yugoslavia, without any serious evidence, but simply trusting the word of an Albanian diplomat dismissed in 1994 for being in the service of the former communists.

What a ridiculous misunderstanding, thought Qorri. How could the members of this parliament, with a reputation as the wisest in the world, believe that the opposition was trying to bring about a revolution to restore the communist regime? He remembered Gumbel's word 'dogged.'

During the dictatorship, the Albanians had considered the West a monolithic deity to which they looked for salvation. Now they discovered that the European left and right, between which at one time they could barely tell the difference, were arguing about the crisis in Albania and interpreting it through the ideological lens of the Cold War. At every meeting with the European right wing, Qorri had tried to explain to them that their so-called anti-communist allies had behaved like communists, and that what the opposition was trying to accomplish, this time on its own, was the overthrow of a regime that had visibly inherited characteristics of the previous one. After every conversation, he would wonder if he had succeeded in convincing them. He had also tried to explain to Western leftists that what they were doing had nothing to do with preserving certain values of Socialism, which they had fought for in Europe when they had idealized the communist regimes of the East, because what was happening in Albania was not a popular revolution against a savage neo-liberal capitalist regime, as some of the left-wing radicals portrayed it.

But the memory of the period before the fall of the Berlin Wall and the divisions of that time continued to colour the new reality. The present was seen as a perpetuation of the past. It was no accident that Berisha insisted on using the term 'left-wing,' and also refused to meet former political prisoners but only representatives of the Socialist Party. In this way he cemented the division he wished to preserve, portraying what was happening as a comeback of the ex-communists.

The European categories of left and right simply did not correspond to the way Albanians used them and did not help to explain what was happening. In fact, this movement did not resemble other popular movements familiar from history. It was peculiar to itself, born out of the specific experience of a society isolated from the world for fifty years.

***

The day after the report on the petition of the British Conservatives, the Forum asked at its news conference at the Rogner for more attention from Europe, and Qorri also said there that the Forum had doubts about some of the aid for Albania that Western governments were planning. 'Berisha has had plenty of aid,' Qorri said, implying that Berisha should now be punished for misusing this aid rather than given more. The next day he saw himself pilloried again by *Albania* and *Rilindja Demokratike* as anti-Albanian.

Chapter XXIV

The Fire Smoulders

In Vlora people passed sleepless nights after the news that special forces had come to put an end to the students' strike. Hundreds and thousands of people gathered round the university and others patrolled the darkened streets in cars. Occasional gunshots could be heard.

Rumours that the SHIK had a plan to evict the students had been circulating round Vlora for some days. The government denied any such intention, but few believed it. The people of Vlora were now convinced that the central government was preparing to reassert the authority of the State in their rebel city. The strike and the university square where the crowd camped out day and night to encourage and protect the students were now the heart of the rebellion. The students had now decided irrevocably to press on with the strike until the government resigned.

Tension increased when the Meksi government accused the strikers of paralysing all the institutions of government. The port and the city's shops had closed down completely. The branch of VEFA had stopped paying back even small sums of $100-$500 because of the confusion created by the strikes and protests. The company's bosses appealed to the population not to cause difficulties, but they took no notice. The government now filed a suit against the strikers at the Tirana Court, calling their strike illegal.

Clearly, this accusation was intended to justify government intervention. The Court put off making its decision and asked the defendants to be informed so that they could be present. The rector of the university was summoned to appear in court on 27th February.

Meanwhile, forty-six students at Gjirokastra University started their own hunger strike in support of Vlora and said that they would continue until the demands of the Vlora strikers were met. In Elbasan, a student was cheered when he called for a boycott of classes in support of Vlora's demands for the resignation of the government.

Hundreds of students of Tirana University had now abandoned their classes and were demonstrating in support of Vlora on the open spaces of the campus. High school students joined them. Reportedly, some of them had tried to start a strike in a lecture theatre, but the police had stopped them with the help of student groups linked to the PD.

The fire kindled at Vlora was spreading throughout the country.

***

As tension grew in Vlora, The Democratic Party's National Council met in Tirana and decided that Sali Berisha would be the party's presidential candidate. Of the council's ninety members, eighty-five were in favour and none were against. The remaining five abstained.

Of the fourteen signatories of the petition within the PD demanding the resignation of the Meksi government, described by Berisha as 'has-beens', only nine had taken part in the voting, because five were not members of the council. Of these nine, four had nevertheless voted in favour of Berisha, and the other five had dared only to abstain. This showed that Berisha was still very powerful in the party. Tritan Shehu, the party chairman, called him the man who had been able to develop democracy and institutions of government, to establish a market economy, and integrate Albania in the North Atlantic Alliance.

The parliament decided that the president would be elected on Monday, 3rd March at ten o'clock.

This decision convinced Vlora that the government would intervene to end the hunger strike. No president could be elected with a city in rebellion, demanding his overthrow day and night.

***

'What we see today is a smouldering fire. The leaves are burning, but the wood has not caught fire yet,' wrote Qorri that day in *Koha Jonë*. His article was a response to criticism within the opposition that the Forum no longer had a role, and it was time for the parties and their leaders to step forward. Qorri insisted that the fire being kindled by the fall of the pyramids would blaze for a long time, and it was important to stay together in the Forum. However, as he reread the article, the metaphor of something smouldering scared him. Had he meant to imply, even threaten, that what was happening was merely the start of a conflagration?

The article's ambiguity in fact illustrated a contradiction that the Forum had never resolved, and nor had Qorri, except through Charles Walsh's judo metaphor. The Forum was trying at the same time to prevent the inferno that this smouldering fire augured and also to drive Berisha from power at all costs. However, to defend himself, Berisha would obviously threaten to set the country ablaze. He had already poured petrol on the wood. He was not going to turn back, especially now that he had hostages with him. He had no way out other than to pursue his adventure to the end, with his hostages. He would demand a route back from the precipice on which he and his hostages now stood. Otherwise they could expect a catastrophe. Everyone supposed that his macho code of behaviour also included the notion of a heroic death.

It was hard to distinguish between empty and genuine menaces, between psychological blackmail and the threat of actual physical violence. The threat of violence could tip over into actual

150

violence. The same analysis applied to the threats of the hunger strike, which could generate real violence. Both sides knew that if they were held back by fear of each other, they would remain hostage to each other. So they needed a lot of courage. Qorri was frightened that it was Berisha, who was looking over the precipice, who had the most courage. By what trick could he be made to shoot himself rather than his hostages?

***

Reuters carried the news first. The spokesman of the Ministry of Public Order tried to deny the report, but its truth was soon established: in Vlora, there had been a gunfight between forces of the SHIK and protesters, and several people had died. Nobody in Tirana knew exactly what had happened, but speculation focused on the strike. So the fire was taking hold.

On the night of 28th February there were more people than ever in the square in front of Vlora University, and some of them did not look peaceful. The news spread among the crowd that police vans were lying in wait in the darkness, ready to move in to forcibly evict the students. The crowd organized themselves, immediately forming a solid human wall facing the direction from which the vehicles might come.

Was there really a plan that night, or was what happened merely the result of accumulated tension, the final confrontation that the crowd expected? Those attackers would not be able to tell the difference. The State denied the existence of any such plan, but nobody believed this after its display of intolerance. All the signs were that Berisha intended to use force to bring this crisis to an end. He had gone beyond blackmail.

As soon as the headlights of an unidentified vehicle became visible in the darkness on one of the streets leading to the university square, the protesters thought that the SHIK had come to reconnoitre an intervention. They hurled themselves against the car. This threat had to be averted. The car accelerated and fled, perhaps in its intended direction, but its headlights alone were the spark that ignited the gunpowder.

A mob ran after it, leaving the square and heading for the SHIK building, where many agents who had come from Tirana were said to be devising a plan to evict the students. This wild mob was not about to hold a peaceful protest. Demonstrations weren't held at night.

Nobody knew where the first shots came from, the SHIK building or the crowd, but it was the crowd who were more exposed to the bullets. Soon there came wails of 'murder!' A SHIK bullet had thrown a protester to the ground. There were shouts calling for revenge. The crowd threw grenades and Molotov cocktails at the building. Tongues of flame enveloped the SHIK headquarters, and the shots from inside died away. A protester signalled that the SHIK were trying to escape the burning building through the back door. The monstrous crowd stretched out a tentacle and seized three of them, while the remainder fled as fast as they could. The prisoners put their hands up and asked for mercy. But if an individual can grant mercy, an angry and vindictive mob cannot. The men were forced to their knees, and in this position were shot in the head. Someone howled that this was not enough. The bodies must be burned like the SHIK building. The petrol was soon found.

But the crowd had no time to savour its victory as the bodies of the SHIK men and their headquarters burned.

'Guns, get the guns!'

This was no longer a rallying cry but an order from the mobsters who had taken command. They had to prepare for war, because the government's retaliation would be swift. Some of the crowd ran through the darkness to the military barracks on the outskirts of the city. The soldiers there were disinclined to mount a heroic defence of their depot. The mob, now bristling with an entire arsenal of heavy weapons, Kalashnikov automatic rifles, hand grenades, pistols, and bayonets, ran through the streets of Vlora from the harbour to Flag Square, looking for the enemy.

When they saw they had nobody to fight against, a few hundred headed for the President's summer villa, where Enver Hoxha had once spent his vacations and Berisha now did the same. The handful of soldiers guarding it put up no resistance. The villa was looted, and everything that could be removed, down to the bathroom tiles and the window frames, was carried off. When there was nothing left to take, the mob attacked the other government villas nearby. That night the ecstatic crowd burned and pillaged everything that belonged to the State.

It was only in the morning when they had sobered up that someone remembered to count the dead. Government sources reported that six SHIK agents had been murdered, four of them burned alive. The director of the Vlora hospital said that his emergency department had received four dead and twenty wounded. Only one of these had been a SHIK employee, and the others had been protesters.

Nobody knew for certain how many had died on the bullet-scarred asphalt of the streets of Vlora, and how many of the killed were SHIK agents.

That afternoon the funerals of three citizens were held. The dead no longer belonged to their families. The armed crowd, most of whom carried a weapon in their hands for the first time in their lives, took over the organization of the ceremony. During the funeral, one of them fired an automatic rifle and accidentally hit someone in the stomach, killing him. Stray bullets fired into the air during the funeral fell from the sky and wounded four more

The city fell totally into the hands of the rebels. They positioned heavy machine guns in front of the entrance to the university. The

State media claimed that the rebellion had followed secret instructions, and that the clearest sign of this was the speed and determination of the attacks on strategic buildings. Radio Tirana repeatedly broadcast an ATA report headlined 'Terrorist Gangs in Vlora attack Arms Depots and SHIK building.' The radio also reported that a number of PD members in Vlora had been abducted from their homes and were being held in unknown locations, and claimed that the rebels were militants of the Socialist Party, the former communists.

Albania claimed that groups of criminals guided by the left-wing opposition were executing people on a 'death list' in Vlora, and that representatives of the government, ordinary Vlora policemen, and the city's intellectuals had been sentenced to death. Allegedly the list was circulating all over Vlora. The terrorists were hunting down everyone on this 'death list,' and the SHIK headquarters had been attacked after the terrorists discovered that three of the people on the list were inside.

The report added that Vlora was without basic foodstuffs such as sugar, rice, and flour, and ordinary people were now the hostages of the city's terrorists and criminals.

Chapter XXV

Doublespeak

The victory of the guns in Vlora created a nightmare for the Tirana Government. Could Berisha weather these events? The government was on the brink of resignation, with dozens of deaths laid at its door. State institutions had collapsed, Vlora was in total rebellion with fighting in the streets, and the nation faced bankruptcy. Moreover, after what had happened, Albania was split in two, and Berisha's people didn't dare set foot in the south. The streets of Gjirokastra, Berat, Fier, and Elbasan, cities dangerously close to the border with Greece, were now seething. Reports came of clashes with the police. Armed men moved along the roads linking these towns, and nobody could tell if they were ordinary bandits or protesters intending to repel any forces sent from Tirana.

Berisha realized that the time had come to throw Meksi to these hungry crowds, in the hope that would pacify them. He announced Meksi's dismissal as Prime Minister and a reshuffle of the government.

Meksi had already sensed that this might happen. A week beforehand, he had threatened: 'If they force me to resign, I'll tell all. Everybody should know that I was always against the pyramid schemes.' The implication of this comment was that Berisha had been responsible, and had failed to act on Meksi's warnings. But it had no effect. Meksi had been Berisha's fellow traveller until the previous week, so his threat merely intensified the hostility between the government and the opposition.

The question now was whether Meksi's removal could prolong Berisha's political life and avert disaster, or was it already too late. The majority felt that Meksi's resignation was not enough. They wanted Berisha's head.

U.S. Ambassador Lino spoke out in support of Berisha. First she expressed her condolences to the families of the victims, and then appealed for rational dialogue that would lead to a realistic solution. 'All sides must show restraint in their words and deeds to reduce the possibility of violence.' 'Extremist language and violence have no place in this process.'

This manner of speaking left scope for both parties to interpret the statement in their own favour, but still ruled out any solution through violence.

The Forum was not in fact a revolutionary party that permitted violence in pursuit of its goals, and neither was Berisha's a dictatorial regime that would dare to suppress any opposition with bloodshed. Both sides were following a kind of middle path. The cult of bloodshed still prevailed among the Albanians, who had just emerged from a regime whose leaders had taught them for thirty-five years that power was won through blood and surrendered only through blood. But on the other hand, the propaganda of the last few years had repudiated this communist slogan, in the name of democracy and pluralism. Neither side was prepared to challenge Albania's Western allies and justify the use of violence. To the north in Serbia too, a protest movement had caused headaches to another dictator, Milošević. Belgrade was buzzing with protests, but Milošević, even though he had gone to war in Bosnia, didn't dare use violence in his own country. It was only in Africa that a violent revolution was currently taking place. In Zaire, Kabila was marching on the capital Kinshasa, and it looked as if violence would be decisive. Deep down the Albanians envied Kabila, but they were aware that they could not behave like him.

So both sides perfected their doublespeak. Berisha condemned more and more strongly acts of terrorism supposedly led by the Forum, as intending to destabilize the country. The Forum talked about its determination to find a settlement through the dialogue that Berisha refused.

156

Chapter XXVI

Second Rally

From Fatos Qorri's Diary
1st March

Despite the heightened tension caused by the events in Vlora, we decided to hold a rally. Ten days before, we had been granted a permit for three o'clock on the field of Ali Demi. The police had issued the permit before the developments in Vlora, but had not dared revoke it.

I set off on foot alone. As I emerged onto the ring road, several people joined me heading in the same direction. I felt more comfortable in a group. They seemed determined people of few words.

At the bridge over the river Lana, we met a sight that left us dumbstruck. Here was an entire army: three or four ranks of policemen with shields, body armour, and truncheons. Alongside them were a large number of frightening-looking trucks. We had never seen such monsters. Their wheels alone were the height of a man. These terrifying creatures ,emerging suddenly from their lair greatly disfigured the aspect of our city and posed a definite threat to the lives of the people. In fact, many people who had come as far as the bridge, turned back when they saw these police behemoths blocking the roadway from one bridge across the Lana to the next.

It was rumoured that the rally had been banned. I was in two minds whether to continue, but my group was determined to go ahead and I went with them, at least to reach the field and see what was happening.

Apparently the police had been given double-edged orders: to mount a show of force to scare people, but not turn them back. After we crossed the bridge, we noticed that some people were avoiding the main road and making their way to the field through alleys. We went down a back lane but at a bend, just as we were about to come out on the square, some plain-clothes men stood in front of us. They were more frightening than the police, because they were at the same time backed up by the State, yet unaccountable.

'You killed our people in Vlora, we're not letting you past,' one of them said.

His dialect showed he was a northerner from the same district as Berisha, what Tirana people had started to call a 'Chechen'. We stood hesitating for a while but we didn't turn back. We turned into a side street between two apartment blocks and emerged on the field itself.

We were astonished by what we saw. On the way here, we had thought that all these hindrances would have broken people's will. We expected to find half a dozen individuals, but here in front of us stretched an unending sea of people. The atmosphere was exhilarating, without any of the fear and tension felt in the streets I had passed through. Joining this crowd made one feel safe from any threat of the police. Once again I felt certain that this mass of humanity was the true hero of this story. I made my way through the crowd to the rostrum of the stadium where the other Forum leaders stood. I climbed the steps and as I turned to face the field, I experienced a strange phenomenon. The sun's rays fell into my eyes and for a moment the strong light and that ocean of people became one. I could not distinguish between them. After a few seconds I discerned the different groups singing and shouting slogans, the placards they were holding, and the true extent of the crowd, which seemed less containable than ten days ago. Again I felt like a little boat tossing on a stormy sea. Shouts of 'Hang Sali the dog' and 'Out with the scumbag!' alternated with the songs 'Vlora,

Vlora', 'Reach for your guns, boys -- freedom or death' and then the most thunderous shout of all, 'To the square! To the square!' The waves of this sea seemed to swell and break as the crowd called for a final showdown on Scanderbeg Square.

I have described these people sometimes as a 'crowd' and sometimes a 'mass.' In fact they were something between the two. A mass recognies its leaders and obeys them. Without leaders it can revert to being a crowd and dissolve into scattered clumps. We were on the cusp, the dividing line between a mass and a crowd, because our authority over these people was minimal, and their respect for us was also slight.

We had no loudspeakers because the police had turned back the vehicles with sound systems. Without loudspeakers to address this mass of people, and under pressure to attack Scanderbeg Square, it became difficult for us to remain where we were. Finally we managed to divert the crowd's uncontainable energy into another direction. For these people, Democracy Square at the university campus was a historic site, and an occupation of this square could also be called a victory.

Reaching Democracy Square meant taking a street with five-storey apartment blocks on each side. This canyon frightened us because in Vlora the SHIK reportedly had thrown stones down on demonstrators from blocks of flats. We had just entered these straits when I heard a gunshot close to me. The mass of people bristled. It was like a shiver passing through the body of an enormous beast. Someone said the shot had been aimed at Neritan Ceka from an apartment block. Another person pointed to a man on a balcony that they thought was the culprit. Some people rushed up to attack him but he escaped to another balcony. He turned out to be the chauffeur of a PD deputy, who had fired into the air to scare us. Seconds later stones were thrown, shattering the windows on his balcony. The crowd's panic and fury reached a new peak.

At that moment, Blendi Gonxhja, who had never been far from me, came up to me and Dash Peza, who was at my side, to tell us that we had better run for it. We were in great danger. There were snipers on the roofs. His face was ashen.

'We have a meeting at the Rogner. Journalists are expecting us.'

It was true that we had a meeting, but later. Seeing Gonxhja's determination, I hesitated. Perhaps I would have gone with him, but at that moment, a protester close to me who had heard what Gonxhja had said turned to me with a serious expression.

'Fatos Qorri, we want you to lead us.'

I told myself to ignore him and keep going, but before moving forward I felt in my guts that familiar conflict between fear and shame at my fear. In the midst of such a mass of people, the shame inevitably won. And so I walked on with a sense of shame which was forcing me to face down the fear. There are some people who say that this shame derives from a sense of self-respect, and perhaps this is the best way to describe it. Dash set off alongside me, and at that moment I felt he was my closest friend.

I have always been averse to merging myself with a mass of people, ever since the time when we were forced to take part in compulsory rallies on Liberation Day or 1st May in Hoxha's time, below the feet of the leadership who waved at us from their rostrum. The dictum 'I think therefore I am' has always been very important to me. It reminds me that I am an autonomous individual, while these compulsory rallies seemed to undermine this conviction, replacing it with, 'I am part of a mass. I am, because I don't think. I allow myself to be led and I shout without thinking.' I think that this is why I also refuse to become the leader of a mass. But now my situation was different. I was neither more nor less than an individual demonstrator, a foot soldier who would cover himself in shame by running away. There are situations in which we run away from ourselves and shed our personal responsibility by joining a mass, but at other times merging with a mass is an act of responsibility and courage. This was a moment in which it was a duty to join the mass and an act of courage to lead it. These people had overcome their fear and passed through ranks of police with body armour and truncheons in order to come this far, and they deserved respect. This was not a demonstration ordered by the regime. It was against a regime.

Gonxhja had vanished. Apparently his fear had got the better of him. We all feel fear. What is important is not to surrender to it. Yet sometimes you have to obey fear to save your skin. Now go figure out the golden mean. Anyhow, it was self-respect that kept me there, or in other words, fear of the shame that haunts you after you commit a squalid act. I could feel that shame, from the look in the face of the protester who said to me, 'Fatos Qorri, we want you to lead us.'

In fact, at the front was a substantial vanguard of people I did not know, who seemed ready to fly in the face of danger. They must have been the ones shouting for Scanderbeg Square. Perhaps they felt important for the first time in their lives, or found this rebellion especially intoxicating. Or perhaps the loss of their money had banished any sense of fear. Whatever their reasons, these people were the true leaders that day.

Soon we faced a barricade of policemen with shields and helmets. What now, I thought. Before I could think of an answer, our vanguard hurled a terrible hail of stones in the direction of the police. The barrage lasted a few seconds, or minutes, I don't know. To me it seemed like the blink of an eye, only long enough to see the trajectory of the stones flying through the air. The police vanished either before the stones reached them or as soon as the first stones fell. Our front line surged forward.

The square was taken and the mass of people celebrated the victory at once by burning the parked car of the director of the Student Union. The black smoke from its burning tyres rose into the sky like the crown of a cypress, and some of the crowd danced with joy

161

around the vehicle as if intoxicated by the stench of burning rubber.

Most of the students had abandoned their dormitories when the disturbances began. But the crowd did not feel their absence. Only one or two windows facing the square were left open, from which a few remaining students watched what was happening. After burning the car groups of protesters danced and shouted slogans.

A group of about ten people surrounded me and almost lifted me aloft to carry me through the seething square to an improvised dais, where there were several other leaders of the Forum. I could sense their need for leaders and symbols in the way they touched me and spoke to me. Somebody shouted about the absence of loudspeakers. We had to speak to them, without fail. These people wanted to hear a message.

There was no way I could speak. I could not even join the rhythmic chorus of 'Hang the dog'. We didn't have loudspeakers. It was better if they just danced and sang, and that is what they did.

Soon a number of men, formerly a part of the vanguard that had put the police to flight, came to the rostrum. One of them, still short of breath, said that they had chased the police a long way, throwing stones at them. They jostled like children in front of us, each of them drawing attention to himself. One man, a ringleader who looked the strongest of all, said he had lost all his money in the pyramids, and was scared of nothing. He was ready to die. How sorry we felt to dampen all this energy.

***

It was time for my meeting at the Rogner. People were still celebrating when I set off with Dash. We crossed Democracy Square, which was totally deserted. We found ourselves in a frightening void. We walked on as far as the railings of the U.S. Embassy. The only person visible on the street was the policeman on guard.

162

To reach the Rogner we took one of the three side streets leading away from the embassy. As soon as we turned the corner, we were faced with the astonishing sight of the entire street packed with armed policemen with truncheons and shields, lined up on both sides. They seemed to be in readiness. We stopped dead in terror. Should we run that frightening gauntlet or turn back? Could anyone pass through and survive? But silently we agreed that turning back would be even more dangerous, and walked on. About half way one of the policemen recognized me, and said to his colleague, 'Isn't it that Qorri guy?'

I pressed on without turning my head, pretending not to care if they recognized me. None of them made a move.

We came out of that frightening tunnel with the thought that the other side roads off Elbasan Street must also be full of Special Forces, and that these squads were there to prevent people coming out on the boulevard and heading for Scanderbeg Square. But that evening I learned that this was not true. These policemen were not there to keep order or even guard the embassy. They were waiting to punish the protesters who had humiliated their colleagues. When the stream of demonstrators came down from Democracy Square to the city at the end of that long afternoon, with their emotions now spent, the squads came out from the three side streets and forced their way among the demonstrators like wedges, separating them into three groups to weaken their numbers. Then they had struck them mercilessly with their truncheons and crushed them under their shields.

Many people suffered broken ribs, Kalakulla among them. When I phoned him he could barely speak for pain, but he was angrier about his wife, whom they had also manhandled and who was in shock.

When I returned to the Kindergarten that evening I turned on the television to hear the official version, which seemed to describe an entirely different event. According to ATA, after the rally on the Ali Demi field, a group of a hundred protesters had attacked the nearby police station and assaulted two officers on duty. One of them had barely escaped with his life. This crowd, composed mainly of teenagers, had broken the police station's doors and windows and stolen some police shields, breaking them in front of the video cameras of foreign correspondents. Some students had tried to come to the aid of the police but the crowd would not let them. The crowd had thrown stones at the dormitories of the women students when they had refused to join the demonstrators. After the intervention of the police the protesters had left Democracy Square and some had gathered round the U.S. Embassy. There they had again attacked the police forces protecting the embassy and the nearby residence of the Italian ambassador.

Chapter XXVII

State of Emergency

There were no more Saturdays, Sundays, or normal days of work and rest. The rally on the Ali Demi field was on 1st March, a Saturday. On the following Sunday, under pressure from the international community, a meeting of all the political parties was held at last at the Palace of Congresses. That same afternoon, the parliament met in an emergency session.

In the Palace of Congresses, besides the parties in the Forum, there were also gathered representatives of the parties allied to Berisha: the National Front, the Monarchists, and the Social Democrats who were Gjinushi's rivals. Godo of the Republicans, who occupied the middle ground, was also there. A PD representative was expected, but nobody knew who it would be, because the party's deputies were at the parliament, where the PD was the sole party after the departure of the Republicans. .

The tables were positioned in a large circle with an empty space in the middle, and chairs and microphones in front of each place. The PD's representative finally arrived, just at the moment when it was decided to start without him. Everybody saw at once that a puppet had been sent, merely to register a presence. It was Albert Brojka, the mayor of Tirana, a man who counted for little in the party and enjoyed the reputation of a petty bureaucrat who had fixed up his friends with building permits for kiosks, depriving Tirana of all its parks and public spaces.

When he saw that all eyes and ears were concentrated on him, he greeted everybody with the grin of a devilish halfwit and hastened to add that he had just arrived from Paris and was present only to listen, because he had no mandate to represent the PD or make decisions. Qorri was irritated by the silly way in which he scattered innocent smiles in all directions, while admitting that he represented nobody.

Nevertheless a discussion started. To the astonishment of the Forum's leaders, even the parties allied to the PD said that they did not want to solve the problem through violence or declare a state of emergency, as it was rumoured the parliament might do that same afternoon. This helped mutual understanding. The parties agreed immediately to sign a declaration opposing any state of emergency and asking for a political solution through dialogue. Qorri wrote the declaration in ballpoint on a loose sheet of paper, incorporating various people's suggestions. He read it out, and passed the sheet round the huge circle to be signed by the party chairmen.

As the paper passed from hand to hand, a whisper also went round the circle, probably started by Brojka, who was talking to his people on his mobile. It was hard to believe at first. The PD, the single party in parliament had just voted for a state of emergency. The declaration they were signing was useless. A single party had taken the decision against the will of all the others.

The representatives of the parties stood up, looked at each other in silence, and filed out. Even Berisha's allies felt the humiliation. Qorri saw Godo making for his car and hurried after him. He knew that Godo was one of the people still in contact with Berisha. He had already got into his car, but when he saw Qorri he left the door open.

'You're still talking to Berisha,' Qorri said. 'Go and tell him not to do what he's planning.'

'I've told him,' Godo said gloomily. 'I told him that nothing will be able to wash his hands clean again. I've got nothing more to say and I'm not going to him again.' He paused for a moment, looked Qorri in the eye even more confidentially, and said, 'But I'm scared

166

of something else, that he'll let loose his northerners in the south and set them looting down there.'

He set off without a further word.

***

At the moment when Godo left Qorri on the pavement by the Palace of Congresses, Albanian television interrupted its programmes for a special bulletin. President Sali Berisha was speaking:

'Groups of terrorists, former communists, and former secret police agents of the old regime, aided by foreign forces, have destroyed our town halls, burned municipal buildings, killed policemen and innocent citizens, attacked banks and stolen money, and now they are looting homes and shops...'

'I have gone to impossible lengths to persuade them to see reason, and will continue to do so. I have spoken to all the leaders of political parties. I invited the opposition, but they did not turn up. They prefer to spread hatred, accusing us of appropriating the money from the pyramids. There is no truth in this accusation. Now is not the moment to discuss this matter...'

'Albanians, we succeeded in building a democracy and we won't allow anybody to take it from us. I ask you to keep calm. Help the police to re-establish the law and stand by the army.'

Berisha's speech was a cold shower for the entire country. It meant that the army would be sent south to quell the rebellion that was no longer just of the 'strong men' of 'the free republic of Vlora' but had spread to Lushnja, Fier, Saranda, and Berat. The army was to take over internal security. The secret services, i.e. the SHIK, would go under the control of the Interior Ministry.

The television next reported that the Public Salvation Committee at Vlora, created in the last few days, had sent an ultimatum to Berisha in the early hours of the morning: 'If you do not agree to early elections and the return of 100 per cent of the money our citizens have lost in the pyramid schemes, our forces will set off for Tirana to re-impose order and liberate the country.'

Who had sent this communiqué to the news agency? Who was behind this 'committee'? Some people believed that it was a fabrication, and others that it was genuine.

The news reports intertwined with each other ever faster as the evening wore on. Some were confirmed and others proved false. The official news broadcast stated that Vlora was in flames, murderous gangs were in control of the city and its surroundings, issuing threats, beating, looting, raping and killing. Foreign news stations too reported that a large number of insurgents armed with Kalashnikovs and with stolen army vehicles were marching on Tirana. They were said to be waiting for reinforcements and heavy weapons near Rrogozhina, about 60 kilometres from the capital.

'Could this really be true?' people asked.

One report was generally believed: Fatos Nano, the former Socialist Prime Minister who was imprisoned for corruption in 1993, and held at a prison in Tepelena, had been transferred to the Tirana gaol. This news too suggested that the South was out of control.

Fear gripped Tirana. The streets of the capital were virtually empty. Hardly a soul ventured out to the little bars and innumerable kiosks. There were more policemen than ordinary citizens in the centre. People shut themselves up in their houses and sat by their televisions and radios trying to work out what fate held in store for them. For some people, a neighbour who had moved in after the fall of the old regime, who had seemed a good friend until now, suddenly became someone to steer clear of.

The countless Mercedes that drove round Tirana dwindled to a few, mostly rented by foreign journalists. Alitalia and Swissair flights arrived full of correspondents, photographers, and film crews from all over the world. There had not been such a massive influx of the 'news force' since the fall of communism. This was another sign that the situation was about to explode.

The first to suffer under the State of Emergency were precisely these foreign journalists. Two groups, from the German TV station *Prosieben* and the BBC, were stopped in the street by military armoured vehicles and ordered to turn back. The journalists demanded an explanation and were told that their broadcasts spoiled Albania's image.

These two incidents turned out to be neither accidents nor the whims of a group of fanatical policemen. The people anxiously waiting by their televisions and radios had another surprise in store that evening. The Albanian-language broadcasts of the BBC, the Voice of America, and Western TV stations were suspended. The European Broadcasting Union, based in Geneva, which distributed the programmes of Western TV stations abroad, ceased co-operation with Albania at half-past five following an order received from the Albanian authorities. Under the State of Emergency, an oral order from a representative of the Albanian Post Office and Telecommunications revoked the licenses of the BBC, CNN, ARD and ZDF, RAI, TF1 and other Western channels that operated through the EBU. They ceased broadcasting immediately.

Only Albanian Television was left. In its first news that evening, a sombre general prosecutor appeared and spoke about a special meeting to discuss 'duties' and 'measures' to do with the State of Emergency. He had ordered the immediate prosecution of armed bands that had looted shops, attacked military units, and burned public buildings in southern cities such as Vlora, Saranda and Delvina. The police also had orders to shoot stone-throwers and to arrest anyone whose papers were not in order. A curfew was imposed from eight o'clock in the evening till seven o'clock in the morning. The President's counsellor told an Austrian radio station that this was a rebellion of common criminals and political criminals trying to overthrow the legitimate government and that armed insurgents would be shot without warning if they did not hand in their weapons by one o'clock on Monday 3rd March.

Armoured vehicles and tanks were now moving on the main highways. According to Albanian television, local headquarters to oversee the State of Emergency had been created in all the towns.

As they went to bed that night, people imagined their country as a slaughterhouse. But nobody could tell what was happening because of the media blackout.

Returning to the Kindergarten that evening, Qorri envied his cat Nusi, who sat down quietly on his chest like on any other day. For her, nothing at all had happened. She had no inkling of what was going on. Usually it calmed him down and relieved the pressure of his thoughts to stroke her soft fur, but that evening it was impossible. His brain thudded like a hammer, imagining what would happen. Albania had entered deep into a dark tunnel. Qorri's eyes stared at a part of the wall where the plaster had fallen most and a patch took the shape of a tank. He fell asleep only towards dawn.

As soon as he woke the next day he went out to see what had happened during the night. His instinct told him that it had not been a quiet one. The first news was that the editorial office of *Koha Jonë* had been burned. Armed civilians had beaten up the guard, terrorized the journalists they found there and smashed the computers and printers before setting fire to the building.

Qorri wanted to see it with his own eyes. He found the building a blackened shell without doors and windows, leaving to the imagination the terrifying operation it had been subjected to. Inside, Qorri surveyed the wreckage of the computers, printers, and photocopiers, whose mangled shapes seemed conscious, striving to convey without success their own amazement at being broken in this way.

170

Chapter XXVIII

The Oath

'I swear by my honour and before the flag to be loyal to the people and the homeland, to the ideals of freedom, democracy, and progress, and the independence and territorial inviolability of Albania.

'I swear to respect the constitutional laws, develop and protect democracy and human rights and freedoms... I swear.'

Berisha tried hard to look confident as he took his second presidential oath. The parliament, composed solely of his own party, had just voted for him with one hundred and thirteen votes in favour, one against, and four abstentions. His mandate was for five more years. Would it last five days?

An intimate of this man had said that if Berisha were ever forced to give up power he would grip the iron railings round the presidency and have to be dragged away with the railings themselves. This prophecy was being proved true, but he was taking with him not just the railings, but the whole of Albania.

Qorri had always been in two minds about Berisha. He did not agree with the widespread view that Albania deserved no better than Berisha, but he saw a certain truth in it. According to Qorri, Berisha could not have come to power if he did not represent a prevalent type in Albanian society, a man brought up in isolation and ignorance who combined a primitive cult of the tough guy with a lackey's subservience, who trampled pitilessly on anyone beneath him but was unhesitatingly obsequious to anyone above. These conflicting impulses sometimes tore personalities apart, but in other cases increased their determination to stand out from the crowd, if without ever freeing them of their fear of someone stronger than themselves.

These 'tough guys' represented a recognizable and frightening type. They came mainly from the Albanian countryside but were now experiencing a second wave of urbanization. They came down from the hills with the mind-sets of mercenaries, materially poor and short of ideals, but ready to do service and to plunder, and with all the aggressiveness an inferiority complex provides. Anyone who succeeded in manipulating these individuals' aggression could become very powerful. Enver Hoxha's Communist Party had done it after World War II. The dictatorship could not have been so fierce if this type had not existed, ruling over a thin stratum of confused and divided city people. But Hoxha did not complete the country's urbanization. It seemed to Qorri that under Berisha Albania was experiencing a reprise of the narrative of the communists' ascent to power, what might be called a 'second urbanization'. The tough guys once again faced a weak stratum of urban citizens, persecuted or corrupted by the communists, of whom the best were hurrying to leave the country for a quieter and better life in the West. Communism had made him even more irresponsible. The only thing that they had not learned, living in a compulsory collective, was a sense of community and responsibility for others. They did not recognize responsibility because this had always belonged to the State. They were now individual intent on seizing what they could for themselves. These types might unite to form a mob of looters but not a community. And so the kind of people who rose to power had no compunction about getting their hands dirty. Politicians created ties with criminals and mafia gangs. The financial pyramids were a racket of this kind.

Berisha's speech to the parliament was a further step in the career of a man who had trampled on everything to arrive where he was. He had been a fanatical communist, and then had seen that the communists would have to leave power. As communism fell, he had unleashed the destructive power of the tough guys. Now came hatred of communism and a *revanche* against it.

Chapter XXIX

The Westerners Flee

A cold wind blew in the Bay of Vlora, raising huge waves and darkening the sea and the western horizon. Weather forecasts warned of storms. But this same horizon still offered the hope of rescue.

A large group of Italians, four Germans, a Dutchman, and several journalists waited anxiously on the runway of Vlora airport for the helicopters that were to evacuate them from the rebel city. In the distance they heard the noise of racing cars, the rattle of gunfire, and sometimes explosions. At the city's little airport, which nobody guarded, armed men came and went, firing nonchalantly into the air.

A group of inhabitants of Vlora who had worked alongside them escorted these people to the airport and begged them, 'Don't leave us alone. Who will tell people what is happening here?'

But the foreigners in Vlora were in total panic. The Tirana government, not without an ulterior motive, had been warning foreigners for days to leave Vlora, telling them they were in danger. The Italian Foreign Ministry had appealed to Italian citizens not to travel to Albania except in cases of absolute necessity, and under no circumstances to go to Vlora or the south. France had also appealed to its citizens to leave, and asked anybody planning a journey not to go to Albania.

The Westerners in Vlora had to be evacuated as fast as possible. How? It would be dangerous and time-consuming to transport them to Tirana airport. There was only one way: a quick intervention from across the sea. Italy was only forty miles from the Bay of Vlora, a short hop. But in Italy they feared that this jump might be fatal, because there were rebels with their guns at the ready on the opposite coast. So the Italian staff counted on surprise and speed. Every second had to be precisely calculated, and the least slip could be disastrous.

For the Albanians escorting the foreigners, the appearance of the huge Chinook transport helicopters something out of the movies. The whole operation lasted eight minutes, from the moment when the Italian marines disembarked in combat readiness to their take-off. Not a shot was fired. By 16.20 hours, 'Operation Vlora' was complete.

The Italian media boasted of the successful rescue mission of the two helicopters sent from the frigate, but nobody pointed out that their swift operation caught nobody by surprise, because the armed rebels in Vlora were preparing to ward off an attack not from the Adriatic but from Tirana.

***

The declaration of the State of Emergency brought tensions in the South to a new pitch. In the hearts of the people of Vlora, fear of reprisals from Berisha fought with their resolution not to surrender. Could they confront an attack by the army? The answer to this question hovered like a trembling needle on a dial.

Again groups stormed the army depots that were packed with weapons and ammunition. Twelve people died, killed not by resisting soldiers, but in accidents caused by others in the crowd who seized guns without knowing how to use them.

The more the danger of armed conflict increased, the more powerful those who were not frightened to fire them became. They were joined by many escaped prisoners from the gaols of the South, who had no intention of going back inside. What the government called 'rebels' were not a uniform category, but an alliance of the broad-based movement of the people, representatives of political parties led by the Forum, and groups of strong-men said to include even former officers

174

pensioned by Berisha, but with links to the Socialist Party. Now the atmosphere of blood and war affected everybody. Some people acted out of savagery. Others were determined not to sell themselves cheap.

***

On 4th March, the chief of the Crime Squad in Vlora and a police officer received orders from the headquarters of the Emergency Staff in Tirana to set off for Saranda and re-establish order there, by which was meant reopening the police station. They were joined by a criminal inspector from Vlora and another policeman, and the four set off in a green Mercedes 2400 without police license plates. They were armed with pistols and Kalashnikovs. The outward journey passed without incident. They stopped for a coffee at Llogara. Now and then they passed cars whose passengers casually pointed guns out of the windows and fired into the air, but did not molest them.

The streets of Saranda were full of armed men. There was not a policeman to be seen. The police station was a burned-out shell. In the port, ships were also full of armed men. Somebody took the team to the Salvation Committee, which had been set up in the town's high school. They introduced themselves and explained the purpose of their trip.

'Berisha's police are not welcome in this town,' was the curt reply. 'And there's no question of surrendering weapons. The police tried to convince them otherwise, but were told to go back where they came from. Otherwise there would be consequences. The crime chief contacted headquarters in Tirana and reported the situation as the team had found it, saying they had decided to return because there was nothing they could do in Saranda.

During the return journey their attention was caught by a dark green Mercedes that came out of a turning in front of them, and neither sped ahead nor allowed them to overtake. At first they put

175

this down to the poor road surface and the many bends, but later, on a straight part of the road where it would be natural to overtake, the dark green Mercedes obstinately blocked their path, and they realized that it meant business. The police team cocked their weapons and went on the alert. The Mercedes stopped. Two young men armed with Kalashnikovs got out of it and signalled to the driver to halt. Clearly these were the tough guys who had taken control of the Saranda-Gjirokastra road. The young men boldly approached, evidently unaware they were dealing with the police. `One of them bent down to the window to speak to them, and found an automatic rifle pointing at his throat. The other officer got out of the car, disarmed both men and bundled them onto the back seat. But meanwhile the green Mercedes had shot ahead.

'Follow it and don't lose it,' said the crime chief to the driver, firing his Kalashnikov at the car. But it was too late. The green Mercedes was faster than their car, now laden with six people.

'What are your names,' the police officer asked them.

'If you want our names, mine's Bubeq, but you'd better release us or you'll regret it,' replied the one who seemed to be the boss. The other kept silent.

'You're a brave lad.' said the crime chief, 'but we'll show you who's brave. What's your name? Bubeq is a nickname.'

'It's Bubeq. Don't you like it?' Silence fell in the car. The road surface worsened.

A few hundred yards later, at the place known as Qafë Gjashtë, their car was forced to stop in front of a truck placed askew across the road. Beside the road was a petrol station that looked abandoned. Some shots fired in the air signalled that they had been ambushed. The driver of the Mercedes had been quick to inform the members of the gang who were patrolling another stretch of the road. The two policemen exchanged glances with their prisoners in the car.

'I told you. Now let us go and keep driving,' Bubeq suggested.

They didn't hesitate. They thought that releasing the men would be enough to let them continue their journey unhindered. They opened the door, and let them get out.

Bubeq, as soon as he was far enough from the police car, talked to his mates in a language the police could not understand.

'*Tufjani*,' was the word they heard.

There was a volley of bullets and the explosion of a grenade. In bandits' slang, this word evidently meant *futjani*, -- zap them.

The crime chief jumped out of the other side of the car and ran into the hills, while the crime inspector tried to shoot. But his Kalashnikov stalled. He darted behind a wall and hid. A bullet caught the police officer, and he could not move. The policeman in the car also remained in a state of shock, with his hands still raised.

When they saw that no reaction came from the car after the gunshots, except a call for help from the wounded police officer, a group of armed young men emerged from their ambush and went up to it. They saw the police officer lying on his stomach on the back seat, groaning. The policeman still sat with his hands up.

'Move,' said Bubeq to the wounded man.

'I can't,' he replied.

'You came to disarm us and put us in prison,' said one of them, who seemed to be the leader of the gang.

The police officer had no time to respond because a second man came up and without a word emptied the entire magazine of his pistol into his body. A third man came up and fired a volley from his Kalashnikov into the corpse.

Was this the bloodlust of war, did they think they were acting out a movie, or were they looking for a human target for the guns they had just started to use? The policeman begged them not to kill him. They kicked him and beat him with the butts of their Kalashnikovs until he lay on the ground covered in blood. Someone suggested tying him up and taking him to Saranda as a prisoner. The crime chief and the inspector had managed to run away.

Meanwhile one member of the gang at Bubeq's orders brought a bucket of petrol from the pump. With this they hurried to douse the car where the police officer's body lay and set it alight. They fled, uninterested in seeing the body reduced to charred bones and a handful of ash.

In Saranda, they displayed the policeman in public, shoving him, spitting on him, accusing him of being a traitor, a provocateur, and a filthy spy. In front of the wild crowd, he confessed that he had come to plan reprisals against them.

***

This news spread fast. Its message was that the South would not surrender.

Barricades had now been erected on many streets of Vlora, with both light and heavy machine guns positioned on top ready to fire. There was also heavy artillery with barrels pointing north. Not a car passed through Tepelena without being checked by armed men.

As preparations for resistance got under way, food stores were also looted. Small shopkeepers closed their stores in fear and took their stocks home, leaving the population without basic foodstuffs. In Vlora the VEFA supermarket was attacked and looted first. Then the State reserves on the outskirts of the city were attacked and thousands of tonnes of flour were stolen. A vocational training centre built by the Danes at a cost of $7 million was looted and set alight. Within a few hours it was burned to ashes.

In Gjirokastra, at the entrance of the town, a depot that supplied the South with petrol was looted and burned. A huge mushroom of smoke rose above it for an entire day, a signal that the South was preparing for war.

Chapter XXX

From Fatos Qorri's Diary
4th March

If the fear in the air of Tirana could be measured like its pollution, it would turn out so laden with particles of panic that 'breathing' it for a long period would be fatal. It is only inside the houses that this 'air' is less foul, and so people have shut themselves up indoors. The emptiness of the Tirana streets is scary, and seems to suggest that the worst is still to come.

The way people react in Vlora and the South will decide a great deal. If they give in, we're sunk. If they stand firm, Berisha will be finished in a few days. There are reports that the army is refusing to go to the South. For the moment, the State of Emergency operates only in Tirana and the North.

Few people visited the Forum today, although movement during daylight is permitted. Some of the Forum's leaders are not sleeping in their own homes and are not saying where they are bedding down. I am still at the Kindergarten, not just because leaving it would feel like an act of panic, but because I have Nusi here and I can't leave her alone. There she is sitting on my desk by the computer, looking at me with her innocent eyes in a way that makes it impossible for me to leave her.

5th March

I had a strange meeting at the Forum's offices today. I was sitting looking out at the sun when the door opened and an old friend from prison came in. I won't mention his name, because who knows what might happen to me and this diary. I hadn't met him for ages. But we spent no time catching up or remembering prison, and launched at once into current events. I don't recall exactly what I was saying to him, but it was more or less what I think, that our situation is very dangerous, and that Berisha has gone too far by declaring the State of Emergency and deciding to send the army to the south. He interrupted me and said something that stopped me in my tracks:

'Listen, I also think that this all this is only going to get worse. There's only one solution. Berisha has to be killed.'

I sat speechless and looked him in the eye.

'And here I am. I'm ready to do it.' Two quite different feelings ran through me. What he had said frightened me, because I thought this might be a provocation, and there was also the thought that here in front of me was a brave and honest man, who had come to me as a trusted friend from prison. Perhaps the fear of a provocation came first, and then this other thought, because the instinct of self-preservation comes before anything else. I don't know how long the silence between us lasted. It can't have been long because he was waiting for an answer. I said to him in a blunt but friendly tone, 'We're not here to kill people. We're looking for a political solution. And we hope that Berisha will go after all this that's happened.'

He did not insist. He considered the conversation closed. He had finished what he had come to say.

I am sure I wouldn't have answered as I did, if I hadn't been suspicious. To a trusted friend, I might have said that this might be done, or not. I might have analysed its pros and cons, the damage such an act would cause, and the difficulties it would involve. But my curt response seemed to convey my mistrust. We had not met for years, and he had come to me unexpectedly with his proposal. Perhaps he had seen me on television and for him I wasn't simply an old friend from prison but the leader of a Forum that needed strong men. Perhaps he was looking for his place in history.

180

I don't know what he made of my reply. If he had been sent as a provocateur, I imagine that this must have been under heavy duress, and he would have been relieved at my answer. If he was sincere in his offer, he no doubt left unconvinced and disappointed in me.

I didn't even think of mentioning this unexpected proposal to anybody else in the Forum. I was concerned to spare this man, and myself. I might have mentioned it to Daut and Kurt, whom I trust, but they weren't present.

In fact, with both Daut and Kurt I share the experience of a second sentence in prison, which marks us out even from this fellow-prisoner of ours who came with his alarming suggestion. It is the difference that separates a prisoner sentenced in perpetuity from another who will be freed in a few years' time, the difference between someone who still hopes that the State might release him, and someone against whom the State has declared total enmity, and who can hope for nothing but its overthrow. I do not forget the day when they came and took Kurt from our line-up on the parade ground at Spaç. As he climbed the steps, with his hands handcuffed, he shouted 'Damn the narks!' Nobody who hoped to be released would have said that.

The survival strategies of those who were sent back to prison with a second sentence in perpetuity were of a different kind. These prisoners had their own subculture within the subculture of the prison itself. As the years passed, they acquired an increasingly stubborn disdain for human weakness, contempt for any surrender to the violence of the state, to the point of an obsession. This now makes them ill-adapted to the present time.

The fact that I thought of nobody but Kurt and Daut to trust shows that I am suspicious of the Forum. We are undergoing an ordeal by this fire that has only now been ignited, and it seems that the Forum is melting even before the flames have taken hold. Just see how everybody has abandoned the office in the last few days.

Chapter XXXI

White Raincoats

The mortal fear created by the events in the South brought
to light an important difference between Berisha and the Forum
leaders. The President had dared to play his final card, that of civil
war, because he was involved in a life or death struggle. But the
Forum leaders did not have this spur. Only the people in the South
were fighting for their lives, and the Forum's attitude towards them
began to change.

'Vlora is the only place safe from these bandits in power'
said Kalakulla. 'Let's all move there and try to take control of this
revolt. It's slipping out of our hands,'

But this idea found no support. In those March days, against
this background of gunfire and anxiety, the members of the Forum
ducked the question of their attitude to the South. They either
disagreed or fell back on ambiguity.

The majority held fast to the position that the Forum had
supported a political solution from the start.

'Yes,' said Qorri, 'but as we try to achieve this solution,
we can't speak for the South. The South should have its own
representatives. We too would be stronger with them beside us.'

But another current was emerging within the Forum that
sought to make decisions on behalf of Vlora, and thus leave Vlora
in the lurch. This tendency spread very fast. In those difficult days
when men with knuckledusters could lurk in any alley, everyone
experienced pendulum swings between fear and self-respect, and for
some people the pendulum came to rest in favour of fear. Many
people turned their backs on Vlora because they were the sort who,

when difficult times came, turned to mush and sought shelter under the wing of someone stronger. But this tendency also included people of another kind, who deep down felt closer to Berisha than to the people in the South. There was a tacit alliance between them and Berisha's people that arose out of their common past. They came from the same stock, the elite of the communist regime, and even if they quarrelled or hated one another they shared a common code that marked them off from the rest. Most of them had belonged to the Party of Labour. They had family ties. They had held privileged positions, and had all behaved in the same way under the old regime, according to a shared morality. They never imagined that outsiders could worm their way among them to take away their power. Just as animals of one species may fight and draw blood, but not go so far as to kill one another, these people too felt an affinity to their own kind.

But even within this category, some were also linked to Berisha by a less well known but much stronger organization, which had secured the peaceful transition from one system to another in 1991. Ever since the formation of the PD and its first rallies, there had been rumours of a secret agreement that its leaders would wear white double-breasted raincoats in order to be recognized by the police and the regime's secret services, and not be touched. White was chosen for visibility, but also because it was the colour of peace. And so the double-breasted white raincoats represented the bridge between two regimes. The secret network that had built this bridge also destroyed the *Sigurimi* personnel files of most of the PD activists before they infiltrated the democratic movement. This network could not simply be called the former *Sigurimi*. It was composed of its former covert operatives who suddenly became more important than its public officers. It was a network that seemed to evaporate as it evolved, something familiar and yet unknown, whose members were not bound by personal ties, but by their compromised past. So, when the anxious wife of one of the top communist leaders had phoned the last communist prime minister in 1991 and said, 'What's going on? We're all done for!' the latter had replied, 'Don't worry. They're all our people.'

In fact the situation had spun out of control because of Berisha's unbridled ambition for power and also a thousand unforeseen events. Now it was time for them to remember that they were all one family. How could they fight one another to the death? In the Parliament, more than half of the PD deputies were former covert *Sigurimi* operatives. They were a symbol of the continuity of power. These same people, as soon as the crisis erupted, had been able to withdraw their deposits from the pyramid schemes, with interest. How could all these things be forgotten?

Events in Vlora were like a cancerous growth that put their survival in danger. Vlora was known to be the stronghold of the Socialist Party, which was the largest party in the Forum, and the leading figures in the Forum were members of this party. But who was this Albert Shyti, a migrant worker who had returned from Greece, and was announced as the chairman of a Salvation Committee for Vlora? Who were these intellectuals in the South, talking to CNN and the BBC and giving interviews without asking Tirana? And what if, once they had settled their accounts with Berisha, this cancer spread and these strangers took over in Tirana, seizing the power that Berisha's people had inherited, and wanting to know all about their collaboration with the former regime?

***

Preç Zogaj, the Democratic Alliance's number two in the Forum, was drinking coffee with the lead correspondent of the Voice of America in the lobby of the Rogner, less than a hundred yards from the President's office. The correspondent was known to be in regular contact with Berisha, and Zogaj was asking him to facilitate a secret meeting between Berisha and his opponents.

'Tell him that otherwise we'll ask for asylum in embassies, and that would be bad for all of us.'

The VoA correspondent listened attentively.

'Is this your personal suggestion, or does it emanate from your people?' he asked.

'Both mine, and from my people,' Zogaj replied.

The correspondent promised to talk to Berisha. If fact he could hardly wait to make this important phone call.

On the next day, 5th March, Zogaj waited for a reply in the lobby of the Rogner. The VoA correspondent turned up at one o'clock in the afternoon. He hadn't met Berisha yet but hoped to do so later that day.

The correspondent was not totally sure that Berisha would meet him to discuss this issue. They had talked only once on the phone.

'How does the situation look?' Berisha had asked.

'Not too good.'

'Why?'

'Preç Zogaj told me that the opposition people are thinking of taking refuge in embassies. Think of the impression this would create abroad.'

Both Berisha and the correspondent knew perfectly well that the Forum had not discussed fleeing to the embassies, and some members of the Forum were in fact waiting for Berisha to take flight. But this confession of weakness from the opposition was a gesture.

There was silence on Berisha's end of the phone.

'Let them go. Nice idea,' he replied at last, pretending to think this would only benefit him.

But the correspondent detected his ploy.

'We should talk a bit,' he said. 'I also have a proposal from some of these opposition people.'

'Come to my office and we'll talk.'

But Berisha had still not phoned back.

185

Zogaj could not wait. He had to find someone else with Berisha's ear. The director of *Albania* was perhaps his closest confidant and Zogaj set off in search of him. He had to act before another of the 'white raincoats' took this initiative. Anyone who succeeded in mediating in this situation would become the man of the moment. Clearly Berisha was going to lose power, but he was still strong enough to choose to whom he would surrender it, and this would certainly be someone who would guarantee he wouldn't be harmed.

Did Berisha trust even the VoA correspondent, the director of *Albania*, or anyone? Was there anyone to whom he confided his true purposes? No, Berisha was not the sort to confide in anyone, even in his closest circle. This was at the same time his strength and his weakness: it created the distance that preserved his authority, but also deprived him of the advice of true friends. He kept his loyal people close to him, to bolster his confidence in his power to retaliate, but not to listen to their advice. When these people pretended to give him their own opinions, they showed their loyalty by emphasizing what they knew he liked to hear. Now they were suggesting it was time for him to settle accounts with his enemies, because they knew that this was what he was thinking. But he was scared to make this decision. Berisha was well aware that he could use the State of Emergency as a threat but he could not send in the army to commit acts of butchery. The reports he had received from the army staff told him that none of the soldiers wanted to shoot. Two pilots who had been sent into the air to bombard the rebels had preferred to seek political asylum in Italy. The international community too had made it plain that they would not tolerate butchery in the middle of Europe.

Berisha had hastened to announce that he would ensure that the State of Emergency encroached as little as possible on the rights and freedoms of his fellow-countrymen, and that the forces suppressing the rebellion would make every effort to protect lives and property. The restrictions on the press would be minimal.

But these words were not enough for the West. Italian Foreign Minister Lamberto Dini phoned to ask for all military operations to be suspended. Berisha was obliged to promise that he would not use force to recover control of the south, an assurance that Dini had immediately made public.

Berisha now felt weaker than ever. They had forced him onto the defensive. Now his aim was to survive, not to win. The phone conversations with the VoA correspondent and the director of *Albania* showed that they read his mind better than anybody. Of course, their own survival was at stake, and if Berisha sank, so would they. Both had been his mouthpieces and had spoken his language, stirring up hatred and urging the use of force, for as long as they thought that the ensuing storm would cast them up high and dry. Now they were carefully suggesting something that he was ready to listen to. The VoA correspondent knew that a rumour was coursing through Tirana that Berisha, not the opposition, was making plans to escape, and of course he did not like to hear this. Nor did Berisha like this rumour, because he interpreted it as an indirect appeal to do this very thing. He had sent his children away, but had decided to stay himself as long as he could.

***

At about half past four, the director of *Albania* asked the VoA correspondent to go urgently to the Rogner, where he was waiting with Zogaj. The correspondent realized at once that Zogaj was also involved in this affair. Zogaj had with him a friend who had recently come back from abroad and was planning to launch a newspaper. They were sitting in an inconspicuous corner of the lobby.

The director of *Albania* told Zogaj that everything was ready, if he could merely promise that his side would participate. The time for the meeting had not been set, but they would be informed of this while they drank their coffee.

At six o'clock the director's mobile rang.

'I'm here at the Rogner with Zogaj,' the director said.

Berisha's voice could be recognized on the phone, but his words were indistinct.

'At the Presidency at nine o'clock,' the director said to Zogaj.

Zogaj had told them that he, Ceka, and Meidani would go to the meeting, but not that the veteran Socialist leader and former editor-in-chief of *Zëri i Popullit*, Namik Dokle, would also be there. The director passed this on to Berisha, who accepted.

'Just remember that this is top secret,' the director said.

Zogaj set off to inform his people. They had only three hours' to spare. The correspondent and the director said that they would wait for him to return to the Rogner, however late he was.

Chapter XXXII

Katowice

Qorri saw a big envelope pushed under his door. It looked very old, as if from an earlier era. He opened it with great curiosity. Inside were some typewritten sheets. On the first page were a few handwritten lines addressed to him. 'Fatos Qorri, you have sold out to the communists and betrayed your fellow-prisoners and your own suffering. Several times you have expressed the suspicion that both political sides are birds of a feather, products of the Party of Labour. We send you this document so that in the future you won't be able to say you didn't know.'

There was a note lower down, 'from a group of your old fellow-prisoners.'

The document was headed 'Katowice.' The text purported to be a copy of a secret speech by Ramiz Alia, the former communist president, made while he was still in power.

'Our system now faces capitulation to the capitalist system... let us change our strategy... creating political pluralism and respect for human rights... in this way we will gain the support of the West and of anti-communist dissidents... let our opponents create right-wing, left-wing, or centre parties. We will even encourage them. The main thing is that all these parties should be controlled by us... people who support our strategy...'

'...beware of the children of those who have been persecuted politically, who are themselves so old or ill that they can barely walk. We will give these people passports to leave Albania, and this will satisfy them. Their property belongs to us, because we created it.'

'We have enough people to fill seven Central Committees, so there's no need to be afraid.'

'Within two or three parliaments we will succeed in creating a capitalist class out of the communist class, which will perpetuate our political power into the future. Rest assured that the future belongs to us. We will never allow our enemies to recover political power.'

Qorri could not understand how, while he was reading the letter, he could see Ramiz Alia reading in a dark hall of the Central Committee. It took him a while to realize that he had been asleep. He rubbed his eyes to be sure it had been a dream, and then opened them.

Katowice. He had heard about this document, a supposed record of a meeting held by Gorbachev in the city of Katowice, which, he remembered, was either in Poland or Ukraine. Qorri had never bothered to find out more, because he had never believed that this document was authentic. It was not the habit of communist leaders to talk so frankly. They always clothed their sinister intentions in fine words about socialism and the people. He was sure that this document had not set these events in motion, but had been written after them.

It was the fact that he had seen this document in a dream that struck him.

Had this dream come from repressed guilt at having joined forces with his former persecutors? No, that wasn't the case. He hadn't repressed this feeling, but analysed it in full awareness. Berisha, more than anyone else, incarnated the spirit of his former persecutors. But the document in his dream made no distinction between Berisha and his allies. Did this dream come from a part of him that had begun to falter? The truth was more complicated than he had thought and more complicated than he had described in his articles. After the fall of the Stalinist communism, a semi-dictatorial regime had come to power in Albania, in which it was nevertheless possible to divide the 'grey' collaborators with communism into the 'dark grey' and 'light grey'. The dark grey had stayed with Berisha, while the light grey had become the first dissidents against authoritarianism. Now he had to differentiate shades of light grey. It was better to admit that it was impossible to categorize this complex reality.

He left Kindergarten 19 and set off for the Forum's office. He found nobody there, or in the offices of Gjinushi's Social Democratic Party underneath. There was a strange emptiness in the air. At least it was a sunny day.

Chapter XXXIII

Agreement of 6th March

Close to midnight, Zogaj appeared again at the entrance to the Rogner, his face even ruddier than usual. He looked pleased. The director of *Albania* and the VoA correspondent were waiting for him.

'We're saved!' he announced with glee. What did he mean? Who was being saved, Albania or themselves?

The director and the correspondent sat down and ordered a coffee.

Zogaj started to describe the meeting between Berisha and his sworn enemies. Ceka and Berisha had absolved each other of responsibility for the past. Ceka had spoken indulgently and in touching tones. Berisha had been self-critical, Dokle mild-mannered, and Meidani courteous and almost silent.

Zogaj said that the next day, 6th March, the leaders of ten political parties would meet Berisha and reach a political agreement to solve the crisis. Ceka had promised to bring his people into line. When they stood up to leave the lobby of the Rogner was almost empty.

'Fingers crossed!' said the director, the correspondent, and Zogaj before they parted.

***

The next afternoon on the 6th of March, Meidani was the first to emerge from the Presidency gates. He refused to make any statement, and looked upset. Paskal Milo came out after him, proclaiming loudly that Berisha had tricked them. Skënder Gjinushi, coming out next, echoed him. Zogaj, blushing, tried to explain.

After them, the chairman of the Monarchists, a party allied

to Berisha, came out with the agreement in his hand. The VoA correspondent grabbed it from him and cast his eye over it: 'The political parties support the re-establishment of the constitutional order, which guarantees public order throughout the country. They ask their supporters and all citizens to surrender their weapons and ammunition within forty-eight hours, starting from 06.00 hours on 7th March 1997...' 'They ask the President of the Republic to pardon all those who surrender weapons during this time, unless they have directly perpetrated crimes. They ask the Defence Council to suspend for forty-eight hours all offensive military operations in areas where they are planned, starting at 06.00 hours on 7th March...'

The correspondent's joy knew no bounds. This was Berisha's victory. He was a great man. He had persuaded his opponents to sign a document asking for the people in the South to surrender their weapons within forty-eight hours, without a word about early elections and with no conditions for the government except that the President would appoint a person who enjoyed as broad a consensus of support as possible. What could be better? The correspondent contacted his Washington studio immediately to arrange a live broadcast. At about a quarter past four, Neritan Ceka emerged from the Presidency building. The correspondent asked him to speak to Voice of America. Ceka agreed with enthusiasm and praised the agreement as historic.

From the Presidency, the group made its way to the Rogner where journalists and opposition members were gathered, including Qorri, whose face was as black as thunder. Still the correspondent asked him for an interview as one of the three leaders of the Forum for Democracy. But Qorri was in the depths of despair at the treachery, cowardice, insincerity, and double-dealing in this agreement. It left the country in the mire. He couldn't express all these things in the interview, but he said that the agreement showed contempt for both the Forum, where the parties were committed to making decisions together, and for the people in the South. How could decisions be made while ignoring the people who had risked and sacrificed most in this whole history?

Qorri was not alone in his anger. More and more people in the Rogner lobby expressed their disgust at the agreement. Journalists of *Koha Jonë* snorted that Berisha had tricked them. Zogaj became the whipping boy, and his old cover name as a *Sigurimi* agent, Çiftelia was passed from one indignant group to the next. The disconsolate Zogaj apparently overheard this.

Meidani and his people, confronted with the resistance of the Socialist militants, were also understood to have repented.

***

That evening a journalist of RAI3 invited Qorri to talk about the agreement in a live broadcast. He had set a meeting at the Italian journalists' hotel. They went outside as little as possible at that hour. Qorri entered the hotel and was told the journalists were waiting for him on the first-floor terrace.

On the terrace he saw the cameras positioned on tall supports, with a view of the deserted Scanderbeg Square behind. He went towards them, and saw Tritan Shehu, the PD chairman, whom the journalist invited to speak first. Qorri was not close enough to hear what he said. He looked round in the terrace and into the empty darkness of Tirana and wondered what he himself would say. He would repeat that they were still a long way from the solution they were looking for: early elections and a new government. He would insist, so that the Italians would be aware, that the South had to be represented in its own right.

At that moment Neritan Ceka arrived, worried that he might be late. He had been invited as a signatory to the agreement and Qorri realized that his own turn as an opponent of it came last.

194

He greeted Ceka coldly but nevertheless drew close to him to hear what he would say after listening to Shehu. He imagined that he would repeat what he had said to VoA, but was surprised to hear Ceka angrily appealing through Italian television to all the Albanians not to trust this agreement, because it was a trick.

Chapter XXXIV

From Fatos Qorri's Diary

Finally after several days' absence we all gathered at a meeting of the Forum.

'He's a cheat. He's deceived us. We won't talk to him any more as a party, but only as the Forum,' Ceka wailed.

'He's deceived himself, not us,' added Zogaj, sitting quietly next to him like his shadow.

Listening to their indignation, I thought that these two genuinely felt to blame for the failure of their enterprise. But I could not tell if they also felt ashamed at having acted secretly behind the Forum's back.

Gjinushi and Meidani sat silent at first. When they spoke, they described what had happened as like being drawn into a trap. But if there had been a trap, it was not clear where. Berisha had not forced them to sign. It seemed that the trap was that Ceka and Zogaj had pressed them into entering Berisha's lair, and there they had been unable to resist his power.

A livid Kalakulla was determined to point out their treachery to the Forum. They explained that Berisha remained adamant about not meeting with the Forum.

'But now, he will have nobody else to meet except the Forum,' Ceka repeated. He had prepared a renunciation of the previous day's declaration.

We passed round Ceka's text, which repudiated everything done and said the previous day, but it was purely emotional and without style or ideas. It mostly reflected Ceka's state of mind. Nobody knows who these people really are or how many different faces they can display. I remembered the Katowice dream. These people are bound by a kind of solidarity that outsiders do not understand, just as I share a feeling with other former prisoners that only people who have been in prison can understand.

I proposed that the entire meeting with Berisha should not be dismissed, as Ceka's statement proposed, but that it should be considered a first step, bearing in mind that the international community is calling for dialogue. They immediately accepted this proposal. We drafted a statement that maintained a critical but moderate attitude to the previous day's meeting, not disowning but downplaying the document that emerged from it. We said that it was only a 'first step' towards finding a real solution to the crisis, not a document that would give a sufficient guarantee to the people in the South that the government had pulled back from using violence. We asked for the removal of the State of Emergency and the restoration of rights and freedoms, especially of the press. These freedoms could only have meaning if early, free elections were held.

In a separate paragraph the Forum protested that the people of the South should not be branded as 'terrorists' and 'bandits' and that their fate should not be decided without hearing them speak. The Forum therefore recommended inviting a representative of the political parties of Vlora to the discussion table. We agreed on all the points and signed. We distributed the statement wherever we could.

In fact, the Forum started to crumble away several days ago. It is now clear to me that some of its leaders have used it as a poker to stoke the fire, useful for a while, but to be set aside when the fire dies down. They have come back to the Forum because they see it is still necessary. The problem is that it was created precisely because these people had no faith in the parties they represented. When they saw that not even they themselves could be trusted, they scurried back to the Forum at once.

So many people have been coming to our little office informing us that they have launched branches of the Forum in their workplaces or towns on their own initiative. I have been obliged to tell them that the idea of the Forum was not that it would be turned into a party, because the parties would continue to exist. But seeing people organize voluntarily around a name, I have come to understand better that genuine movements begin when there is a vacuum and a lack of trust. But we are no such movement. These poor people do not understand what a fragile construction of politicians this is, no longer united even by their common hostility to Berisha.

Chapter XXXV

The Internationals in Action

The capital city lost contact with the South. Reports of what was happening there came from people arriving in Tirana, from private Greek television stations, and a few correspondents of the Albanian Telegraphic Agency. ATA was now the only national medium that still functioned. Its reports were increasingly distrusted, though they were news of a sort.

After the statement of 6th March, all sources, including ATA, reported that the ultimatum to surrender weapons within forty-eight hours had further inflamed the rebellious South. There were no signs anywhere of weapons being handed in.

In the streets of Vlora there were even more barricades with weapons in combat positions. The population remained shut within their houses and only armed men moved about the city. According to ATA, many Vlora families who were known to be linked to the Democrats had left and sought refuge in Tirana, Elbasan, and other quieter cities. All the shops were shut and there were rumours of a bread shortage.

In Saranda, hundreds of people, mostly armed, had gathered in the city square, where orators repeated their demands. Armed men still patrolled the city. Armoured vehicles in the hands of the insurgents were moving on the Saranda-Delvina road. Emergency medical teams had been set up at the Saranda hospital, which was also in the insurgents' hands. A policeman from Vlora was being treated there, handcuffed to the bed.

No weapons were being surrendered in Tepelena either. Men armed with high-calibre weapons and heavy artillery had taken up key positions, expecting a confrontation.

In Gjirokastra, a crowd of two or three hundred people gave a hostile reception to a number of army helicopters. ATA claimed they were on a routine mission. The rumours that soldiers from Tirana were coming to occupy the city enraged the townspeople, who attacked the helicopters and forced them away before they could land.

***

While some in the South prepared for war, others were looking for escape routes. The Italian News Agency ANSA reported that a sailing boat with fifty Albanians on board, including fifteen women and eleven children had been stopped twenty-five miles north of Otranto, off the shores of Lecce. A few hours later, RAI reported that the women and children had now been brought to land. They were all friends and relatives of the crew of the ship, who had left Vlora out of fear of the situation there. They told the Italian journalists that many people were planning to escape.

The Greek Defence Ministry reported that seven Albanian soldiers had sought political asylum in Greece. They would be considered political refugees until the Foreign Ministry and the Public Order Ministry decided if they should be granted asylum status. ATA commented, 'These are the first Albanian soldiers to seek political asylum in Greece since the rebels first clashed with the Albanian Army at the beginning of this week.'

The prospect of a new mass exodus of Albanians frightened the internationals. One delegation after another was sent to Tirana to defuse the situation. The public spaces of the Rogner filled with ruddy-faced statesmen in expensive suits, whose pale, well-shaven necks bulged over their shirt collars. Rene van der Linden of the Council of Europe arrived in the capital the day after the agreement of 6th March. He met with Berisha immediately and expressed his satisfaction at the establishment of dialogue and the amnesty in exchange for the surrender of weapons.

He announced after the meeting that Berisha has assured him he would appoint a prime minister who enjoyed the broadest possible support.

So events were turning in Berisha's favour. He had various options. He started to show magnanimity, leaving the tough work to the chairman of the Parliament, who told the Westerners that despite the imposition of the State of Emergency the government forces had not killed a single rebel and were still asking for the surrender of weapons without bloodshed.

There was no way the foreigners could know that in fact Berisha and his parliament no longer had an army that obeyed their commands.

But the person who would lead the foreigners in their decisions would be the former Austrian chancellor Franz Vranitzky, who arrived in Tirana at the head of a large delegation. He spoke in the same tones as his colleagues, but added a demand for Berisha to extend the ceasefire to give people a chance to hand in their weapons. Berisha conceded another forty-eight hours.

But who would collect these weapons? What institutions enjoyed such trust? Whoever collected the weapons would in fact hold power, and it was a struggle for this power that was going on. Vranitzky thought that a transitional government could do it, stabilizing pubic order and preparing for early elections. The Forum had asked for a transitional government before any weapons had appeared on the scene.

The idea of a transitional government was gaining ground even though it was not mentioned in the 6th March agreement. Berisha could see that it would be hard for him to oppose this idea, even though it was a way of easing him out of power. He told Vranitzky that the elections could be held within forty-five days if the rebels handed in their arms. He felt that the longer they were postponed, the more difficult it would be to maintain control, because his people were become increasingly discouraged as the days passed. But if the weapons were handed in quickly, he would know what to do in those forty-five days. Of course, he had gained most from Vranitzky's visit, bearing in mind how close to the abyss he had been: to secure the elections, and enter them as an electable choice, even remaining as president -- this was the maximum that was within his grasp now that the overwhelming majority of Albanians wanted to see him ousted.

***

Qorri was indignant to see that the Westerners did not even think of looking for who was responsible for the country's tragedy. Their policies were dictated purely by fear that Albania might explode, and their own countries be swamped by emigrants. So they talked about national reconciliation. Berisha had succeeded in touting the myth that the conflict was between the ex-communist South and the anti-communist North, whereas in fact it was merely a conflict between the deceived people and the government, which had not merely failed to protect them from the fraudsters of the pyramids, but had been complicit in fleecing them. Instead of forcing the culprits to face up to their responsibilities under the law, the Westerners were endorsing them, for the sake of their own interests and out of their fear of regional instability. So the Albanian body politic would not be purged, and injustice would be condoned. The Albanians, instead of being helped to grow up, would be kept in the role of obedient children, not mature enough to create a court of law or appear before one.

This was Qorri's worry in those days, even though he also felt his reasoning was faulty. It was not the fault of the Westerners. This injustice was taking place because the main culprit, Berisha, was powerful enough to disguise his personal responsibility as a national tragedy. As the internationals saw it, the prospects of holding a fair trial in Albania were poor. It was much more likely that the turmoil would continue. It was less the short-sightedness of the internationals than the weakness of the opposition that led to this conclusion. When

Vranitzky arrived in Tirana, there was still a possibility that Berisha would be forced to resign. This could be achieved by making the insurgents in the South participants in the dialogue. But the people who had talked to Berisha did not want them to take part, some because the discussions would then slide out of their control, and others because they lacked the courage to enter the unknown territory that the discussions would then enter. So Vranitzky did not even ask to meet the Forum, who themselves again forgot the promise they had made after the debacle of 6th March, that they would go to meetings only as a Forum. Vranitzky confined his attentions to those who had talked to Berisha. When foreign journalists asked Vranitzky about the chances of inducing the 'third party', meaning the armed men of the South, to lay down their weapons, he said that some representatives of the opposition had told him they believed that the south would surrender its weapons if a political settlement were achieved. Many people attached no importance to Vranitzky's reply, because after the repudiation of the statement of 6th March there was an increasing belief that the 'political settlement' could not be in the teeth of the South's opposition. This was the decisive point. Qorri insisted that the Forum should tell Vranitzky that the South would not give up its weapons without Berisha's resignation because with the imposition of the State Emergency, the South had lost all trust in him. Or at least the Forum should tell him that they could not speak for the South, and the South should be invited to the table, instead of implying that their own decision would be sufficient and acceptable to everyone. The exclusion of the South was the betrayal of a struggle, which, despite the dangerous anarchy it had caused, was in essence a just one, because for the first time in their history the Albanians were showing their rulers that they were able to punish them for the havoc they had caused. This could open a new era and create a new type of politician.

However, if the South yielded up its weapons, and was left leaderless, did it not mean that this was as much as they deserved, and that they were not capable of creating their own leadership? Qorri was afraid that this second interpretation was closer to the truth. But still, he argued, this did not mean that the Forum had no chance to change this reality. By asking that the south should speak for itself, they would be taking a step towards democracy and breaking the habit of expecting decisions from above.

***

Vranitzky did not know for sure if this opposition represented the opinion of the majority, especially in the South. For him it was more important to know if he could dictate the course of events with these protagonists, or if he should summon others onto the stage. He seemed satisfied with the cast of characters he had. Why complicate the scene unnecessarily? But he did not exclude the possibility of others appearing in a later act. When asked what he thought should be done if Berisha agreed to extend the ceasefire another forty-eight hours, but the south still did not hand in its weapons, he opened the prospect of a different solution: 'When we make a proposal,' he replied, 'we believe that it will be an effective one, and, if it is not effective, that means that we are dealing with a different situation that will require another proposal.'

Nobody, least of all Vranitzky, could imagine what kind of situation might be created if, while Tirana insisted on the surrender of weapons, the South still refused to hand them in.

Chapter XXXVI

The Agreement of 9th March

On the morning of 9th March, Qorri set off early for the Forum's office. He found nobody there. No meeting was set for that day. The rays of the sun, already warm in those March days, drew him to the French windows opening onto the terrace. Whenever he stepped out onto this terrace he liked to imagine himself on the left-hand wing of a soaring bird. Surely the architect had been inspired by the vision of a bird with outstretched wings. Qorri identified this bird with the Forum, whose offices occupied its head. But that day he did not think of the bird, but of the Forum's empty office on the floor below. There was nobody in Gjinushi's office in the right wing either. After half an hour the phone rang. When he lifted the receiver, he heard Ceka's voice.

'We're meeting here at my house,' he said. 'Come round, we've got something important.'

Ceka's serious tone made him think that relations with Berisha must have deteriorated still further since his repudiation of the declaration of 6th March.

So why don't these people come to the Forum, he wondered as he unlocked his bicycle and set off.

The roads of Tirana were not as deserted as in the evening, but still there was plenty of room for cyclists. In less than ten minutes Qorri arrived at the stairwell of Ceka's apartment block. He locked his bicycle at the foot of the stairs and climbed up.

Ceka lived in a typical apartment from the time of the dictatorship with two or three small rooms and a kitchen. When Qorri entered he noticed in passing the furniture of the sixties manufactured

205

by the Misto Mame Combine, so often found in intellectual households. In the living room, he found Zogaj and Perikli Teta, both leading figures in the Alliance, and also Gjinushi. The atmosphere was conspiratorial.

He had no time appraise Ceka's furniture in detail or look at the pictures on the walls, because Zogaj started explaining why they were there.

'Berisha has set another meeting for us. This morning, in about an hour's time.'

Qorri did not speak, but Zogaj saw his spasm of surprise, and began to explain what had happened that day. The situation had taken a turn for the worse. They had made several attempts to reach Berisha before in the end finding suitable go-betweens.

'He absolutely refuses to meet us as a Forum,' he added, as if reading Qorri's mind.

The others did not speak.

Qorri realized why he had been summoned there. They were going to meet Berisha again, but this time they wanted to avoid what had happened two days before, when they had come up against the Forum's opposition. The fact that it was Zogaj who was explaining what they had done reinforced Qorri's suspicion that he was the principal mediator.

He felt powerless to remind them that only two days before they had declared they would act only as a Forum. He could not identify the precise source of this helplessness. Was it because he had no authority over these people? Because he was merely an individual with no party to back him up? Because he was not sure that he should stand in their way? Because the international pressure for dialogue also gave them the right to act outside the Forum in the interests of everybody? Or was he afraid he might appear slighted at not being invited himself?

'At least let Kalakulla go, as the chairman of a party,' he said.

'There are certain people Berisha refuses to meet,' Ceka

interrupted. Then he seemed to think again and turned to Zogaj, 'Phone the Presidency again, and mention Kalakulla.'

Ceka had regained his confidence in making decisions without considering others. This annoyed Qorri.

Zogaj phoned. The secretary answered. Zogaj asked him to convey to the President the request for Kalakulla also to attend the meeting.

'... of the Right-Wing Democratic Party,' Zogaj added.

After a while, the secretary returned with a brief reply. Zogaj laid down the receiver.

'It's no use,' he said. 'He won't meet Kalakulla.'

Qorri saw that they were going to this meeting whatever happened. They were even looking at their watches, worried at being late. They were meeting up with the representatives of the Socialists, to set off together.

'Ask for representatives of the South to come to the talks,' Qorri said as they made ready to leave. 'That's what we decided. Say that without them there's no way we can make decisions. He won't accept them ever, but there can't be any agreement without them. He should be clear about that. With the situation as it is, in a few days he'll have to flee anyway.'

They set off, expressing the view that, in the end, these talks were necessary to reduce tension, and for the sake of the internationals, but without it occurring to them that they might repeat their first mistake of signing an agreement on behalf of people they didn't represent.

***

About an hour after he left Ceka's house he saw at the entrance to a bar an unusual gathering of people, grouped round a television screen. He went up out of curiosity. He could not believe his eyes.

This crowd was watching Berisha's meeting with representatives of the opposition. How could this be broadcast live? This meant that there would be no laying down of conditions at this meeting, he thought. This was a *fait accompli*. There had been no mention of any such thing at Ceka's house.

Even the television presentation showed that Berisha totally dominated the occasion. He was at the head of a long table. On one side were representatives of the opposition parties, including Meidani, Majko, Gjinushi, Ceka, and Zogaj. On the other side were Godo of the Republicans, the chairman of the National Front, the fraction of the Social Democratic Party, and the chairman on the Legality monarchists.

Everybody was listening in silence to Berisha's speech:

'From this room, we state together that what Albania needs most today is a platform for national reconciliation.'

How could he dare speak of national reconciliation after all that had happened? Why were these people sitting there listening like schoolchildren?

'In the last few days, many different solutions have occurred to me, but I ultimately reached the conclusion that an act of national reconciliation is the most imperative need and the most honourable settlement. In this reconciliation, there are no losers. Nothing lost in national reconciliation deserves to be kept.

'An immediate end to acts of violence demands that we should all rise above party pressures and interests. This is a noble and civilized cause.

Berisha spoke with the assurance of someone who had the last word. Clearly, nobody round that table intended to raise objections.

'I think that to achieve this step, the parliament must declare an amnesty for all servicemen and civilians who were involved in the revolts of the pyramids.

'Sunday will be declared a day of national mourning and prayer for all those who lost their lives in this period.

'Let us agree to have a Government of National Reconciliation including all the political parties.

'Let parliamentary elections be held within two months.

'I invite the Socialists to come to the parliament.

'Citizens are to hand in their weapons within one week.

'The Government of National Reconciliation that will also prepare for the elections must make serious efforts alongside international institutions and friendly countries to assist the areas of the country that have suffered the most damage.

'These were some of my ideas. .'

Qorri left the bar and set off for the headquarters of the Socialist Party in the hope of finding somebody he could work with to stop anybody signing a document of the kind Berisha envisaged. How could he elevate himself above all parties, when he himself was a party and the worst of all parties? He was deeply discredited, morally and politically, and yet he was now claiming the privileged high ground. He was asking for an amnesty and a day of mourning without considering that the dead called for justice. Ceka and his friends were responsible for this too. It was enough to drive you out of your mind.

In the Socialist Party office, he found only a few secretaries, also watching the television with disgust.

He left and headed for the Rogner.

Chapter XXXVII

From Fatos Qorri's Diary
10th March 1997

It's all over. I've fallen out with them. Yesterday afternoon Paskal Milo came to me at the Rogner and gave me a copy of the statement. I read it and asked him:

'And you signed this?'

'Yes,' he replied.

I gave it back to him and said to everybody round about, 'These people have always been rubbish, and always will be.' And I stalked out.

I can't even begin to understand this feebleness. After the dictatorship, we all have weakened backbones, but these people seem totally spineless. Yes, it was a frightening moment, but this was not the time to disgrace ourselves and abandon all those people who were looking to us for their salvation.

The chess game was almost over. A few more moves, and checkmate would have been inevitable. Then these people sat down and put their signature to a stalemate. Did they do this out of fear or self-interest? The two are hard to distinguish. People with little courage also have petty interests.

The only person in the Socialist Party worth talking to is Meidani. I went to meet him in the party chairman's office. I told him we had been on the threshold of a historic breakthrough when the Albanians would at last do something to give them faith in the future, after they had succeeded in clearing a poison from their system by their own efforts. But in the event, we were more like abortionists strangling a healthy infant ready to be born.

He listened to me carefully.

'I'm not for a revolution,' he said. 'If this is a revolution, I'm going home.'

'There's no question of a revolution,' I said. I think he wanted to shame me, because this word has become a synonym for communism.

I don't know myself exactly what I wanted from them. Perhaps a bit more resilience, keeping the promise they had made two days before. A little more respect for the people in the South who had sacrificed so much, who had been attacked, and were now threatened with reprisals.

I am for elections too, but does Berisha deserve to be considered a legitimate candidate in these elections? After all that he has done, is he not a threat to them? If not even Berisha is convicted for what has happened, then nobody can be brought to justice ever again in this country, and this will be worse than the failure to punish the crimes of communism. In such a semi-democracy, the state will be able to commit any kind of crime.

I left Meidani, casting an eye at the enormous table where the chairman held his presidium meetings. I recalled that on one occasion when I had entered that office Majko had shown me with special pride the head of the table, with the chair of the imprisoned chairman Fatos Nano. 'None of us sits in that chair,' he said to me.

How can you expect people who don't dare to sit in an empty chair to unseat Berisha?

Chapter XXXVIII

After the Agreement

'We want guns!'

'We want guns!'

'We want guns!'

A wave of shouting crested and broke, and the human flood surged forward to engulf the largest arsenal in Berat.

People plundered what they could, Kalashnikovs, heavy machine guns, bullets, mines, bombs, grenades. They came out ecstatic. Some, with Kalashnikovs over their shoulders, jumped into trucks that set off with a roar to the nearest town, Poliçan. When they reached the main square they fired volley after volley into the air, as if to show they were masters of the town. After this invasion, they set off towards Skrapar.

But the agreement of 9th March did not persuade the South to surrender its weapons, but sparked a chain reaction of attacks on arms depots and occupations of towns by armed men.

In Skrapar, the insurgents from Berat joined a section of armed inhabitants of the town. Someone pointed them to the police station, claiming that police units would be deployed to unblock a road for the passage of troops from Tirana. The insurgents attacked the police station and set fire to it.

Gunfire of the same kind could be heard all over Fier, Lushnja, and Levan.

The next day the entire South apart from the city of Korça went out of all control, with attacks on arms depots, the looting of food reserves and the destruction of public buildings. At least ten people were killed and twenty wounded.

Did this so-called uprising have leaders? Who would dare to direct it, now that Tirana had issued an act of reconciliation? Or was it spontaneous? Berisha's people argued that it was not, and produced conspiracy theories that sometimes contradicted one other. On the 'map of the rebellion' they pointed their fingers at important strategic centres like Berat, which had also been the air base from which the two MIGs had taken off to seek refuge in Italy. This must be a military plan, they said, devised by foreign intelligence services, the Greeks above all, even the CIA itself, which was under the influence of the Greek lobby. These fictions were conveyed to Western journalists, some of whom processed them into interesting news for the Western public. 'The Nightmare of Northern Epirus: Albania in Danger' was the headline of an article in *Corriere della Sera* on 12th March, in which the writer claimed that a well-known Greek lawyer, one of the best-known leaders of the Epirus movement in Greece whose aim was to attach the southern part of Albania to Greece, was trying to co-ordinate the efforts of the Albanian insurgents in the south. He was travelling unhindered from Saranda to Gjirokastra, Delvina, and Tepelena, and meeting with rebel leaders. The article concluded, 'The international community must ensure that Albania's borders are guarded and secured from the infiltration of destructive elements. The Albanian people must be vigilant and not fall for trickery.'

This scenario had been concocted by Berisha's people during the last few days, after they had seen that the opposition in Tirana had sat down with Berisha, while the South continued with its own business. But in Berisha's propaganda, the old narrative of communist reaction still prevailed. According to this script, former *Sigurimi* agents and officers of the old regime who did not obey Tirana had organized this uprising in an attempt to turn back the clock and restore communism. Had not the communists repeated for fifty years that they had come to power with bloodshed, and would only let it go with bloodshed? Now it was time for blood to flow.

Some Western journalists swallowed this scenario, blaming their own countries' diplomats for not reacting properly to the terrorism of the former communists at the beginning of February, when the arsenals at Vlora were opened. The name of Kiço Mustaqi appeared in the Western press. This senior officer, once Enver Hoxha's defence minister, and convicted of genocide, had taken refuge in Greece, and was allegedly the mastermind controlling the rebellion in the South.

These conspiracy theories made Qorri furious. He knew how they operated, and this annoyed him more than their absurdity. Berisha's people served up these explanations to Westerners, who were inclined to believe them because of their limited knowledge and their reliance on stereotypes. And so these interpretations, invested with the style and authority of the supposedly impartial and reputable Western press, were recycled on State television, to convince the Albanians themselves of their truth.

The reality of the chain reaction that ran through the South after 9th March was complicated and quite different.

After all that had happened, the people of the South could not trust the agreement of 9th March. Berisha had tried everything against them. After police violence failed, he had tried the State of Emergency, sending the army and even aircraft to bombard them. After even this failed, he had suddenly announced, 'Let's sit down and talk about peace and reconciliation.' Who could swallow this? The opposition in Tirana had stretched out a hand to him at what should have been his moment of capitulation. Worse, it had reached a deal by selling out the South. According to the agreement, the people in the South had to hand in their weapons within a week without any guarantee of what would happen next. Of course they were scared of Tirana. The instinct of self-preservation told them to defend themselves.

This dismay of the South was compounded by the fact that the agreement of 9th March weakened still further the authority of institutions. Nobody knew any more who was responsible for the

214

State. The criminal world came to the fore, in all its power, and filled this vacuum. The prisons had been thrown open and their liberated inmates were exploiting the turmoil to steal and pillage.

The people had to defend themselves from an army that might disarm and imprison them. They had to secure food and protect themselves from criminals. So most of them thought they would be safer with a gun.

No leader was coordinating these actions in the South. Precisely because they were weak and leaderless, people fired into the air, to feel strong and protected, and to scare anyone who dared approach: in fact, to scare away their own fear. People also headed for the arms depots in the hope of looting something worth selling.

As Qorri had read somewhere, the most perverse turns of events cannot be foreseen but are the product of coincidences.

Chapter XXXIX

An Alarmed Priest

Tirana appeared calmer on the day after the agreement. On his way to the Forum's offices, Qorri was struck by the greater numbers in the streets. He headed for the Forum out of habit. He knew that nothing would happen there. Nobody had declared the Forum's mission complete, but opposition politics had now shifted to the headquarters of the parties that had signed the agreement. Even those who were against, like Kalakulla, had gone back to their own party bases. Kurt Kola had resumed his struggle to repossess the Association's headquarters.

There was nobody in Gjinushi's office. He and Milo were now spending more time at the Socialist Party offices.

Qorri walked along the corridor of the wing of this bird which looked ever less likely to fly. The phone rang in the Forum's office. A BBC correspondent wanted an interview about the agreement. Qorri made an appointment for a few hours later, and fired up the computer with the idea of setting down his objections to the agreement, which seethed in his brain. The program had still not loaded onto the screen when a knock came on the door. Clearly whoever it was would not enter uninvited.

'Come in,' he said.

The door opened and he saw a stranger, looking very shaken.

'What's happened?' Qorri asked.

'Good morning,' the person said in a quiet voice, not to be overheard.

'Who are you?'

'It doesn't matter. I'm a citizen of Tirana.'

'And what are you worried about?'

'I don't know if you've been told, but some people in my neighbourhood, SHIK agents or PD people, are handing out guns.'

Qorri was speechless.

'That's all I have to say. I'll go now,' the man said, obviously frightened. He hadn't even mentioned which neighbourhood.

Qorri started phoning people he knew. He tried Kurt, but there was no reply. Soon a second person arrived. This man was much more outspoken, declaring in a loud voice that weapons had been handed out at PD headquarters and at the United Officers School. He mentioned the names of the deputies of Berisha's party who were organizing the distribution.

'And you sit down to discuss reconciliation with these criminals,' he said, and stalked off.

Qorri had not foreseen anything like this. He had thought that the double- game would continue, with on one hand a supposed dialogue to form a new Government of National Reconciliation, and on the other hand intrigue and treachery. But this duplicity was an unexpected move by Berisha, his last and most desperate and dangerous one.

Qorri met the BBC correspondent and asked if he knew anything about such reports. The correspondent said he had no information, but believed that these reports could be true. Qorri could not mention these things in an interview, because the sources were unconfirmed, but he spoke out even more angrily against the agreement. It would not work, even in the short term, let alone stand the test of history. The agreement asked for weapons to be surrendered within a week, but still more people were arming themselves: The politicians, from their behaviour at the discussion table, were not to be trusted. History would not call this step an act of national reconciliation, because the Albanian people were not divided among themselves.

***

That evening the State television carried a news item that looked very peculiar to those who did not know what was happening.

The television cameras had gone to a village near Kukës in the North and filmed a crowd of people storming two arms depots and stripping them of their contents. The screen showed people brandishing Kalashnikovs, gleeful at having secured such trophies and full of the elation of battle.

This was a strange report because there had been no protests in the North over the losses in the pyramids, nor police reprisals and threats. What need did these people have to attack the arms depots? Why was this happening? How did the television crews happen to be there?

It wasn't hard to understand that this incident had been staged.

***

The next day, a Catholic priest from the village of Bushat near Shkodra was trying to find a foreign journalist. He got a man to stand by the main highway to flag down cars coming from Tirana and ask any who stopped if they had a foreign journalist with them. Few people were daring to drive to Shkodra these days. Finally an old Mercedes stopped and a German journalist with his Albanian fixer and a photographer got out. The man took them to the church.

The priest told them that he had certain information that the army had orders from Tirana to leave the arms depots open. They shouldn't ask him about his source, but should take it on trust. The order was first to supply PD members with weapons in an orderly fashion, and then to leave the arsenals open for anybody.

'What do you think the purpose of this operation is?' the journalist asked.

The priest said that the people in the North were agitating to be armed to counterbalance the south. The PD militants had to

218

be ready for any eventuality. As for the others, perhaps they did not intend to send these people into battle against the South, but merely create the impression that Berisha too had his supporters. But armed men of any kind were totally unpredictable. The priest therefore begged the journalist to warn the world that a catastrophe was imminent in his country.

As the priest spoke, gunshots and explosions were audible in the distance. In Shkodra and its surrounding villages and in Lezha further south, the arms depots were being opened.

***

The arsenals in the North were looted one after another. In Berisha's birthplace of Tropoja not only Kalashnikovs but artillery and heavy munitions were taken. The army put up no resistance. The State television cameras were there too. The armed men were not heard to shout slogans against the South, but the unspoken message of these scenes was clear.

The shots into the northern sky continued all night. Many people were killed and wounded from random firing. The attacks were organized to give an impression of spontaneity. Wherever people gathered, at petrol stations, shops, or in the centre of villages, rumours were spread that at a given time there would be an attack on a certain depot. This was enough for people to head towards it. At the appointed time they would gather outside the depot, and rush in without meeting any resistance.

From the North, this operation moved to the middle of the country. Chaos spread from one town to the next, fuelled by rumours that were carefully planted and impossible to control. The military depots at Burrel were attacked and looted. The mob there also stormed a VEFA branch and the private warehouse of a hotel owner. The looting lasted several hours while armed men ran through the town, firing into the air.

In the little town of Gramsh the crowds set fire to the police station, attacked the arsenal and State reserves, plundering all they could.

A little further east in Prrenjas, close to the Macedonian border, armed crowds looted a tobacco factory that contained several million dollars' worth of tobacco. After stealing what they could, even the doors and bathroom fittings, they set it on fire.

In Elbasan too the crowds stormed the military depots and took everything they found: grenades, mines, and artillery shells. Then the tumult finally reached Korça, a city famous for its high culture. Groups of armed men attacked all the arms depots round the city. A military division with its vehicles and a military hospital with its ambulances were looted. So were the State reserves of flour and foodstuffs in the outskirts, a supermarket, and the education authority.

Then the city's electricity supply was cut off and the population was left in total darkness. The noise of tanks and armoured vehicles in the streets at first terrified the inhabitants until they realised they were being used to transport plunder.

Many children took part in the attacks on the arms depots. They had no idea how to use weapons and no conception of their danger, and there were many tragic accidents. Some depots exploded, blowing up the looters too. The explosions in tunnels used as depots were the most lethal.

A hundred people died and many hundreds were wounded on this first chaotic day. But this disorder spread beyond what the imagination could conceive.

Chapter XL

From Fatos Qorri's Diary
Tirana, 11th March 1997

Yesterday afternoon I gave an interview for the BBC that was broadcast in the evening. I spoke against the agreement of 9th March. No more than half an hour later, I saw on the State television news Perikli Teta, the number three in the Democratic Alliance, appearing before the cameras with a rather odd expression. He looked as if he had been forcibly summoned to the television studios. He held a sheet of paper in his hand, from which he read a declaration by the three parties of the Forum that had signed the agreement, saying that from this time on any statement against the agreement was not a statement of the Forum, or at least not of these three parties. They fully stood by the agreement, which fulfilled the main demands for which the Forum was created.

This was clearly a response to my interview. It meant that the Forum now had to be dissolved, or nobody would be able to say anything that the three parties did not agree to. But I was astonished at the speed of the reaction.

This was why a meeting of the Forum was called today. Everybody came.

Teta, looking both smug and guilty, produced the statement and read it out, as if to show it meant no harm.

It soon came out that this statement had been drafted hastily under pressure from Berisha, who, after hearing my interview, had accused the parties of first signing the agreement and then using the Forum to repudiate it. I said that my interview was my own and not a statement by the Forum and that I couldn't say things I didn't think.

Also, in my interview I had dissociated myself from these people, not spoken in co-ordination with them.

They told me that I inevitably represented the Forum of which they were also a part.

'But the Forum also has other parties,' Kalakulla interrupted.

They said that the demands for which the Forum was created had been met. I told them that the demands had changed as the situation had evolved. For instance, the Forum had not at the beginning asked for Berisha's resignation, but after all that happened this had become a fundamental demand. Kurt reminded them that only two days ago they had said that they would only go to Berisha to speak as a Forum. Daut Gumeni added that they had signed a statement prepared by Berisha, to which they had been unable to change a comma, let alone stand up for the people in the South.

At one point in this exchange, Paskal Milo butted in and said that I had announced in the Rogner, 'These people have always been rubbish, and always will be.' Silence fell for a moment, which was interrupted by Kalakulla, who shouted:

'He's right. You're turncoats, cowards, and double-crossers. You've gone back on what you said only two days ago.'

Deep down they know that they've committed an act of weakness. They know that the agreement has caused more disorder than it has settled, and that the South has rejected the agreement, while Berisha has distributed weapons and opened the depots in Tirana and the North. They therefore feel that they still need the Forum just as Berisha needs armed men in the North.

The spat ended with a compromise statement. The Forum considered the 9th March agreement to be a step forward out of the crisis into which Sali Berisha had plunged the country, but it also had reservations. The Forum agreed to say that representatives of the insurgents should also have been invited to the table. This demand was also in the declaration of 7th March that they had approved, but at the meeting with Berisha two days later it was forgotten. I'm sure they will forget it again.

We also added that we had serious reservations about calling the new government one of 'national reconciliation' because there is no conflict among the people. There is a conflict between the government and the people and it makes no sense to talk about reconciliation in a conflict of this kind.

'A compromise is a good umbrella but a poor roof.' We have an extraordinary ability to unfurl umbrellas like this, often because we are unable to face a storm with courage. But we also have to survive in this little society where everyone knows everyone else, as if we were all related. It seems that neither the law nor justice nor the truth can function in a society like this because our familial relationships distort all these things. A person does something disgraceful and then gives you a smile in your regular café, and you grin back because you know his brother, because he once did you a favour, or because he's a friend of your friends. The prison guard who beat you comes up and embraces you as if he were your big brother who thrashed you when you were little, because he was told to do so by his father who is your grandfather's friend. Your father dies in peace because you are obliged to respect him as your father but also because you behave exactly as he did. This is a society without genuine communication; people do not face up to other people or to themselves, but behave according to a code in which all that counts is who wins, who cheats, and who loses. That is how these people behaved in the agreement with Berisha, and how they are behaving now. They say one thing and do the opposite. They did not for instance say a word about Italian Foreign Minister Dini, who met several of them at Foresti's residence before he left on 9th March. No doubt they promised him different things to what they signed today. This cannot even be called compromise, because a compromise may be a healthy thing when it is reached by two honest sides that genuinely communicate with one another. This is duplicity elevated to a principle of survival. This is pure irresponsibility.

I said these things to them just as plainly as I am writing them, but then went on to sign double-dealing documents with them. We are all products of this culture of survival at all costs, which became our second nature under communism.

Chapter XLI

Bullets in Tirana

At dawn on 12th March, Tirana finally erupted, like some forest finally engulfed by surrounding flames. Volleys of gunshots were heard from all sides, sometimes obscured by the dreadful detonations of shells or mines.

Huge crowds of people ran to the arms depots, both above and below ground. The depot in the Kombinat neighbourhood, one of the capital's largest, was emptied in a few hours. Children were loaded up like mules with weapons of every kind: Kalashnikovs, rifles, pistols, machine guns, hand grenades, mines, bullets, shells. The same scene was enacted at Brar on the opposite side of the city. The soldiers guarding the depots had left the gates open.

After all these depots were emptied the crowds stormed the food reserves. Nobody stopped them from entering, and they loaded sacks of flour and wheat onto cars, bicycles, and old carts or even carried them away on their backs.

Nobody knows how, but while this was going on the gaols were opened and all the prisoners released. The simplest explanation was that the guards were no longer able to do their duty. Within a few hours nothing was left that resembled a State, neither an army nor a police force, but only armed groups, mostly teenagers and young men, who wandered the streets of Tirana with guns in their hands.

The shops and offices all closed and the banks stored their deposits in safe places. The gunfire was continual, with barely a second between one rattle of automatic rifle fire and the next. Handguns and artillery were fired in a senseless orgy of shooting in the hills round Tirana, in the outskirts, and in the streets of the centre. Nobody had expected this. The toll of casualties rose fast.

The city hospital reported that the morgue could no longer hold the dead, and the doctors could not cope with the numbers injured by stray bullets falling from the sky. One of the city's best-known cardiologists appeared on television almost in tears and appealed for an end to the shooting,

Immediately after National Reconciliation, the Albanian state crumbled to dust.

***

On 13th March, the day after Tirana exploded, Qorri, Petrit Kalakulla, Kurt Kola, Daut Gumeni and a group of others not included in the agreement met in the Forum's office in the head of the bird, which to Qorri now seemed to have been killed. They had to act, but how? They felt powerless to do anything but draft an appeal, dissociating themselves from any responsibility for what was happening.

It did not take long to prepare a text. They pointed out that the situation was precipitating towards total chaos by the hour, and appealed to people not to turn the arms they had seized against one other. Citizens' committees, where they existed, should preserve the peace and protect cultural assets.

They then noted down the points that distinguished them most from the signatories of the agreement.

'Considering that the main culprit for the creation of this situation is Sali Berisha, and that calls for his resignation are growing louder from all sides, even from the international community, the Forum insists that he must leave politics as soon as possible.

'His office must be replaced by a presidential council until elections. The basis of the new government should be extended, turning it into a Government of National Salvation that will also have the support of the insurgents.

'The work of the Government of National Salvation must be supported by a political panel to include, besides the parties in the agreement, a broad representation of the Forum and the insurgents.

'The Forum welcomes every form of sincere assistance from abroad to bring the country out of its present situation, but opposes any intervention that would affect its territorial integrity.'

At the end they noted that the Socialist Party and the Social Democratic Party had not taken part in this meeting.

There was now nowhere the Forum could send its statements because the newspapers had shut down. Only foreign radio stations were operating. For the Forum only the BBC was left. Qorri phoned its Albanian correspondent, who said he was very busy and told him to bring the statement to his office. Kalakulla carried it to him and the correspondent said he would try to include it in his broadcast, but could not promise to do so because of the pressure of events.

***

The gunfire subsided early in the afternoon, but it was still dangerous to stay out in the street. Qorri ate, tried to rest a little, and set off on his bicycle for the Hotel Rogner. He might learn more news there. Foreign journalists were trying to move around and find out what was happening. The hotel seemed to be the only island where one could feel physically safe. The Bar West had been virtually abandoned, and Noel's was rarely open.

At the Rogner, Qorri was drawn into a diverse group of journalists trading news. An Italian was describing his adventure travelling to Rinas Airport, which was closed. He had just returned, and said there was no traffic at all on the motorway. You could have driven at 200 kilometres an hour, were it not for the potholes. Even the checkpoints had gone. He had seen only one near the airport with about twenty armed men, some in uniform, some in plain clothes, standing by obstacles they had placed across the road. On the runway there was only an ancient twin-engine Albanian Airlines plane, and all around was an incessant concert of gunfire.

Another journalist described anarchy at the port of Durrës. Thousands of people had taken to the sea, climbing onto anything that floated.

At this point someone entered the Rogner and announced that Berisha was taking flight. It was a matter of minutes, he said.

People rushed out into the hotel forecourt not to miss the sight of Berisha's helicopter rising above the Presidency building.

Reportedly, Americans, Germans, and Italians had been trying to persuade him all day, 'Escape while you still have time. You are the problem. Find some pretext.' But nobody knew if he had paid any heed. The only certain news was that he had sent his eighteen-year-old son and twenty-five year-old daughter to Italy on the last ferry that had left Durrës that day for Bari. Heavy machine guns were prominently positioned near Berisha's house on Fortuz Street and on the roof of the Presidency building, in the care of a handful of trusted men to discourage anybody from attempting some *coup de grâce*.

One Western diplomat, a tall man of fifty-one with a ruddy face and a loud, distressed voice, expressed scepticism of this report. He had been at the Presidency that very morning, evidently among the group trying to persuade him to leave. He had found Berisha alone in his office, deserted by his staff. 'I talked to him about the looted arsenals and the gunfire everywhere in the city,' he was telling a journalist, 'but his first concern was how to bring foreign troops to deal with the looters who had destroyed the Coca-Cola factory.'

'You've got to do something. They've burned it,' Berisha

228

insisted. 'This factory is one of the few multinational investments in Albania. It's very dear to me.'

The diplomat couldn't contain his laughter as he tried to imitate Berisha.

***

Qorri's heart quickened. Wasn't this the moment that Charles Walsh had talked about, when Berisha would turn his weapon against himself? Qorri too went outside to see the helicopter lift this culprit-in-chief from the Presidency and away from Albania. But as he watched, the less likely this prospect seemed. The day after his 'act of reconciliation', Berisha had armed his own people and opened the arsenals throughout Albania. Would he flee the next day? Now that he no longer bore responsibility for what was happening, but was sharing it with the opposition, he could act out the scenario that his instinct for self-preservation suggested to him. No, the moment that Walsh had hoped for had passed. Walsh had said that they would need skill and courage if Berisha were to turn the weapon against himself. But they had not shown these qualities. On the contrary, by opening the arsenals in Tirana and the north, he had fired his weapon and killed the innocent people who were his hostages. Now it was not just Berisha but both sides who were murderers.

If the uprising in the South had been leaderless and chaotic, the chaos that had now enveloped the entire country was organized by Berisha and the people around him.

In the midst of such mayhem, it was not hard, with the help of the SHIK and his trusted militants, to incite people to seize hundreds of thousands of weapons from open arsenals. The armed men would precipitate total chaos. In the darkness, all cats are black. Moreover, Berisha could easily describe this turmoil as a response

229

of his supporters in Tirana and the north to the insurgents in the south. Then he could raise the alarm to the outside world, 'We are in civil war, help us.'

***

Qorri had to return to his refuge in the Kindergarten before eight o'clock, the curfew under the State of Emergency. It was dark when he left the Rogner. The din of the firing was growing louder. As soon as he stepped out, he came across two armoured vehicles on which the word 'police' had been written crookedly in white oil paint. They were parading up and down the main boulevard of Tirana and round Scanderbeg Square. They were manned not by uniformed soldiers but a ragged crew with scarves round their heads brandishing automatic rifles and firing into the air. It was impossible to say if they supported Berisha or the new government, or were merely part of the confusion. The fact that no government buildings were attacked and burned, nor the state television studio, suggested they were Berisha's men.

Qorri held the handlebar of his bicycle with one hand and instinctively protected his head with the other. This was an absurd reaction, because a bullet would pierce his hand like a sheet of paper. So he pressed down on the pedals as hard as he could and raced home.

The route he usually followed passed along the boulevard into the 'Milky Way' where Noel's was situated and then along Qemal Stafa Street. Passing Noel's he saw its wooden door closed. The last time he had been there, he had met Shvarc who was in the company of Dita. Shvarc was worried about his heart trouble, but he hadn't given up smoking. His conversation was rambling and disconnected.

'Look at you!' He had shouted. 'Killing each other! That story about Albania being the only country in Europe that didn't hand over the Jews has a simple explanation. The Nazis didn't impose racial laws

230

in Albania. Otherwise they would have handed us all in like lambs. In Kosovo there was an SS Division named after Scanderbeg, and two hundred Jews disappeared from the camp in Prishtina. The guards were Albanians.'

'Are you talking about the Albanians then or now?' asked Qorri, smiling.

'At any time.'

It was almost eight o'clock when he reached the Kindergarten. He turned on the television news. The first item was a strange statement read by the announcer, that a Committee of National Salvation had been created in Tirana with branches in all the northern regions of Albania. This committee stated that forces of destruction at home and abroad were trying to divide the country, but the committee would re-establish the constitutional order and national integrity. 'Every part of Albania is sacred to us and we will defend it with our lives.' The committee of the North vilified the committees of the South as 'the spawn of the unbridled egotism of anti-national cliques trying to divide Albania, setting one region against another.' The committee warned that any armed attack or resistance against it would be punishable under military law, as would any act against the nation or the people. It appealed to all officers, servicemen of all ranks and reservists to take up arms to save the country and to obey military discipline and regulations.

Oddly, this statement had no named signatories. Qorri recalled that in the Rogner he had seen Berisha's adviser talking to a PD deputy, known as a hardliner within the party, with the ability to mobilize hoodlums. It struck him that the emergence of this committee must have something to do with the meeting of these two people. This was another document that fed the myth of a north-south civil war.

Chapter XLII

Untitled

'Albania Implodes... President's Men Flee Country... Government Fails To Disarm Gangs.' The headlines of *The New York Times* went round the world.

On 14th March the defence minister, who was accused of having given orders to bomb the South, left for Italy with his wife and 14-year-old daughters in a ship that had arrived to evacuate Italians. His farewell to his escorts was overshadowed by the tears of one of his daughters who wanted to take her dog with her.

Berisha's people were fleeing the country one by one. A number of officers of the National Guard that protected public buildings and Berisha himself were making preparations to leave. For some of these people, the agreement and the creation of a new government were steps on a slippery slope. Some had already sent ahead their wives and children. Rumour had it that the only office still working, and on overtime at that, was in the Foreign Ministry, where diplomatic passports were issued.

As a riposte to reports of this kind, one Italian television channel reported Berisha's press office as denying that the President intended to flee.

Berisha had been invited to take part in diplomatic talks that day, to include Ambassador Foresti, on board an Italian frigate somewhere off the coast of Durrës. However he did not want to venture so far out, fearful that this might be a ploy to persuade him to flee abroad.

***

The firing in Tirana became more intense and reports of the catastrophe engulfing the entire country came thick and fast. Several tunnels used as weapons depots had exploded with people inside, turning them into mass graves. In Vlora, there was panic at reports that the drinking water was poisoned, and the inhabitants let their taps run for a long time, and made sure to boil the water. In Korça, the tanks and armoured vehicles seized from the army were being used as taxis, and anyone wishing to travel safely from the city to a village had to pay the plunderers. Further south in the little town of Erseka, six thousand guns were looted. In Shkodra, armed groups robbed and set fire to two state banks, the office of the SHIK, the prefecture, and Radio Shkodra, as well as the ancient shopping street that was a national monument.

Public buildings stood empty, especially those of the army and police. All the country's prisons were open. People known to have money were being kidnapped.

The newly appointed Prime Minister of the Government of Reconciliation, with the patriotic call 'The homeland is in danger,' appealed to all soldiers and officers, wherever on active service or not, to report to the ministry, the military units, or other bases where they had served. But few responded.

Finally at a quarter to five on the afternoon of 14th March, after a day of terrified appeals, something happened that the internationals did not expect, although Berisha had planned it. The prime minister of a government that governed nothing appealed to the outside world:

'We are on the brink of civil war, help us.'

For the Westerners, this was the final act of a tragedy foretold. Its episodes had included the rebellion of the South, the agreements, their mediation, and the Government of Reconciliation. All in vain. The events of the last few days had persuaded even the

233

most sceptical that only foreign intervention could save Albania from final destruction.

Berisha's plan was working, although the flight of his staff had caused hitches. He had now ensured that the call for the intervention of Western armies came from his political opponents.

In this situation, many people who had been asking for Berisha's head shrugged their shoulders when asked who would take his place. One Western observer claimed that even the leader of the Socialists, the strongest rival party, had called Berisha 'a necessary evil.'

However, the NATO spokesman rejected Berisha's appeals for intervention and said that the main problem was that the government did not enjoy confidence.

Vranitzky held a meeting with the newly appointed members of the government, emerging in despair to say that the European states should consider sending military and police forces to help Albania suppress the violence. The Albanians had made it clear they were unable to establish order themselves.

In response, NATO diplomats said that they would not send help until Vranitzky reached a political solution. The OSCE would have to devise a credible framework for this solution and then make a specific request to NATO.

Chapter XLIII

The Exodus Begins

The first alarm was raised in Bari. A ferry with dozens of Albanians on board had set off from Durrës. 'These people are armed,' the Italian Navy warned. 'Be careful.'

All the Albanian ships had been stormed by armed crowds seeking a sea route out of the chaos. Two fishing boats that left the port of Shëngjin to protect themselves from the armed mob arriving from the North were caught in a storm. They were dashed against the rocky coast, and sank.

The situation was even more complicated at the port of Durrës. The *San Giorgio* amphibious craft had set off for the Albanian coast, with marines of the San Marco Battalion on board and orders to evacuate all the Italians. When it arrived it was attacked by dozens of people armed with Kalashnikovs, iron bars and staves. A short time before, they had attacked the *Annamaria Lauro* ferry that plied the Otranto-Durrës route and attempted to board it by force. The captain had succeeded in closing the main portal and had departed at full speed, but both ships headed for Italy carrying more Albanians than Italians.

The flight of the foreigners increased the panic among the Albanians, who resorted more and more to violence in their attempts to join them.

Now that evacuation by sea was difficult, the Italians attempted an operation with helicopters, which landed on a sports field in the middle of the city, and aircraft, using a runway in the chaotic port of Durrës. Here too crowds of despairing Albanians fought to board the helicopters and planes, and soldiers had to drive them back by force. One Italian helicopter as it took off was struck by a bullet fired from among the crowd left behind, but was not brought down.

The Italian press of 14th March reported a sea of Albanians in the reception camps in Apulia, expecting to make a future life in Italy. The journalists highlighted the case of fifty young men dressed in blue Italian uniforms. These were sailors of the Albanian Navy who until three days before had worn Albanian uniforms. They had left the shores of Albania in their ship without taking even a change of clothes. Their officers were in another corner of the room.

'We came here to save our ships and their crew, not just our own skins,' they said to Italian journalists.

'And what is happening now in Albania?'

'We have no idea either, we promise you.'

***

From morning to late afternoon, helicopters took off from Tirana carrying westward the Americans, the Italians, the Dutch, and other foreigners, economic and military advisers, experts in law, agriculture, health, human rights, culture, the environment, and animal protection. Berisha's people said, 'For five years they gave us valuable advice, helping Albania change to a market economy. But now they're being forced out by the communist rebels.'

That same day the U.S. ambassador, Marisa Lino, appeared on State television to speak to the Albanians on behalf of the U.S. Government and people. She wished to assure them that the United States was not abandoning their country. She and a part of her staff would remain to tackle the many problems together with the government. Only American citizens who wished to leave were being evacuated, with the families of embassy employees and some non-essential staff. 'This is our duty to our citizens and I ask all Albanians to cooperate with us at this time to assist U.S. citizens who wish to leave the country.'

But despite Lino's appeal the attempt to evacuate the Americans was suspended when two helicopters waiting to take away the families assembled on the field in the embassy compound were fired on. Only four hundred and eight of the two thousand Americans in Albania had been evacuated. The Pentagon expressed its concern at leaving Americans to spend another night in the city, exposed to the dangers of stray bullets and looting.

***

Qorri learned that many of his friends had also fled. Phone calls came from Italy, France, the United States, Germany, Spain, and Greece, urging him to escape. Most of the intellectuals who had signed the petition against Berisha six weeks before had already fled. An international association that helped writers and artists in danger had come to their aid. Ben Kumbaro and his wife had left to join Edi Rama in Paris. Many *Koha Jonë* journalists had gone, but some from *Albania* too. Qorri told people who phoned him that he had been in the public eye and couldn't run away. But the deeper reason was that he was kept in Albania by curiosity to see what happened next, a curiosity that could probably be swept away at any time by rising panic. But he felt no panic. He had been more frightened earlier. Now it was obvious that this was not a civil war. Nobody had taken up weapons against anyone else. Everybody was firing into the air. The greatest danger was the lunacy and desperation of people who didn't know what was going on or what would happen to them the next day. It resembled an apocalyptic drama, but it was a false apocalypse, a revelation that revealed nothing. It would leave everything just as it was.

So, his writer's and journalist's instinct told him that it would be a great loss not to live through this false apocalypse that one day he might describe. In fact, all historical calamities had been like this, false apocalypses to which God's angels had failed to turn up. This one was perhaps more farcical than most, but maybe for this reason slightly more truthful.

***

Nusi was distressed by the gunfire and wandered from one window of the Kindergarten to the next.

As Qorri went to bed, curious about what the next day would bring, a message in capital letters was spreading on the internet:

TO: ALL READERS ON THE WEB AND ALL
ALBANIANS ABROAD

TODAY MAY BE THE LAST DAY I CAN WRITE. OUR LIVES ARE IN DANGER. ALBANIA IS IN CIVIL WAR. THE WHOLE COUNTRY. ALL OF THE TOWNS AND VILLAGES. TIRANA IS IN CHAOS. THERE ARE REPORTS OF DEATHS AND A LOT OF WOUNDED. DURRËS TOO. THERE HAS BEEN GUNFIRE ALL OVER MY CITY OF KAVAJA FOR THE LAST 24 HOURS WITH BULLETS FLYING LIKE CRAZY.
WE HAVE NO LIGHTS AND NO PHONE.
I DON'T HAVE ANYTHING ELSE TO SAY.

I CAN'T STOP CRYING AND ASKING WHY. WHY THIS SHOULD HAPPEN. I TRY TO GO OUTSIDE TO SEE WHAT PEOPLE ARE DOING BUT I ONLY SEE PEOPLE RUNNING, CHILDREN CRYING IN FEAR OF THE SHOOTING. I DON'T SEE ANY POLICE ANYWHERE.

I CAN'T SEE ANYTHING. IT'S A GHOST TOWN. WE'RE ASKING FOR HELP. WE WANT THE OUTSIDE WORLD TO HELP US. MY FRIENDS TELL ME THEY'RE FLEEING THE COUNTRY AND THEY WANT ME TO GO WITH THEM. BUT HOW CAN I? WHO WILL BE LEFT? I HAVE MY FAMILY. WHERE WILL THEY GO? MY HUSBAND IS TRYING TO BRING TOGETHER THE PEOPLE OF KAVAJA TO FORM A COMMITTEE TO STOP THIS CRAZY SHOOTING. WE'VE JUST HEARD THAT THERE IS A LITTLE VILLAGE CALLED LEKAJ WHERE THERE ARE TONNES OF TNT. IT THIS EXPLODES IT WILL BLOW UP THE VILLAGE AND ALL KAVAJA WITH IT.

WE MUST SAVE OUR CHILDREN AND ALL OUR PEOPLE. I APPEAL TO ALL FOREIGN STATES TO HELP US SO WE DON'T DIE LIKE ANIMALS. WE ARE HUMAN BEINGS STRUGGLING TO SURVIVE. WE WANT A FUTURE FOR OUR CHILDREN.

AS A MOTHER, A WOMAN, AND AN ALBANIAN I APPEAL TO ALL MY ALBANIAN BROTHERS AND SISTERS THROUGHOUT THE WORLD TO BE STRONG AND TO PRAY FOR A FREE ALBANIA. MAY GOD BE WITH US.
I PROMISE YOU THAT AS LONG AS I AM ONLINE AND HAVE ELECTRICITY I WILL KEEP YOU INFORMED ABOUT EVENTS. THE LATEST NEWS IS THAT THE CHAIRMAN OF THE DEMOCRATIC PARTY, THE DEFENCE MINISTER, AND THE PRESIDENT'S CHILDREN HAVE FLED THE COUNTRY TO SAVE THEIR SKINS, LEAVING US HERE.

ALL THE BEST AND PEACE TO YOU ALL.
DONIKA

Epilogue 1

Tirana, 29th March (ATA) –

Yesterday an Albanian boat sank thirty miles off Brindisi while attempting to reach the Italian coast. According to information from survivors, military vessel No. 405 left the port of Vlora at three p.m. Near Sazan island it took on board three more people who were fleeing in a small boat. The ship was small, of about 30 tonnes and designed only for harbour use. The ship was full of women and children and there were no weapons. Before it entered international waters, Italian frigate No. 577 appeared and shadowed it for a long time, sailing alongside it and preventing the Albanian vessel from manoeuvring. The Italian frigate informed the ship by megaphone that its crew would be arrested and its passengers returned to Albania. The Albanian vessel responded by hoisting a white flag and pointing to the presence of children. The frigate shadowed the boat until six p.m. and then vanished.

Shortly afterwards another Italian frigate No. 558 appeared accompanied by a helicopter. The frigate blocked the path of the Albanian vessel, making it difficult for this ship to move in the rough seas. At about seven p.m. the Italian frigate, several times larger than the Albanian boat, after calling to this ship once again, approached from the stern and rammed the Albanian vessel first amidships and then in the bow. The Albanian vessel filled with water and sank at once. An unknown number of lives were lost. Thirty-four survivors have been held in isolation and questioned. In interviews, they denounced the Italians as criminals. The Italian side has not taken into account the testimonies of the Albanians. The explanations given by Admiral Angelo Mariani, chief of the Naval General Staff, entirely contradict the statements of witnesses, both regarding the deterrent manoeuvres performed by the Italian frigates and the ramming of the Albanian ship, which witnesses claim were both deliberate.

A few days ago several well-known Italian politicians declared that 'the Albanians should be thrown into the sea.'

'Murderers, murderers.' The shouts came from faces contorted in agony.

'They rammed us,' they yelled. A young man of twenty-five, at the end of his endurance, says in an exhausted voice, 'I lost my wife and son. He was only two months old. I saw him drown before my very eyes.'

'How did you survive?' we asked him.

'It was so cold and all the men were on deck, to leave room below for the women and children.'

La Stampa, 30th March 1997.

Tirana, 30th March (ATA) –

Italian Defence Minister Beniamino Andreatta has sent a telegram of condolences to his Albanian counterpart.

'I have learned with deep shock the news of the tragic accident at sea in which your fellow-countrymen lost their lives. At this sad time I ask you to accept the deepest sympathies of the Italian Armed Forces. I also express my personal grief and share the sorrow of the families of the victims and the Albanian people. I send to these families my sincere condolences and my best wishes to the injured for a fast recovery.'

Epilogue 2

From Fatos Qorri's Diary
April 1997

Today I was in Vlora with some Italian human rights activists. I have known one of them, Bruno, for a long time and he asked me to go with him. I was curious to see what was happening in the city. We set off in two cars that we decided never to let out of each other's sight, because the roads are extremely unsafe. I didn't take with me either my wallet or wristwatch, but only put a little money into my trouser pocket. The danger comes from the 'hoods', as the masked bandits who ambush cars on the main roads are now called. There are more on the roads to the north, but plenty on the roads of the south too. They come out especially at night. Generally they position a large rock in the middle of the road, to look as if it has rolled down from above. When the driver gets out to move it aside, he finds Kalashnikov barrels pointing at him. If the hoods fancy the car, they make all the passengers get out, rob them, take their car, and leave them standing in the middle of the road. Otherwise they merely rob the passengers.

We decided to go and return in one day, coming back before nightfall. We saw very little traffic on the roads, and even less the further we went from Tirana.

We met with no unpleasant incidents.

Along the entire road we saw destruction and burned buildings, but when we arrived at the Mifol bridge I seemed to absorb through all my senses the atmosphere that prevailed in Vlora. Perhaps my imagination was working too, because a bridge is always a crossing to an imagined other side. Entering the bridge from the

Tirana end, I saw the marks of the government's tanks on the asphalt, and on the other side the Vlora people's checkpoints. The tanks and the checkpoints had confronted one another for a long time. A part of the bridge's railings had been torn up. A checkpoint boom still pointed in the air but there was no one to lower or raise it.

The beauty of the olive groves that start when you cross the Mifol bridge and descend into the town made no impression on me. Neither did the sea, because my eyes were fixed on the burned car bodies along the road. Some of these were still smoking and emitting a horrible stench. I felt I was heading towards a dangerous, smouldering ash heap.

When we entered the town I phoned on my mobile my old prison friend Kujtim to whom I'd spoken before we left Tirana. Kujtim told me that he was with two or three other ex-prisoners in a café in the city centre. The café was hard to find, in a hut hidden behind an apartment block.

Our reunion was an emotional one, but we started talking immediately about the news of the day, with no mention of the memories, either nostalgic or bitter, that are the favourite topic when ex-prisoners meet.

'What's happening? What are people saying here?' I asked.

'What can we say?' came the automatic reply.

Kujtim looked me in the eye.

He told me that he had been a police officer recruited by Berisha's government. But he had resigned when he saw that instead of talking to the outraged people, the government was giving orders to use violence. 'Then,' he said, 'when Berisha announced the State of Emergency, we were all ready to fight against the army, with weapons.'

'And now?' I asked.

'Now we'd call on the devil himself, if he could get us out of this mess.'

'What? Why?'

He explained that the city was in the hands of bandits who were kidnapping men and raping women. Nobody dared go out in the streets. It was horrible. We had arrived at noon and had seen that the city was virtually empty. Kujtim and his friends too would go home in about half an hour.

'What about the Italian troops and Operation Alba?'

'They've taken charge of the harbour to prevent migrants but they don't come into the city. A few days ago an Albanian and an Italian went to them and knocked on their door because the gangs had threatened them with death if they didn't pay money. The Italians said they were sorry, but they didn't have any orders to intervene in public order problems in the city. They were there only to distribute humanitarian aid. Both these men were shot in the end.'

I asked him about the Salvation Committee. Was it still leading the protest movement? Was it doing anything to take control of the situation?

'There's no more protest movement,' they told me, 'The Committee still meets. You'll find them in the high school. But they don't send anyone out onto the streets any more. Zani and his gang control the city now.'

Who Zani was, I found out a little later. He and his gang were talked about in Tirana too. He had appeared on the scene after the agreement of 9th March and the storming of the arsenals. He had been a migrant worker in Greece and had been imprisoned there for delinquency. Who knows how he reached Vlora, whether he was released from prison or escaped. Berisha's people say that the Greeks released him on purpose to stir up trouble in the south. The Italian press has portrayed him as a Robin Hood figure, because he distributes money to the poor. He has also met with Italian Army officers.

'Who is he?' I asked.

'An ordinary criminal. He's now at war against another gang, Kakami's. They've been fighting every day to control the city and the traffic in women and drugs, but they also kill innocent people. Zani says he's on the side of your lot in the opposition, and Kakami is with Berisha.'

I left my friends, who showed me the way to the high school. They told me not to take my Italian friends with me because the Salvation Committee no longer received foreigners. Bruno and his people set off to meet their own contacts in Vlora.

***

The Committee had gathered in the head teacher's office. Here too was a T-shaped table, like in the days of communism. At the head of the T, I recognized from television Albert Shyti with his bouffant hair and characteristic long sideburns. Next to him on the two arms of the T sat seven or eight other members of the Salvation Committee.

As soon as the conversation began I understood what they thought of the agreement.

'This government is a two-headed snake,' said one of them, who had the look of an intellectual.

'And one of those heads is going to bite us,' Albert Shyti said, completing the other man's thought.

The others nodded in agreement.

Albert Shyti was not concentrating on the conversation. He had in front of him a copy of *Koha Jonë*, which had resumed publication, and he was reading it with close attention.

I don't know for how long I talked to them or what I said, perhaps because of the shock I experienced at the moment when I stood up to go.

I was about to leave the room when the door flew open at a mighty kick from outside. In front of me stood a tall young man with filthy matted hair, dressed in military kit and boots. He held a gun that looked bigger and longer than a Kalashnikov. An entourage of young men with Kalashnikovs came after him. He didn't pay me any attention and perhaps didn't know me. This must be Zani, I said to myself and stood rooted to the spot.

He headed straight for the person he wanted, Albert Shyti.

'Who's boss in Vlora, you scumbag?' he bellowed. He knocked him to the floor with his fist and kicked him.

None of us made any response. We all felt powerless, terrified by the armed gang. The man who had said that the government was a two-headed snake put his arm around my shoulder and said it was better if I left, and they would settle the business themselves.

'It's the fault of *Koha Jonë*,' I heard him say as I left.

I left the schoolyard and came out on the main road, past a line of parked armoured vehicles with military camouflage paintwork. I hadn't seen them when I arrived. A jeep, more impressive than the others, led them with tall antennas on its bonnet. Clearly these were the cars of Zani's gang, with their boss's in front.

The streets of Vlora were totally deserted.

I met Bruno and the other Italians at the café. Through their contacts they had found a powerfully built young man who told us that he belonged to the Socialist Party. I told him where I'd been and what had happened. He understood the reason immediately. He explained that *Koha Jonë* had reprinted that day an article published two or three days earlier in *Corriere Della Sera*, whose correspondent had visited Vlora to report on the deployment of the Italian troops in Operation Alba. He had also interviewed Albert Shyti. The article mentioned what he had said about Zani: 'He isn't the boss of Vlora. He's a bandit and a murderer and the Italian officers who shook hands with him should wash their hands well afterwards.' This was

246

why Albert Shyti had looked so worried when I found him with *Koha Jonë* in front of him. He was wondering if Zani had been sent a copy.

It was now entirely clear to me who was boss in Vlora.

'But how do you put up with him?' I asked the young man.

'He doesn't bother us,' he replied. 'But don't worry. They'll get rid of him when the time comes.'

The young man led us through the city centre to see the damaged buildings -- the city hall, the prefecture, and the SHIK headquarters, their blackened façades saddening and horrific.

The University where the students had held their hunger strike was not burned but was deserted. We went in to see the strikers' room. Our guide took us to eat at a restaurant by the sea called the Bologna, where foreigners went because it was safe from bandits. Zani had surrounded it a few days before at a time when it was full of Italians, but had come to an agreement with the proprietor, who no doubt paid to be left in peace.

When we entered we noticed a table full of Italian servicemen of the Alba mission. One of them had acquired some Albanian.

'Good morning -- *mirëmëngjesi*, goodbye -- *tungjatjeta*; food -- *ushqim*; medicines -- *ilaçe*,' he said, rehearsing the lessons he must have received before leaving Brindisi.

'Throw down your weapons -- *hidhni armët*; stop or I shoot -- *ndalo ose qëllova*' another soldier butted in dramatically and laughed.

'Thank you -- *faleminderit*,' another interrupted.

The proprietor of the restaurant, with a gold chain round his fat neck, laughed as they rehearsed the key Albanian vocabulary they had learned.

We ate fresh fish. We asked where the fish was from and our guide said with a smile that it was probably blown out of the water with dynamite and sold to the owner for five leks.

We didn't stay long because we had to leave in order to be home before dark.

But first we visited the city cemetery. Our guide told us we would see an unusual sight. There were so many new graves. There seemed to be more piles of fresh earth, some covered with flowers and some not, than old graves that had accumulated down the years. There were up to ten burials each day accompanied by keening, flowers, and gunshots.

So many new graves had been added that the paths between the plots had been narrowed to make room for the number of dead. Most of these paths were now blocked, leaving only the main alleys. Then they used the plots reserved for the political victims of Vlora killed under the dictatorship, whose bones have yet to be found. When these were full they had dug graves where they could and without permission, because the authorities were not working.

There were cases in which, during the burial, mourners had been killed by stray bullets, or by people out for revenge who had stalked the dead man's friends. Even in this cemetery, one death led to another. This afternoon we found only one group of mourners leaving after burying one of their family. The sexton who had just finished his work came up to us. For some reason I didn't look at his face but the soles of his rubber boot with their accumulated layers of mud. He thought that we had come to ask for a plot. Apparently he made a business out of graves. When he saw that foreigners were with us and weren't burying anyone, he set aside his serious expression and perked up.

'How many burials today?' our guide asked.

'Not many, six.'

He suspected that Bruno was a journalist and, without prompting, began telling us of extraordinary things that had happened there.

A few days previously, a woman who came regularly to mourn her husband was seized by two bandits and forced to transfer her grief a few graves down the line, to weep for their friend. After she had lamented the deceased with an automatic rifle pointing at her head, the bandits took her with them. The sexton was worried for her sake, but did not dare to interfere. The next day, she appeared again at her husband's grave, and the sexton asked her what had happened. She said they had liked her performance and so had driven her home and even paid her. Evidently the sexton's favourite tales were about the bandits who organized funerals. He had tried to persuade two of them that every grave had to be 1.4 metres wide and 2.4 metres long, and that he couldn't make them any larger. But they had pointed a revolver at his head and forced him to dig the enormous grave they wanted.

The sexton had more stories to tell but we had to leave. Our guide followed us in his car as far as the Mifol bridge and we parted company there.

Throughout the homeward journey I could not help thinking about the cemetery. Unconsciously, I had fixed in my mind the memory of the plot set aside for my former fellow-prisoners, whose bones were still missing. Surprisingly, I felt more sorry for the delay in finding these bones and commemorating these victims than for the recent dead. Those piles of fresh earth seemed like usurpers, violating a sacred space. These new deaths had occurred before the old victims had been properly buried. But then I thought that they were only a new twist in the same tragedy, new plots in an old graveyard.

Afterword

Early elections were held on 29th June 1997, and these were won by the Socialist Party and its allies.

Sali Berisha, having lost the elections, remained leader of the opposition for eight years. In 2005, his Democratic Party won the elections and he became the country's Prime Minister. In 2009, when this book was finished, he was appointed Prime Minister for the second time.

After the 1997 elections, Rexhep Meidani became President of Albania, elected for five years. After completing his term, he stood for the leadership of the Socialist Party, but did not win. At the time of writing, he enjoys the status of a former president, writes in the newspapers, and teaches at the university.

Skënder Gjinushi, after the 1997 elections, became parliamentary speaker. He subsequently became Education Minister in the Socialist governments. He still writes for the newspapers, and is respected as a former parliamentary deputy.

Neritan Ceka became Interior Minister after the opposition victory in June 1997. He was elected a deputy in two parliaments in coalition with the Socialist Party. At the time of writing, his small party, the Democratic Alliance, has now entered a coalition with Berisha's party.

Preç Zogaj became Meidani's adviser for a while. After several years in coalition with the Socialists, he transferred, with Ceka, to a coalition with Berisha's party. He has written several books about the development of democracy in Albania.

Pandeli Majko was elected a Socialist Party deputy in 1997, and became Prime Minister for a short time in 1999. He has also been defence minister. He is currently a Socialist Party deputy.

Paskal Milo became Foreign Minister in the government that emerged from the 1997 elections, and was a deputy in three parliaments until 2008.

Foresti remained Italian ambassador to Albania for only two months after the agreement of 9th March. In May the Italian Government was obliged to recall him after the Albanian press published transcripts of recorded conversations between him and Tritan Shehu, the chairman of the Democratic Party, which exposed his efforts to rescue Berisha and also to subvert the work of Franz Vranitzky. This obliged the Italian Government to recall him. It is still unknown which secret service gave to the Albanian newspaper the recordings in this scandal, which was christened 'Forestigate'.

Charles Walsh left Albania and according to unofficial information was declared *persona non grata* at the request of Ambassador Lino. He started working at the United States' mission to the OSCE in Vienna.

Edi Rama returned from Paris at the start of 1998 and became Minister of Culture in the Socialist-led government. Two years later he became mayor of Tirana and later chairman on the Socialist Party, a post he retains at the time of writing.

Blendi Gonxhja became Edi Rama's chief of cabinet when he was appointed Minister of Culture, and deputy chairman of the municipality when Rama became mayor of Tirana. He later fled abroad following accusations of corruption in the city hall. He is now a private businessman.

Arben Kumbaro returned to Albania after staying one year in France. For a short time he became adviser to one of the Socialist ministers of culture. He had been active as a theatre producer. He now teaches drama at the Academy of Arts.

Zani Çaushi, after a time at large, continued his serial murders among rival gangs and was arrested and sentenced to life imprisonment. At the time of writing he is still in gaol.

Kurt Kola became director of the Institute for the Victims of Political Persecution, and remained in this post for several years.

Daut Gumeni, after the 1997 elections, became an adviser to President Meidani. He was later consul in Ioannina and subsequently at the Albanian Embassy in Croatia. He was removed from the embassy after Berisha became Prime Minister. He now works as a translator and journalist.

After the victory of the Socialists, Fatos Qorri was offered the post of director of Albanian Television, which he did not accept. He continued to work as a freelance writer and journalist, as he still does today as he finishes this book.

About three thousand people died in the events that followed the agreement of 9th March, although this figure has never officially been confirmed.

THE END

FREEDOM
TO **WRITE**
FREEDOM
TO **READ**

This book has been selected to receive financial assistance from English PEN's Writers in Translation programme supported by loomberg and Arts Council England. English PEN exists to promote literature and its understanding, uphold writers' freedoms around the world, campaign against the persecution and imprisonment of writers for stating their views, and promote the friendly co-operation of writers and free exchange of ideas.

Each year, a dedicated committee of professionals selects books that are translated into English from a wide variety of foreign languages. We award grants to UK publishers to help translate, promote, market and champion these titles. Our aim is to celebrate books of outstanding literary quality, which have a clear link to the PEN charter and promote free speech and intercultural understanding.

In 2011, Writers in Translation's outstanding work and contribution to diversity in the UK literary scene was recognised by Arts Council England. English PEN was awarded a threefold increase in funding to develop its support for world writing in translation.

www.englishpen.org